THE
BLOCKADE
RUNNERS

DAVID C. REED

PRAISE FOR DAVID C. REED'S COLD, DARK, AND SILENT:

"This is a wonderfully written mystery. The author grabbed my attention from the first page (not many authors are able to do that). The characters are very well drawn. The story and the way it is told is captivating. Well done!"

"Such a compelling page-turner! No way could you quit reading to tend to your daily life. Each character was described in ways you could almost smell their perfume or cologne. A combination of mystery, crime, of love, grief of a parent, along with finding your purpose in life whether it be what you'd expect."

"The book was well written and kept me intrigued as the story went along. The talents of the writer were definitely on display in this novel. The characters developed in a manner that brought the story to life. I would totally recommend this book to everyone that enjoys a good investigative story."

"Excellently written adventure. Exciting and suspenseful. David C. Reed is a master of the law enforcement story. I was a deputy with a small county sheriff's office. He captures the essence of working with limited resources in small regional counties. I can't wait for his next book."

"Not only enjoyed the read, relooked the cover after the read and enjoyed the "tease" (in police work we call that a clue) luring the reader into discovering details about solving the disappearance."

For The Blockade Runners:

"Fast, intriguing, and filled with the snappy dialogue and realistic police scenes and action Reed does so well! Easily 5 Stars!" - *J. D. Anders*

"The Blockade Runners is a fascinating follow-up to Cold, Dark and Silent with action, intrigue, and mystery. David C. Reed does well in keeping the stakes high and the plot payoff satisfying, while keeping you on the edge of your seat the whole time!" - *Addison Williams, Editor*

"Boomers need heroes too!

David C. Reed has given us a great one in Chig Ashe. The Blockade Runners, the second in his new Chig Ashe mystery series, is a taut procedural thriller written by a man who knows procedures. Not since the Matthew Scudder novels of Lawrence Block has there been a better or more accurate offering in the noir genre.

Sexually charged, entertaining dialogue from challenging, complex, and believably flawed characters make for an enthralling, fast-paced read -- and for a potentially great TV series starring an aging boomer filled with wisdom, panache, and Viagra. In other words, the PERFECT Nick Searcy vehicle! 5 stars."

– *Nick Searcy, Actor, Director, Producer.* Star of television and motion pictures.

 "The "Chig" Ashe series is proving to be a good one! Looking forward to further adventures!"

"Excellent sequel to Cold, Dark and Silent! Fast paced action written by an author with years of real-life experience!"

"The Blockade Runners. Great and steady read! Got it done in two days! It flowed and had great signature characters (from the 1st Book Cold Dark & Silent) which were a huge welcome and compliment to the flow of the story line. DC's knowledge of investigative tactics and procedures lent to the validity of what happens in real homicides - having credible "tried and true" police practices deepen the story. It has suspense and intrigue. I am looking forward to the next book as it's been teased and I NEED to see Ashe get his justice!"

Library of Congress Control Number: 2025905251

Publishing Coordinator – Sharon Kizziah-Holmes
Cover Design – Jaycee DeLorenzo

Paperback-Press
an imprint of A & S Publishing
Paperback Press, LLC
Springfield, Missouri

ISBN 978-1-964559-52-0 (Paperback)
ISBN 978-1-964559-53-7 (Hardback)
ISBN 978-1-964559-54-4 (eBook)

DEDICATION

Again, and always,
For Audrey

CHAPTER 1

Ashe stepped back from the metal table in the basement of the Seacord Family Funeral Home to let the coroner run down his checklist. Hurrt County didn't have a morgue, nor a local pathologist, but it had a dead body.

The coroner, who had been recently elected to fill a vacancy, was a former licensed practical nurse at a clinic. As Ashe watched him, it was apparent the man had little actual experience with unnatural deaths.

Much less one that was shot and left in the lake.

Ashe was present at the request of Sheriff Larry Jacobs, who paced in small circles in the room with his cell phone to his ear.

The man's body before them wore a still-damp, muddy, and heavily wrinkled suit. He was found washed up on the shoreline just over eight hours ago, and Ashe calculated from the looks of him, he'd been in the lake almost a week; minimally.

The dead man wore a black suit and had what was left of a clear, coiled wire earpiece that went to a radio. No radio, though.

Ashe looked at the whole body first. Men who dress for the day in suits have plans, ideas, a schedule, *dreams*. Then suddenly, all his plans and appointments and dreams were gone. Stolen, violently by the look of things, in a matter of seconds.

Did he have children? Did he have places to be for work, or plans with his friends and family?

Someone else, someone who did not give a damn about all that had canceled his appointments, stealing his last seconds. Like all murderers, they had cruelly, violently, robbed him of his next thought, his next kiss, his next meal. His next dream.

A representative of the funeral home stood silently in a corner of the room, his hands clasped in front and his head lowered respectfully. Ashe assumed this was his practiced posture.

"This is, well...I do not believe this is a natural death," the coroner said to Ashe. He fidgeted with an electronic pen and a digital tablet.

"You think?" shouted Sheriff Jacobs, who held his hand over his cell. He scoffed, looked at Ashe, then circled back away from the table.

The coroner shot Jacobs a hard look then gave the same one to Ashe.

Ashe just shrugged. "I think that's a fair observation, Mister...um, I'm sorry, once again, please?"

"Canaday. Eric Canaday."

"Mister Canaday. Given the body has three huge exit wounds from a large caliber rifle and no face left," Ashe said. "The sheriff has a point."

"Yes, of course, Mister Ashe. Or is it...what is everyone calling you? *Chig*?"

It was Ashe's childhood nickname. Canaday must have heard it from someone older around town because as he was half Ashe's age, and there was no way he would have known that name.

As a kid tagging along behind his father in his small home town of Seacord, the seat of Hurrt County, his dad had given him a nickname.

C'mon, Chigger Bug! he'd say. Or, *Let's go, Chig!*

Once Ashe had left home, he never revealed that familiar name to anyone, but ever since he'd moved back to Seacord, his old school friends seemed bent on revising it.

"No, just Ashe. A few people here that I went to school with still call me that, but I'm just Ashe. Last names are kind of a military and cop thing. At my age it's a habit."

"Yeah, you know my dad knew your dad I believe, and..."

Ashe gestured at the body. "Nice suit. Some kind of earpiece. This man was working."

Canaday blinked, looked at the body, then said, "Yes, you're probably right. But, first...can you please tell me why *you* are here?"

Before Ashe could answer, the funeral home director

interrupted. "We were *most* honored to handle your father's final arrangements here," he said.

"Yes, um, thanks for Dad," Ashe said. Then back to Coroner Canaday, he said, "Sheriff Jacobs asked I take a look at this. I have over twenty-four years of criminal investigation experience up in Metro. In fact, I was in charge of the Major Crimes Unit and homicide until I retired."

"Yeah, I guess I heard about you recently. Small town and all. You were dating that young lady lawyer, and that whole gunfight business last year on the town square. So…" Canaday leaned in and spoke more quietly. "You care to tell me anything you think I should know?"

Ashe leaned forward as well. "Sure," he answered quietly back. "Normally the pathologist will determine the exact cause of death, once *you* determine it's suspicious, or like this one, obviously unnatural. But to aid the investigation while we're waiting on transport, allow me to look at him a little more."

Canaday nodded. "Of course. It'll be about forty-five minutes I think, before we're ready to move him."

Ashe nodded and returned his attention to the exam table. The body was of a Caucasian man approximately six foot and looked to weigh about 200 pounds. Being in the water so long, his skin was mostly ashen but bright red in places. All across the skin was the typical blueish spider-webbed mottling of the skin, and in places, it was pale green-white and had separated from the tissue below.

In another few days in the lake, large sections of his flesh would have floated off.

Ashe put on nitrile gloves and reached across the body to take a pen out of Canaday's shirt pocket, to point as he spoke.

"As you've noted, death was by multiple gunshot wounds. Two shots into the body from the rear and one to the head, also from the rear. He was standing, or sitting upright, by the approximate angle of entry."

Ashe stuck the pen into the rear of the head wound to illustrate the angle as he talked.

"The shooter had a small superior elevation evidenced by the slight ten-to-fifteen-degree downward angle of the entry wounds. There are two entry wounds close together in the mid dorsal, ah…the *center* of his back. The tight grouping of the shots, large exit wounds, and missing tissue and organs, mean likely a high caliber rifle."

"Not possibly a shotgun?" Canaday asked. He dabbed some medicated menthol gel into his nostrils.

Ashe shook his head patiently. *Easy. This guy is new.*

"Actually as coroner, you should just be focused on whether this is a natural, accidental, or unnatural death. The pathologist in Metro will be better able to examine him, and the crime laboratory will look at things like blood, DNA, and the tiny algae *on* and embedded *in* his body and help with a timeline."

"No shotgun?"

"No. Rifled slugs would be required to get a group like that from a shotgun and the entry holes are too small. See, since there's no shot pattern on his back, these are not from a shotshell. The extreme damage to the body is too great for a handgun, even a magnum."

Ashe removed the pen from the body's head wound and stuck it back in Canaday's pocket, who visibly cringed and walked over to a trash can. Holding the pen with the tips of his fingers, he dropped it in.

Ashe carefully moved the body's clothing to search for further wounds. There didn't seem to be any more he could find.

"It could be a boating accident, maybe?" Canaday said, reading off his tablet. "Propellers from a boat might cause similar tissue damage."

Sheriff Jacobs heard him and covered his phone with a hand again. "Oh...for the love of..." Then he shot Ashe a look and rolled his eyes. "Shit, Canaday!" Jacobs said. "I've not met too many people who go boating on Minor Hills Lake in the heat of summer wearing a black suit."

Ashe smiled to himself. "No, Mr. Canaday, absent any evidence to the contrary this is a high caliber rifle, and fired from some distance."

"Distance?"

"No burn marks we can see with the naked eye on the clothing; make sure to ask the pathologist and the lab to look microscopically for that. I see fairly clean-cut holes in the rear of his head, suit jacket, and shirt. So, absent any conflicting info from the lab, this was *not* a close-in shooting," Ashe said.

"I see. I, ah, am supposed to identify the body if possible," Canaday said, reading his checklist off his tablet.

Ashe frowned. "I don't see anything, no identification, no business cards, nothing. Where are his personal possessions?"

"On the table there, but nothing that will immediately ID him."

"DNA will take a couple of days, but we need to know now. You'll have to get fingerprints."

Canaday recoiled at that. "Prints? My...my God, the skin on his hands is rotting. It's all but falling off."

"Yeah, well, you can't get dental records, can you?" Ashe said, pointing at the blown-out cavity that once was a face. Then, seeing the look of shock on Canaday's face, he could tell his grim cop humor hadn't landed.

"Sorry. You ever handled a drowning vic or waterborne corpse before?"

"No. As an LPN, I saw my share of people who were dying, but...well this is my first time as coroner."

"Okay, well in the old days, we would either cut the fingers off one at a time, print them, and then bag them in order. Or...use a scalpel and cut the skin around the circumference of a finger at the base, below the main knuckle. Then, very carefully, maintaining the shape of the finger, slide the skin off to..."

Canaday was looking wide-eyed, so Ashe shrugged.

"You know what, it's all digital these days, they can get good enough high-resolution photos to print. I've even seen it done by a smartphone. Why don't you let the pathologist get the prints for you?"

"Yes. That would be best I think," Canaday said, grabbing a paper towel to wipe his forehead.

Ashe started to say something else cute but looked at Canaday and took a little pity on him.

"Hey, Canaday. Body is really starting to smell, huh? You know, that menthol stuff you're putting in your nose will just open up your sinuses more. It actually doesn't help much, I've found."

"But, my God the stench. It's getting worse," Canaday said.

"He's drying out a little. Put on some strong coffee."

"Really? I don't think I want any..."

"It's not for drinking. Make it strong and put it in a pan. Fry the grounds, too."

"Really? That works?"

"Uh-huh, sometimes," Ashe said, and returned to his exam as the funeral home guy went to make the coffee for them.

Ashe continued. "This head wound, obviously also immediately fatal, has roughly the same size entry wound. Also clean, sharp with no powder burning, at least as much as we can tell, given this dude's been in the lake so long. Probably the same gun. High power, took off the entire front of his face as it exited."

"How long do you think he was in the lake?" Canaday asked. "Sorry, I know I'm supposed to be telling you all this."

"That's okay. It's hard to tell just us looking here, but based on my experience, I'd say better part of a week. The lack of bloodstains, for instance. A week in the water and bright early summer sun really changes things. Take these wounds for instance, they would produce a torrent of blood, but even his shirt doesn't seem to have any."

"That's actually kind of, well, *morbidly* fascinating," Canaday said.

"Also, I'm guessing this all happened really fast, not like with a bolt gun but a semi-auto. All these entry wounds are all from about the same angle. He didn't have time to react, or the wounds would be from different angles as he twisted or fell."

Canaday took the pot of coffee from the funeral rep and set it on the table. "I see. I hadn't thought of that."

"*Bang-bang* half second maybe; then *bang*, assuming the headshot was last. Then, *spaloosh*! Into the water. If he'd fallen on dry land, there would have been serious blood on his clothes. Make sure the lab checks for deep, penetrating blood in the fibers."

"Yes, I'm sure they do that. I've collected his personal possessions there on the desk. I will sign for the body from the sheriff and escort it to Metro for the autopsy. Then they sign for it from me, maintaining chain of custody," Canaday said, reading from his tablet.

Ashe walked over to the desk and went through what possessions were there. Water-logged corpses often lost wallets, phones, jewelry, and the assorted stuff people carried in their pockets, either through the motion of the water, or as the body itself decayed and clothing came apart.

In a zippered, clear plastic bag was only a completely bleached and water-damaged photograph, a generic masonic ring—no inscription on the inside—and a small bleached-out rectangular lapel pin. A closer inspection of the pin revealed tiny markings where once enameled color had been. It was a flag but not a U.S. flag. What flag it was, Ashe couldn't tell.

Ashe walked back and looked at the dead man's head again. There was something, though. Something familiar.

Dad.

He drew in a quick breath. Canaday began talking into his tablet, describing the wounds, but Ashe didn't pay attention. He was thinking how he had retired from Metro Police and returned to his home town of Seacord to care for his elderly father while he was in hospice. It wasn't a long wait; barely enough time to get the legalities done with a young local attorney he'd wound up dating.

He jumped as he felt a sudden hand on his shoulder. The funeral home rep had walked up behind him.

"This must look so sadly familiar to you. I'm so sorry, but don't hold it against your father. His was an act of selflessness and courage. He did not want you to have to give up your life to care for him, and he did not want to languish…"

"Thank you, but not now. Please," Ashe interrupted. "Dad just killed himself there at the end. Nothing more."

But the face of this body from the lake, or rather the absence of a face or anything below the eyes, did bring his father's suicide to mind. Ashe had been the one to discover what his father had done, and that memory ran a fresh chill down his back. He tried to shake those thoughts off. They weren't helpful and Sheriff Jacobs needed him to be focused.

There was one key difference, though. His father, knowing he was terminal, decided to end his life. But, for whoever this man was, that decision had been made for him. Three rifle shots, precision grouping, and all quickly on target.

Three kill shots before the body could even flinch or fall over. Professional. Trouble. This guy was somebody very important to someone.

That thought struck a chord with him. *Someone important…or perhaps, someone* with *someone important.*

Ashe looked differently at the body; this time not for wounds. He began to look around the suit coat collar where the lapel pin must have been. Beneath it on the body's shirt was the length of broken clear plastic coiled wire they'd noted before. It ran down toward his beltline and, being clear, had at first blended with rotting clothes and loosening flesh.

It might have just been for a cell phone; but looking at it closely, he realized he'd worn this type of wire before. It was a wire from a two-way radio to an earpiece. Ashe looked and found a separate but flat wire that ran down the body's coat sleeve to a microphone near the cuff. It was loose and no longer attached to anything, but it was there.

Ashe followed the clear wire but found no earpiece; it had likely been blown off when the shot impacted and destroyed the man's skull. Looking lower on what was left of his belt, he found no radio. But beneath his rotting clothes and loose flesh barely clinging to bone, on what was left of a leather belt, sat a piece of what might have been a black leather pistol holster.

Empty. No wonder Canaday had missed it.

"Sheriff!" Ashe shouted. Jacobs was still on his cell but turned and looked at Ashe.

Ashe crossed to the other side of the exam table, quickly pushing past Canaday. Using his gloved hands, he lifted away more of the disintegrating clothing. Barely clinging to the inside of his decomposing pants belt was a leather clip-on pouch for a pistol magazine.

In the pouch was a loaded fifteen round 9mm Glock mag.

Canaday had missed this when looking for identification in the clothes.

"Sheriff!" Ashe shouted again. Jacobs hung up his phone and walked over to the table.

"We maybe need to get this out on the net, fast. This guy might have been a cop, or a protective service agent!"

Ashe showed him the earpiece and mic wire then the holster and magazine.

"Hey, Canaday, we need to bag this stuff, especially that magazine and cartridges. We may get fingerprints off them!" Jacobs said. "Damn, I guess I assumed it was a cell phone ear thing!"

Canaday used his tablet to photograph the gun magazine and pouch.

"Ashe, if this guy's some kind of fed or state investigator, we'd have heard about it when he went missing," Jacobs said. "The lake would've been buzzing with people searching."

"Mostly those guys don't have this nice of a suit, much less use earpieces with sleeve mics. This looks more like protective services to me, Sheriff."

Jacobs nodded. "Then even more what I said. They'd be all over, swarming into the office, helicopters searching. We've heard *nada*."

"Possibly a private contractor? I'm guessing, of course."

"Yeah, good guess. Damn, though. Hard way to die."

Ashe nodded. "I want to go to the crime scene."

"Sure, but the state lab team is all over out there. I called the attorney general's office to have a state police CIB investigator handle this. I only asked you here as a favor to me, knowing Canaday's a rookie."

"I understand, but hey…you've got my curiosity up now," Ashe said.

Jacobs looked at his feet. "I'm sorry, buddy. I didn't know if after last year, with what happened to you and all, if you'd even want to jump back into a homicide."

"I appreciate that, Larry."

"If what we think is so, that he's some kind of bodyguard, then this is not all of it, is it?"

"No. It won't be all, Sheriff. If he was a bodyguard, who was he protecting?"

CHAPTER 2

◆

Stephanie Collins sat at her desk in the storefront office of Lifenablers, a nonprofit organization which everyone mispronounced, including the state auditor sitting across her desk from her. Twice so far.

The office was in an older strip mall, and she'd been told by the man who'd given her the office keys that it had originally been built assuming the population and traffic was shifting. The bet had been things would be moving from the touristy, historic town of Seacord in Hurrt County toward the direction of the artsy, eclectic, cozy town of Harmony, in Carson County. It hadn't and it wasn't, she was sure, to some real estate speculator's chagrin. It likely never would.

The small row of storefronts on State Route 593 had been sold a couple of times and was in a perpetual state of "make us an offer." It consisted of the Lifenablers office, a vape shop, a check cashing and car title loan place, three empty storefronts, and a fairly decent Korean restaurant.

"Miss Collins, I'm sorry, I know I've asked this before, but…you go by *Stevie*, don't you?"

"Yes, since I was a little girl. I think Daddy wanted a boy," she said, and tried a disarming smile, but it wasn't working on the auditor.

"Oh, good, I guess. Anyway, *Stevie*, um, Life-And-Ablers, LLC seems to be funded almost wholly by this supporting charitable foundation, Able Keys, that are themselves resourced by trust funds. They don't seem to even try to raise a lot of money publicly."

Stevie smiled her best, albeit fake, smile. "It's just Life Enablers, Mrs. Garrett, but all one word. It's a play on enabling the lives of the so many disadvantaged, and in some cases physically challenged, children."

"I see."

"I think they just skipped an 'e' to save on the sign maybe."

Mrs. Garrett looked at Stevie politely as she spoke, but must not have gotten her little joke. She looked down and made a note on her pad.

Stevie held her smile a beat longer before giving up. Mentally she estimated the state auditor was probably sixty-ish, heavy in the way her mother would have called "sturdy," and by the looks of her, had simply not aged well. Her gray hair was up and tinted silver-white. She wore a heavy-for-the-weather knee-length dress, and to Stevie, her jewelry looked old. Her over-applied perfume was drugstore caliber, and also old.

Mrs. Garrett was fanning herself with a file folder in a way Stevie assumed she meant to be obvious about it. But the air-conditioning had never worked very well if it got over eighty outside, and it had to be at least ninety-five. Stevie stood and walked around to stretch some while Mrs. Garrett looked through the files, fanned herself vigorously, and made notes.

The floors were concrete with dull, thin carpet tiles, so walking around in the office required cushioned running shoes or her back would be hurting by five p.m. Of course, *today*, she'd worn four-inch heels.

The big front window, where the other volunteer normally sat, had yellow stains in the corners and a small pile of fly and bug carcasses on the sill near the floor. The glass and aluminum front door hadn't closed right without significant pushing and tugging in the six months she'd been here. Despite using odor spray and even plug-in deodorizers, a strange sour and moldy smell lingered just below awareness. If you thought about it, *there it was*.

After stretching and circling the front of the office for a few minutes, Stevie returned to her chair.

"So, Mrs. Garrett, you received our self-inspection, we sent the required supporting documentation and the affidavits of the LLC owners, is there anything else here I can show you?"

Mrs. Garrett set down her pen and huffed a bit, looking up at the air vent in the room then back at Stevie. "Well, you know my boss and I were talking. I mean, all that sad stuff that happened last year in Hurrt County—Seacord, you know. I mean, that all was just terrible."

"Yes. It was."

"And poor you! You were right in the middle of it all. I mean, up on the town square, your boyfriend getting shot and all!"

Stevie looked down at her desk, counted to five, then back up. "Technically he wasn't my boyfriend then, but yes, it was *dramatic* to say the least."

"Well, we were talking, like I said, and we remembered you were part of that land deal that was going on, people losing their homes, I heard. We were logically concerned, since you were in the thick of all that."

Stevie dropped her pretend smile. *Is she trying to be a bitch, or does it just come naturally?*

"Ma'am, I was an alcoholic, *am* an alcoholic, but I'm doing well in recovery, I think. Those responsible took advantage of me back then. The state board suspended my law license, but even *they* said I was not culpable. And, just to be accurate, nobody *lost* their homes or land. They all sold voluntarily, and were all paid. Anyway, I'm trying to do good for the community *today* by administering this very important charity."

"Oh, well." Mrs. Garrett increased her fanning. She was obviously hot; Stevie was hot. The air-conditioning sucked, and Stevie decided she'd worn the wrong bra to be dealing with all this.

"Tell me, Miss Stevie, do you have *anything* to drink here in the office?" Garrett asked.

"I…beg your pardon!"

Garrett seemed to realize her poor choice of words. "Oh no! I meant like a bottle of water or tea or something. It's so hot!"

"Ah, I might have a diet soda in the little fridge there," Stevie said.

Garrett shook her head. "No, I never drink them. They're habit form…no, thank you."

"Can we get back to our audit now?" Stevie said, a tad more curtly than she'd intended.

Mrs. Garrett nodded. After a minute or two of looking at her papers, she said, "So, you don't handle the money, then? I mean, you don't control the *money* that comes in and out by yourself, right?"

Oh, I see. So you are *a bitch.*

Stevie counted to herself again. "It's all online, there is no cash, and no. I don't *handle* the charity's money."

"I don't mean to suggest anything," Garrett said, but Stevie was unconvinced. She'd heard this crap before.

"I execute the charity's directives only by notifying the various facility and resource managers that their funds are available in previously set-up bank accounts. I don't determine who gets what, or how much. I ensure the accounts are resourced, then I track expenditures to ensure our monies are spent appropriately, and within the scope of our various written agreements."

"Okay, good," Garrett said without looking at Stevie. Then after completing a note, she sat back and lifted her nose a little.

"Well I…I mean, *we* at the auditors' office thought given how you were in court last year over a big land swindle, it was kind of unusual for you to be running this charity, that's all."

"Is that one of the audit's compliance indicators? I must have missed that one! I just explained how I couldn't rearrange money, even if I wanted to, Mrs. Garrett. I'm a volunteer, and given I have nine years of family and business law experience, they are lucky to have me!"

Stevie pushed back her chair and got up and walked back to the front of the office to stand in front of the big tinted glass window that looked out over the parking lot. She made sure her heels spoke loudly on the hard floor as she walked. Behind her, she could hear Mrs. Garrett collecting her things.

In the window's reflection, Stevie looked at herself. She'd dressed to go out that evening with her fiancé without having to go home first. She reached down and tugged at her short black faux-leather skirt, and even in the window, she could see her lacy black bra she'd worn beneath a white cotton blouse. She'd worn it that way on purpose; so he'd look at her. When he arrived this afternoon, she'd undo a button. She wanted him to look.

He hasn't been looking as much, then she shook off that thought.

But since she'd sweated a good bit this afternoon from the

sweltering combination of the heat *and* this audit, her shirt was wet in places, clingy and all but transparent.

Jesus, no wonder Mrs. Garrett's been stink-eyeing me. This is a little too *steamy.* She tried to fan at her shirt and thought about wet paper towels.

Damn, I should've worn something else today and just brought this to change into. But how could I know old Miz Judgy Battleaxe would show up the day the A/C *took a dump.*

Looking deeper into the reflection, she could see Mrs. Garrett shaking her head and mouthing words behind her back. The woman huffed and made small exertion noises as she hoisted up her stuff and walked with her arms full of papers and folders, while packing a big black briefcase and her own giant purse to the front door. Stevie sighed to herself, watching her.

This Garrett is a piece of work.

She must have been lugging fifty pounds of crap she didn't need or use. Why? In the two hours she'd been in Stevie's office, she hadn't even touched the big padded briefcase stuffed with papers. *So silly!*

Then she took a second look at the dead fly cemetery and the mis-fitting door. It was an old crummy office in an old crummy building.

Is this it for me? Have I screwed up my life so bad, this is the best I'll ever have?

Stevie remembered her law office with the expensive furniture and her receptionist who called her "ma'am." She looked at herself again. She wouldn't be this young or in this shape forever.

Has he stopped wanting to look at me? Then another thought came to her. *In a few years, will I be a Mrs. Garrett?*

At the door, Mrs. Garrett paused and turned to Stevie, who decided not to face her. There was a full five-second pause where Garrett was apparently working herself up to say something.

"I'm...glad you're sober now. My husband is too, almost thirty years. Good for you, and good for these children you're helping. They need you straight. I didn't mean to be rude; I just have to do my job."

Stevie let out a breath and opened the door for her. "I know. So do I."

CHAPTER 3

Ashe rode with Sheriff Jacobs out to the lakeshore where the body had been discovered. On the way, Jacobs used his phone and gave orders to someone on how to handle the dead man's pistol magazine.

"Call me when you know something on those prints," Jacobs said over the phone.

Ashe was about to ask him about the call when they pulled off a gravel road and headed across a field to where a state van and a collection of official vehicles were parked.

There were a couple of unmarked cars, the forensic team's van, a state police trooper marked Explorer, and a Dodge pickup with Hurrt County Sheriff markings.

There wasn't much of a crowd of onlookers, just a few curious people who looked to be out on a walk. This wasn't part of the park, and the road they were on had only recently been built.

Jacobs checked out on the radio then pitched the mic up onto the dash.

First-term sheriff, his first cop job, and he's learned that move already.

Before walking over, Jacobs wanted a cigarette, so they leaned against the hood of the cruiser as the State Police Mobile Crime Scene Unit technicians did their work just a few yards away.

As Jacobs smoked, Ashe watched the techs operate in slow, deliberate moves behind what must have been a whole roll of yellow crime scene tape. They had used everything they could to create a boundary; trees, a power line pole, and their own portable light stands. It wouldn't be a simple job to work a crime scene in the sand and in the water.

Jacobs lit a second cigarette off his first then shot Ashe a quick look. "Sorry, but they won't let me smoke once we go over the line," he said. Ashe nodded and knew Jacobs wasn't really apologizing.

He recalled how they'd met, less than a year ago over breakfast at Roger's Café. Larry Jacobs asked him to help with a two-year-old missing person and probable murder case that had ties to Metro, where at the time, Ashe was head of the Major Crimes Unit. At first, Ashe wasn't sure about getting involved after retiring, but there was something about Jacobs; something that Ashe picked up on quickly.

You trusted him.

He'd come to know Jacobs well after spending damn near every hour of two months with him last fall. Behind the spiderweb of wrinkles around Jacobs' eyes was a sharp, honest mind.

"*You* about ready, there?" Jacobs asked as he stubbed out his smoke, although it had been he who slowed them down.

Damn retired first sergeants.

"Of course, sorry for holding *you* back, there, boss-man!" Ashe said, grinning.

They ducked under the crime scene tape and walked closer to the water's edge. Scuba divers were coming up from the water and onto a launch just off shore. Looking at the markers, Ashe saw a few footprints in the mud that'd been made by sneakers, and likely made by those who'd found the body. They were too fresh to have been there more than a day.

The body had been discovered half in and half out of the lake, on a very small sandy stretch mostly hidden between tree roots jutting out from the bank. To even see the body, a person would have to climb down the steep bank through some trees and tall grass, climb over a couple of recliner-sized boulders, then finally hop off them to the edge of the water.

Ashe looked behind him. Where Jacobs had parked the cruiser was forty yards away and on a grassy area. The gravel road that led to a public area about a half mile farther, curved away from this spot about fifteen to twenty more yards distant. From where he stood, Ashe estimated they were just over sixty yards from the road. From where the body had been, would be nearer seventy.

"So, Sheriff, how did anyone even find this body? I mean, who would be around here? Bank fishers?"

Jacobs looked around to where Ashe was looking then said, "Couple of early morning boaters pulled into this little cove. Spotted it from the water."

"Okay. That makes sense. They handy to talk to?"

"Well, the state police investigator wants to interview them here in a bit. It's a guy and his girlfriend. They're young, kind of shook up."

Ashe nodded and looked around at the forensics technicians again. They mostly appeared to be rechecking their checklists and conferring with one another. Ashe checked his watch; they'd been at the scene at least several hours.

There were about a dozen small white tentlike markers on the ground to indicate where evidence or something of interest had been found. Ashe frowned. Having seen maybe a hundred homicide crime scenes over the years, there just weren't as many markers as he'd hoped. That could only mean what he'd feared was correct. At this location, there would not be much evidence to find.

Jacobs was watching Ashe carefully. "You're looking at them evidence markers," he said. "I know. Not much to see."

"Well, the state team is good at their jobs and they're not leaving just yet. I've seen tougher nuts to crack. When you hit the wall at a difficult homicide scene, you don't rush. You slow down, take a break, discuss what you've found, vice what you *should have* found, then go at it again."

But at an outdoor scene like this, we truly only get one shot at it. So take your time, guys, as long as the weather allows.

Then Ashe looked at a weather app on his phone. It was going to be hot and clear for another couple of days. "At least it's not going to rain soon."

Jacobs's cell phone rang, so he answered it and walked a few steps away to talk. Ashe looked at a couple of the evidence markers and saw nothing promising. No bloody business card of an assassin, no beer bottle covered in prints. So instead of looking for himself, he tried to see what the techs were focused on.

Amidst the small group of technicians, most wearing navy nylon windbreakers with "State Police" imprinted in bold yellow across the back, he saw a familiar face that brought a smile.

Special Agent Rachel Hume was on the job. She spotted Ashe and Jacobs and walked over.

"In a mediocre novel, there'd be a cigarette butt with lipstick on it, and incriminating DNA," Ashe said.

"Ha! Still looking for that. How are you, Ashe?" They shook hands; hers were small and strong and calloused.

"Nice grip," he said.

"Farm girl. Horses," she said and squeezed his hand harder.

She was short, fit-looking, and in her mid to late forties. He recalled she'd been a state trooper before college and then made it to the criminal investigation bureau of the state police. Ashe had worked with her on a homicide recently, and despite their friendliness, they were not always on the same channel.

He'd been a lot like her when he worked as head of the MCU in Metro. Serious, detail oriented, and focused. But going by the book occasionally raised barriers and limited your options. His goal back then was also hers now: a clean, successful prosecution. And as odd as it seemed, that was sometimes contrary to getting at the whole truth.

I'm retired and my only book is my own. That irritates Rachel. I'll try to behave more around her. She's one of the good ones.

Jacobs got off the phone and came over to say hello to Rachel.

"Sheriff, I think we're looking for a cigarette with lipstick on it. Then we'll know what's what," she said, and winked at Ashe.

"Huh?" Jacobs said.

"Never mind, Sheriff," Ashe said. "Rachel, have you found anything important here?"

"Lots of stuff. Mostly trash from hikers, kids parking, and the like. We'll have to print it all, of course, but it's a big waste of time."

"Plus, it didn't happen here. My guess? There'll be nothing more to find here we don't already have," Ashe said. "And surely nothing to indicate our man in the black suit died right here, because he didn't."

"Which means we have another crime scene somewhere," Jacobs said. "Just like you said, Ashe."

"Yes, there'll be another site that no one's found or reported yet," Rachel said. "We have to find it."

Jacobs shook his head. "Damn."

"Exactly, Sheriff. This was a hit. A murder of a man who looks to me to be some kind a bodyguard," she said. "We have to be fast. I need to be out here about another half hour, then I want to interview the boaters who found the body."

"That was the call I just took. My deputy, Ed Bell, has them at the sheriff's office and separated for now. The girl's parents are with her."

"Okay, then I'll break off soon and head that way. See you there?"

"Sure," Ashe said, but that seemed to catch her off guard. She'd meant Sheriff Jacobs.

She looked at Ashe with her bright but steely blue eyes. *"You're not looking into this, are you?"*

"I'm...just curious. The sheriff asked me to look over the shoulder of our rookie coroner."

"I met him," she said, and huffed a little.

"We have a man in an expensive-label suit with an earpiece and a loaded G19 magazine."

"What?" she said and took out her pad. "When did Canaday find this?"

"Ashe found it," Jacobs said. "See why I let him hang around?"

"We have it bagged and off with the body to Metro. They'll print the mag and the ammo as they post the body," Ashe said. "Your divers haven't found a pistol or a radio, have they?"

Jacobs interrupted before Rachel could answer. "Actually I had one of the deputies grab a couple of prints from the outside of the mag. He should have uploaded them to the system by now."

Rachel made a note on her pad then shouted over to one of the senior technicians. "Jim, we're looking for a handheld radio and a Glock pistol!"

Jim waved back as one of the dive team on shore shook his head and made a slicing motion in from of his chin to indicate they hadn't found anything like that.

"Water is shallow and pretty clear today. They would've found them," Jacobs said.

"They'll keep trying," Rachel said and reached for her cell phone.

Ashe lowered his voice. "Pretty cool, Sheriff, getting the prints uploaded. Your guys are stepping up."

Jacobs smiled. "Well, since you and I jailed our last detective, everybody's bucking for the job."

Rachel hung up her phone and came back over. "Got the prints. Didn't take but a second, we already had him in the state system. We were right, this guy had to be working."

"Oh?" Ashe said.

"Yes. He's a Charles Carter. Retired Deputy U.S. Marshal."

"Chuck Carter? Well, shit!" Ashe turned and walked off in a long circle.

"You know him?" Jacobs asked Ashe.

"Seriously?" Rachel added.

Ashe took a long breath and blew it out. Then kicked a rock hard across the grass.

"Yep. Pat Keagan and I worked with him several times up in Metro," he said.

"Our Pat Keagan? Lieutenant Keagan from Metro? Your old partner?" Jacobs asked.

"Oh boy," Rachel said under her breath. Then to Ashe, said, "This is a state investigation, Ashe. I have lead. Sorry, Sheriff, but the DA's office has already taken jurisdiction."

"I am still the senior..." Jacobs started, but Rachel interrupted him to point at Ashe.

"Ashe, *anything* you know you have to bring straight to me. I prefer you stay at home and do...whatever the hell you've been doing all winter and spring."

Jacobs scoffed and said, "Or report to me. Ashe is my new detective, Rachel. He'll be working this *with you.* And dammit, as sheriff I have that authority!"

Ashe didn't say anything while they'd argued, especially considering Jacobs had just lied to a state criminal investigator. *Detective? Since when?*

The sheriff likely just wants to know what all is going on in his county. He has to start running for reelection in another year or so.

Rachel sighed and didn't take her eyes off Ashe. "Walk with me, Ashe."

Jacobs smiled and started back to his cruiser, shaking out another cigarette as he went. Ashe and Rachel walked over to the shoreline to where no one was working.

As they walked, Ashe said, "I was thinking, we should check the currents. Talk to charter boat skippers and the like. We need to backtrack as best we can where a body in this water would drift *from*. That's where we'll find out what happened to Chuck."

She took his arm by the elbow and they stopped. "*Are* you the new Hurrt County detective?" she said.

Ashe paused then said, "You heard him." He tried not to look her in the face, but *he* knew that *she* knew. So the less said, the better.

She must have decided not to pick at it. The high sheriff can make whomever he wants a detective.

"How well did you and Pat know Carter?"

"Reasonably well. I mean, I never met his family, but he worked protective assignments on federal judges and witnesses and the like. We coordinated operations, assisted with people when we could. Intelligence sharing, logistical support, you know. He got to know us and trusted us, even with confidential jobs."

"Okay."

"Pat will be pissed. I think he and Chuck were closer."

Rachel sighed. "There's another complication. Pat and I...have been dating, you probably knew."

"What? You're kidding me?" Ashe said with a big smile. "Say it ain't so!"

She couldn't stop a small smile herself. "You've always known."

"I knew before either of you did. You know Pat is my brother 'in-law' and I'm happy for him and you, too."

"Listen, I have to go by state procedure here. If this develops like it might, I cannot have you going off on your own like you did with...oh, what's her name last year."

"You know her name. Stevie. And I've only seen her briefly since then. She's dating a lawyer and works out of town."

"But you understand, Ashe, this is a retired marshal so it deals them in. Plus, if he was killed while working, this could be a very complex case. Especially as we really have no idea what the fuck is going on!"

"Rachel, if he was protecting someone, then *who*? Where is...or hell, *are* they? Is there another body or bodies floating around?"

"I know, I know," she said, looking out at the lake.

"He had an earpiece and a hand mic to a radio. Who was he in contact with? The sheriff put this out hours ago, but so far nobody is claiming Chuck as theirs."

"Right. I need to contact the AG's office and my SAC. We have a name and indirect evidence he was on a job. Maybe private, but somebody has to know."

"I'll get with the lake patrol and work the currents angle. Try to backtrack him."

"Ashe, look…I, we, I mean…"

"Rachel, I gotcha. I'll behave. It likely won't help you, but you should go interview the kids who found him."

"Okay, *detective*." She cocked an eyebrow as she said that. "I guess I should call Pat as well."

"Better you than me."

She took his elbow again. "Meet me at the S.O. in the morning. Call me or text me anytime with anything you find out. We coordinate every morning and every evening, got it?"

"Sure," Ashe said and smiled.

She shook her head and went toward her car while Ashe joined Jacobs, who was finishing up his smoke.

"You get everything worked out?" Jacobs asked, gesturing toward Rachel.

"Uh, yeah and I want a pay raise."

"Huh! You aren't being paid now."

"Better double it, then."

They got in the car and headed back toward the sheriff's office.

"Ashe, is it petty or lazy of me to wish wherever this guy bought it, it's in another county?"

Ashe shook his head. "No, not at all. But you're not that damn lucky."

CHAPTER 4

Stevie arrived at the apartment she shared with her fiancé, Tom Fischer. It was a newly built complex designed to be upscale, and located along the river that ran through the center of Harmony township.

Tom hadn't met her at her office as planned.

I sweated my ass off and wore these heels and this bra for nothing?

She dropped her laptop bag and kicked out of her heels then walked to the bedroom stripping as she went. Her shirt she'd sweated through was still damp in spots, so she dropped it to the floor and turned on the shower. As she finished, she heard the front door slam.

This had better be good.

"Stevie? Jeez, I almost tripped over your heels at the front door," Tom said as he entered the bedroom.

She turned off the water, and as she toweled off, she could hear him fumbling around in the closet. She got dressed in shorts and a tank top and was about to walk past him to the living room when he caught her arm.

"Hey, I was trapped in a thing at work. Sorry, babe."

Tom was blonde with fashionably long hair on top he combed to one side, and shorter hair on the sides. He was a couple of years younger than her and about her height.

"I waited nearly an hour in that damn sweat box you rented for me! We were going out to that new fish place tonight!"

Tom shrugged and took off his tie without untying it and hung it in the closet beside other still-tied ties. "Couldn't be helped. I was online and my phone was out of reach." He paused with his tailored shirt half unbuttoned. "Oh, um…you want to go out now?"

"Nope!" she said. And went to find a glass of wine.

After a few minutes he came out in athletic shorts and a T-shirt and sat on the couch beside her, but she ignored him for a full minute more.

He sighed. "Okay. I apologize. I wanted to at least text you, but I left my phone over in the law library. I was the only rep on our side of the video call, and I couldn't just break and run get it. By the time I did call you at work, you didn't answer, so I came home."

"Whatever, Tom. Jeez, this is not the first time." Stevie picked up the remote and started flipping through channels on the TV with the sound off.

"I am building what I pray is a successful practice. Sure, it takes up a lot of my time, but it will someday all be worth it. You of all people should get that."

Stevie took a long sip of wine. "We were supposed to be planning a wedding. We were going to call my daughter in the city to tell her about it."

Tom paused. By the look on his face, she could tell he'd forgotten that part. "I know. We can still do that tomorrow. I hate it, but I need to do some research tonight and…"

"*Tonight?* Friday night? You have to do work?"

Tom pointed at her near-empty wineglass. "Given you…given, ah, things like they are with your…should you be…"

Stevie cut her eyes at him. *Get off that!*

He sat back and after another minute or two, gently took the remote from her hand like it was a bomb detonator, and turned the TV off. "So. Other than me *unavoidably* standing you up, how did it go today?"

She still stared at the blank TV. "The AC in the office is out. Gina didn't come in today; I know she just didn't want to be there for the audit, so I was alone. I wore one of my best outfits, *for you*, and while listening to Mrs. *Carrot*, or whatever her name was, I sweated five pounds off."

"But did it go okay?"

Stevie had a feeling of where he wanted to steer their conversation, but she wasn't off of being mad at him and *her* conversation yet.

"You know my black bra? The one you like that pushes the girls up and out?"

"Um. Sure, yeah."

"I wore that under my white silky blouse."

Tom looked back toward the bedroom. "Really? I bet it…"

"It's probably ruined."

"Oh, come on!"

"Mrs. *Ferret* probably thought I dressed like that all the time for work."

"Maybe…just maybe, you shouldn't have been so confrontational with her. She just wants to ensure the Foundation's money is well executed and all accounted…"

"Whoa, wait." Stevie set down her wineglass and turned to face him. "You talked with her?"

Tom got up and got himself a glass of wine. "Ms. *Garrett* notified the Foundation, one of the directors spoke with her. He called me."

"You?"

"I'm the legal counsel for both Lifenablers and the Able Keys Foundation that resources the whole deal. Look, the idea was that you could administer this charity, make enough friends, and do enough good deeds that I could petition the court to release you from your probation early. Maybe even help get your law license back."

Stevie sat back hard. "I was as nice and patient with that old battle axe as I could be!"

"You're not making any friends. Anyway, there were no errors in the accounting. Just one of your supported facilities is not expending their funds in a timely matter. You need to look into it."

"She asked about why I was even working there after *what all happened*, and my being *involved in people losing their homes*! None of her damn business. The bitch!"

"Well, the Foundation heard from her and *that* is why I couldn't meet you tonight. I was on line with the entire Foundation board, plus the director! Look, I stick my neck out for you, then I come home to your…little fit! And find out you're drinking!"

Stevie felt her mouth open but nothing came out. She stared at him, angry, but also shocked.

She saw that Tom seemed to realize he'd crossed a line. "I just...expected you to be more responsible...now."

"*Now?*"

"Never mind. Just...don't make things harder for me to..." He stopped and drank some of his wine.

"I interviewed for this job and got it on my own. Mrs. Garrett did not say a word to me about any execution errors and..." She paused. "Or *did I?* Exactly how am I making things harder for *you?*"

"Babe, just check what she said about HCCS not executing their funds for the past couple of weeks. Please. Other than her complaint about attitude, that's the only real issue. Then I can get the board back on our side."

She wrinkled her brow. She knew HCCS; Hurrt County Children's Sanctuary. It was in Seacord where she'd lived and practiced law, up to a few months ago.

"That's impossible. They burn, oh, four thousand a week or so there."

Tom nodded as he looked at his phone. "Look, I'm ordering dinner, can you just fix it, please? We'll talk about the other thing in the morning."

"I'm not done with this, Tom. You didn't answer my question!"

He picked up his wine and went to the spare bedroom they'd turned into a home office.

Stevie stared after him. *The other thing? Our wedding? You ass.*

She got up and poured herself more wine then held her glass up as if mock-toasting his closed office door. Taking a big sip, she had a thought.

HCCS is usually punctual. Boringly so. What was their administrator's name? Young girl.

The thought bothered her. *Carol something-or-other.*

Then she remembered Mrs. Garrett's comment. *I'm glad you're sober now. Good for you and good for these children you're helping. They need you straight.*

She dumped out her wine in the sink and grabbed her phone to look up Carol's number and texted her.

Carol, call me as soon as you get this - Stevie.

Then she got dressed in jeans and a sleeveless top, grabbed her keys and purse, and headed for the door.

"I'm going out!" she shouted at the closed office door.

"What?" Tom shouted back.

She ignored him and let the front door slam behind her.

· · · ·

It was a thirty-minute drive along the lakeshore road from Harmony to Seacord. She had a decent cell signal the whole way, unlike taking the highway past her office. She knew that Carol most likely wouldn't still be at work, but she wanted out of the apartment after her tiff with Tom and…well, *he had* said for her to fix it.

Carol hadn't returned her text, which was strange because she always had in the past, so when Stevie got to Hurrt County, she called her.

No answer, right to voicemail. Stevie frowned. Carol was young, in her early twenties, and single. Like everybody else her age, Stevie knew she'd have her phone in her hand. She *had* to have seen the text and the call. She might be on a date, Stevie figured; so she could be ignoring her text.

Stevie drove her six-year-old BMW with her left hand and texted Carol again with her right; being sure to look at the road on the curves. It was still daylight out but the sun had just gone down.

C, 5 min please. Text or call. S

An oncoming car horn sounded; she was half in the wrong lane, so she jerked her car back.

"Dammit!" she shouted to herself as she swerved then checked her phone. It showed the text was not delivered, so she dropped the phone into a cup holder on her console and looked up her name and number on her car's dashboard screen, and pressed the call button.

She heard over the car's speakers Carol's phone ring once, then it went straight to voicemail as before. So she pulled up Carol on the screen again, and this time called the HCCS business number listed beside her name.

It rang and rang, but then it was answered.

"Hello?" said a young girl's voice Stevie didn't recognize.

Stevie said, "Hi, I'm trying to find Carol Buckram, do you know where she is? Is she by chance still there?"

"No. Who is this?"

"I'm Stephanie Collins, I work for the foundation that funds the sanctuary there. Who have I got?"

"Brianna."

"Hi, Brianna. Do you know how I can get a hold of Carol? I need to talk with her tonight or in the morning. It's real important."

"Oh." There was a lengthy pause. "Ma'am, she hasn't been here in a long time; I don't know where she went."

Stevie noticed there was worry in Brianna's voice by the way she'd said, *in a long time.*

Wait, I didn't know Carol had resigned. Did she? Who took her place?

"Did she quit there? Who's in charge then, honey? You...do you *work* there at the HCCS?"

"Um...no. I don't think she quit. I was a resident here but, now I'm more of a *volunteer*, I guess."

Uh-oh. Something is wrong. Stevie sped up a little. There were maybe ten to twelve disabled or developmentally challenged girls there.

"Okay, honey, where is the night shift lead person?"

"I don't know. They quit when they didn't get paid. There's one woman who comes here sometimes, and was supposed to be back this afternoon, but she didn't show up."

What?

"Brianna, listen. My name's Stephanie, but everybody calls me Stevie. I'll be there in ten minutes." Then she punched it.

Stevie pulled up in eight minutes at the Hurrt County Children's Sanctuary that was in an old house built in a long-ago time. It was big and two-storied with a wide wraparound porch and red painted wooden shutters. What had likely once been a big side yard, had been flattened and graveled into a parking lot where a compact Nissan sat. There were no other cars there at this time of day.

In the center of the parking lot was a huge tree that had to be a hundred or more years old. It towered higher than the two-story house and its high long boughs spread so wide as to shade a good part of the parking lot and some of the front yard. Stevie guessed the trunk to be four feet around at its base, where a short brick ring encircled it to protect it from cars. When they'd made the HCCS and this lot twenty years or more ago, someone had probably insisted they keep the tree.

As she parked and got out of her car, she noticed there were leaves plastered all over the Nissan. The car hadn't been moved in quite a while it seemed.

A freshly stained wooden ramp led from the lot up to the front porch and there were handicap parking signs all along that side of the facility. Stevie parked away from them and walked up an old sidewalk to the front porch. The front stairs' original handrails had been replaced with sturdy metal ones, and wide, nonslip traction tape covered the stairs. The porch floor had been recently painted with enough sand in the mix to prevent slips.

Beside the front door was a sign that held the name of the place and an after-hours phone number. Below that was a plastic "No Trespassing- No Soliciting" sign.

Huh. The after-hours number is Carol's cell.

Stevie rang the bell and knocked, and after several minutes, she saw a nearby window curtain part maybe an inch then quickly close. A girl, or perhaps a young woman, opened the front door a few inches, but kept the storm door closed.

"Are you…her?" the girl asked. From what Stevie could see through the crack, the girl looked to be maybe seventeen or eighteen and wore a long dress. Her brownish-blonde hair hung long and straight and down the front of her dress. Her eyes had the look of a cornered dog and stared at Stevie.

"I'm Stevie, are you Brianna? I promise, sweetheart, I'm here to help."

Dead-eyed stare. Brianna seemed to ponder Stevie's statement, but didn't budge.

"Do you know where Carol is?"

Brianna moved her head back and forth slowly. "Are you with them?"

Them? Them who? "Who, Brianna?"

"Just Brie. The men who come here sometimes at night for the basement."

What the hell is this girl talking about?

"I have no idea what men you mean. Plumbers, you mean? Or workers of some kind?"

Brie stared at Stevie without answering for a few seconds more then threw open the big metal front door and unlocked the glass storm door to let her in.

Stevie stepped into a foyer with a high ceiling and polished wood floors. It was functioning as an outer lobby of sorts with a small table that held informational brochures.

As she stepped in and Brie closed the door behind her, Stevie saw that a room immediately to her right, probably originally a sitting room, was an office. There were file cabinets, a big copy machine, a table with wire baskets for documents and mail, and Carol's nameboard on a desk.

"Brie, what happened here, and when was Carol here last?"

Brie pulled at her own hair and began twisting it. Stevie could tell she didn't like her walking into Carol's office, and that's when she noticed Brie's arm.

Her left arm was disfigured, and at least half the size of her right one. It was functioning, Brie twisted at her hair with it, but it was shrunken and paler that her other.

Stevie smiled and tried not to look at it; she didn't want to make Brie self-conscious.

Brie shrugged and said, "Carol left one afternoon with some men, the men that use the basement at night sometimes. She said she'd be back to lock up the office, and for me to make sure the girls got their dinner."

Looking over Brie's shoulder back out into the front foyer, Stevie noticed several younger girls had begun to peek around the corner at her.

"How long ago? How far back was it she left with the men?"

"A week. Maybe week and a half by now."

"Oh my god!" Stevie said. "Is that her brown Nissan outside?"

Brie nodded. Stevie walked over and put her arms out to Brie, who recoiled at first then let Stevie give her a small hug. She guided her to a chair and pulled another one over to sit and face her.

"You can look at my arm if you've never seen one. It's okay."

"Oh, I'm sorry if I..."

"It's called Phocomelia."

Stevie changed the subject. "Brie, who are these men? Do you know any of them? How did Carol know them?"

Brie sat there for a minute then got up and started giving out instructions to the other girls who had been creeping up to get a look at Stevie. They all looked considerably younger than Brie and obviously knew who was in charge. They quickly began moving about, doing their chores, so Brie returned and closed the door so they could talk.

"I don't know their names, but it's five or six men, sometimes more, all of them old. They come every couple of weeks, usually after dinner, and Carol makes us all go upstairs and watch TV or play games while they go to the basement. Sometimes they invited her to come down too, like to a meeting or a club or something. But mostly she stayed here in her office to be sure we didn't try to look."

Stevie frowned. "How long has this been going on?"

"Since I was a little girl here. My mom and dad are dead, and because I need special medicine and my arm and all, I wasn't adopted."

Wow. Someone was using the HCCS for some kind of meeting, even back when I worked three blocks from here. "These men, they never…um, bothered anyone, did they? I mean, the residents here? Did they hurt anyone?"

Brie shrugged. "No. They only ever talked with Carol. And Miss Lynn when she was in charge before that."

"You say you think Carol left with these men? You mean voluntarily—on her own. They didn't force her, did they?"

"Oh, no. She left on her own with two of them. She was laughing and silly acting. They were dressed up nice. One was an older man, and another was not as old a guy. A little older than you, I guess."

Stevie was only in her late thirties, but decided to a teenager she'd be "old" too.

"And she never came back? Who's been taking care of this place?"

"I've been cooking mostly. A couple of the staff stayed even though the new work schedule wasn't up and they didn't get their checks. But, day before yesterday was the last time I saw anyone…"

Stevie sighed and shot up out of her chair to go to Carol's desk. It was locked, but after a couple of minutes, she found a screwdriver and pried it open.

In the top left drawer was the HCCS checkbook; one of the big notebook-sized types, so Stevie flipped through the pages. The last check was a week and two days ago, to a painter whose name she recognized from town.

Porch and ramp had been freshly painted or stained.

She looked for any signs of paychecks then realized it'd probably be digital through the bank. That's when Stevie noticed what wasn't there.

No computer. There were loose cables and a printer connection, though. Probably for a laptop, that was missing.

Brie had joined her at Carol's desk. Stevie checked her phone, but there was no response from Carol. She texted her again.

Carol, call me immediately. Stevie.

Then she looked back at Brie. "Sweetie, has anyone reported Carol missing? How do I call the lead person on the staff?"

Brie looked around. "Numbers are just on Carol's cell phone. Wait, there's a bad weather recall thing over here." Brie went to a bulletin board on a wall. "Here," she said.

Stevie walked over and with her phone began calling the names on the list from the top down, skipping Carol's. She said the same thing to everyone she got from the seven numbers she dialed.

"I represent Lifenablers and the foundation that pays for this place. If you are not wanting to be charged with child endangerment, you better get your *butt* down here now!"

Then she dialed the Hurrt County Sheriff's Office. "This is Stephanie Collins. I need to file a missing person report."

After talking with the dispatcher for several minutes, Stevie hung up and turned to Brie.

"A deputy will be here in a little while, but while we're waiting, honey, show me where these men meet in the basement."

CHAPTER 5

Ashe woke before daylight but stayed in bed, his eyes only half open. He tried to look at the dimly illuminated flip-number clock on his nightstand but couldn't focus on the numbers. They flipped over several times as he tried to see the time in the dark bedroom, lit only by a nightlight from the bathroom. He wasn't sure why he'd woke up so early, as he could hear only the comforting sound of the old oscillating fan in the corner.

The metal blades hummed softly and the base ticked off each degree of movement in its arc. From down the hall, Ashe thought he smelled coffee brewing.

That can't be right, can it?

Heavy footsteps; his father's cologne.

No. Not right.

More heavy footsteps. Then he heard an impossibly loud *bang!* It shook the walls as it echoed from down the hall into the bedroom, and Ashe sat bolt up in bed.

Not again, no!

"Dad!" he yelled as he threw back the covers and jumped from bed. He caught himself halfway across the room; his father had ended his life years ago.

He drew in a shaky breath and decided he was fully awake, as he stood on the old hardwood floor that creaked beneath his feet. The peaceful mood he'd had just seconds ago was gone, replaced by a darker feeling.

It took almost a full minute for Ashe to calm himself, then he padded into the master bath to run some water over his face. As he went, he noted there was no old metal oscillating fan anymore. There was no illuminated flip-number clock. Only his smartphone plugged in by the bed. This was now, not then. There was nothing to dread down the hall.

As he stepped from the bathroom, he heard another loud set of *bang! Bang!*

Ashe picked up his compact Smith and Wesson 9mm and a powerful handheld flashlight, and walked quietly to the front door. He stepped away at an angle from the door, ensuring he wasn't directly in front of it, and turned on the porch light. He peeked cautiously out a side window and saw the large figure of a man who stood on the porch; just back from it, and at an angle, from the front door. Not square on it but more like…

A cop. Dammit.

There was really only one guy that size he knew who would bang on the door then step back like that, instead of using the doorbell. Ashe threw open the front door and turned to walk toward the kitchen to make coffee.

"What the hell, Pat?"

"What the hell, Chig? I've been beating on your damn door for five minutes?"

Pat Keagan. All six foot three, two hundred-twenty pounds of him. He was off duty, or so Ashe presumed, given what he was wearing. He had on a navy polo and lightweight cargo pants with boat shoes. His big Colt 1911 .45 was in a synthetic holster with a stiff-looking heavy nylon belt. Ashe suspected the big man had his lighter, shorter Colt Defender somewhere out of sight. He'd seen Pat wear a shoulder holster under his shirts before, or maybe in a thin urethane holster inside his pants. Either way, Pat almost always carried two, sometimes three guns. Not paranoia but experience.

"You could get shot that way, asshole. Beating on a door out in the country at…whatever time it is."

"Blow me, I was standing still. You'd miss me by a yard!"

Pat had been about a year ahead of Ashe at the Metropolitan Police, but they'd wound up as detective partners for several years. Eventually, Ashe had been his boss at the Major Crimes Unit.

Pat strolled in, kicking the door closed behind him, and followed Ashe into the kitchen. "You're in your old gym shorts. I get you out of bed? I'll make coffee then we're going to talk some."

Ashe yawned widely then squinted without his glasses at the

clock on the stove.

"Shit, Pat, it's five thirty!"

"Is it? So go shower and get dressed. Cloudy today, but warm. I take it we'll be on a boat today."

"A boat? How'd you…ah, never mind," Ashe said and threw a dismissive hand at Pat. After the over twenty-plus years they'd known each other, they could almost read each other's mind.

A convenient ability for detective partners, one that had come in handy more than a few times.

Speaking of partners… "Danny Breslin with you?"

Pat sighed. "He's lost his head. He quit Metro and took a job with the stateys."

"Why would he do that?" Ashe said, then yawned again.

Pat went right to the silverware drawer then opened the cupboard where the coffee was, without asking. He'd been to this house a hundred times over the years, and now that it was Ashe's place, he'd stayed over a time or two. In both good times and bad.

"Politics. Him and Captain Speakes, they just can't seem to…well, you know Speakes."

Ashe nodded. There was no love between his old boss and him, either. The state would be less pay but likely more opportunity for advancement. Ashe shrugged and left Pat to himself and went to get cleaned up.

Thirty minutes later, Ashe reappeared wearing grayish knee-length cargo shorts and a lightweight khaki fishing shirt with the sleeves rolled. He grabbed a windbreaker out of the closet and a mesh-back "TAG" ballcap.

"So?" Ashe asked.

"What do you want? Applause?" Pat drank from the biggest mug in the house and was eating both a granola bar and an apple. A bottle of water sat on the counter, open in front of him. "Talk to me about Chuck."

Ashe got his own coffee, a half mug, which emptied the pot, so he started another one. "Yeah. This sucks. I know you and he were friends, probably more so than I was with him."

Pat just nodded.

Ashe drew in a breath. "So. Charles Carter, U.S. Marshal, retired. Washed up on the southeast shore of Minor Hills Lake a couple of days ago. Shot twice in the back and once in the head, all from the rear. Large caliber rifle. Couldn't ID him at first since he was missing almost all of his face. The sheriff's office got prints off a Glock 19 mag he was wearing. Then Rachel, well, you know all this, I guess. He was in a hell of a nice suit, wearing an earpiece, and was strapped. We didn't find his gun or radio."

Pat didn't speak for a minute or two, which was actually very powerful to Ashe.

Finally Pat nodded to himself. "Yeah, she told me most of that. You're right, he had to be working. Something important, too, because of the suit. Chuck was good people, a good friend, and good at his job. Damn good."

"You remember that guy, a protectee or informant he was watching; he brought him to Dad's cabin to sit on him for a few days to be out of the city?"

Pat smiled for a half second. "Yeah, I forget his name. Me, you, Chuck, the damn informant…we fished the whole time."

"Yeah," Ashe said. "He was worried he'd get fired over that, but I guess the informant made it to court okay. The cabin was pretty secluded back then."

Pat drew in a deep breath and then seemingly put parts of what he was feeling aside. His face changed. "But drifting in a lake, I dunno, Chig." He started rapping his big knuckles on the countertop as he thought.

"Like you said, I want to try and figure out where this actually happened. He'd been drifting awhile in the lake," Ashe said.

"He could've bought it somewhere else and just been dumped," Pat said. He finished both the protein bar and the apple and was poking around through Ashe's cupboards.

"That's possible."

Pat thought for a second. "Yeah, sure. I mean why would he be at the lake in a cabin or on a boat wearing a suit? Makes more sense he was dumped."

"Unless," Ashe said. "It was an important client, or…an important meeting. If he were at one of those expensive condos or weekly rental cabins on the north shore?"

Pat appeared to have a new thought. "Or your cabin. He knew that from before. If he was working, he'd want the advantage of knowing the ground."

"Regardless, we haven't found the real crime scene yet. I think the stateys are going to search today, even use drones."

"Maybe. Anyway, Rachel figures you were going to look yourself, no matter what, and since it's *her* case *not yours*, and since I've got a day or two off, she sent...she *asked* me to...come assist."

"Babysitter? Seriously?"

"Hey! After the junk you pulled last fall, you sort of have a reputation with her, buddy."

Ashe shrugged. "That's actually fair."

"I think I know a friend who can help," Ashe said. He had an old map of the lake folded on the counter.

Pat looked at his watch. "No, let's go to Roger's and eat first. Hell, it's only six fifteen."

. . . .

Roger's Café, originally The Town Café, was a Seacord tradition, and Ashe had hung out there since he was in high school. Roger Clancy bought the place from the original owner years ago and still ran the place, and showed no signs of slowing down. He'd recently built an expansion and broadened his menu past breakfast and sandwiches to jump aboard the growth in the Hurrt County/Seacord area and its revitalized tourist status.

He greeted Ashe and Pat from across the tiny lobby with a shrug. The place was packed this morning and customers were standing in line, so he pointed to the front register at a "To-Go Orders" sign. Behind the counter stood a tall, fit-looking waitress named Tilly, whom Ashe had also known all his life.

"Hey, boy, come over here!" she called out above the hubbub of the crowd.

Ashe made his way over to her and she gave him a big, familiar hug.

Then she spied Pat. "Uh-oh," she said.

"He has that effect often on women," Ashe said, smiling.

Tilly already had a dark, tanning-bed tan and her hair a much lighter shade of blonde for the summer. She wore a pair of very short shorts, but thanks to a lifetime of working out, from cheerleading, to hiking, to yoga, and all the years on her feet waitressing, Ashe thought she wore them pretty damn well.

"Hi, Tilly, how are you?" Pat said.

"Fine," she said with a slight frown, and pointed back and forth at the two men.

"Yeah," was all Pat said. He knew what she meant by the gesture. Business.

"Never mind that," Ashe said when she appeared to be about to ask a question. "Breakfast, my usual times two," Ashe said.

The slight gray in her hair that showed was only where it had grown out between hair appointments, but today, she had it all up in a ball on top of her head. A pair of pencils were playfully stuck in the ball, and she plucked one out to take their order.

"Fine, whatever. You coming to the street fair tomorrow night? There's a live band."

"I hadn't heard about it. I may be…kind of tied up," Ashe said.

She cut her eyes at Pat again. "You shouldn't make him work so much, he's retired and he owes me at least one dance."

"Tell your husband, Tommy, *who I don't want after me with a shotgun*, I said hi," Ashe said.

Tilly just said, "Ah!" and bopped Ashe over the head with a menu. "I do want to talk to you about something, when you can fit me in." She turned and went to put in their order.

Pat looked at Ashe and winked. Ashe shrugged and said, "I've known her since…"

"Yeah, I know, I know. High school," Pat said.

. . . .

In Pat's charcoal-gray Dodge SUV, they drove to the larger of the two marinas on Minor Hills Lake, and parked outside the state conservation office to eat as they waited.

Ashe ate most of his then handed the extra biscuit and bacon to Pat so he could open up the lake map.

"Fifty bucks still says he was killed elsewhere and dumped here," Pat said.

"No bet, you could be right. He was found about, oh, a half mile or so from my old cabin."

"You got it sold? For sure?" Pat asked as Ashe studied the map.

"Yeah, it's not mine anymore. Dad would hate that, but it's getting too damn crowded along the shoreline. Too much new development." Ashe traced a finger from his former cabin across to where Terrible Creek entered the lake.

"What's that?" Pat asked.

"The current runs the wrong way. If he'd been at the cabin and fallen in or been dumped, his body would have drifted the other way."

"We don't know this happened on your property; it was just a guess that Chuck would use familiar ground if he were protecting someone."

Ashe sighed. "It was a good guess. But surely he'd have called me, or even you, first."

Pat reached over and with a sausage-sized finger pointed out a road on the map. "He could've been killed anywhere and then rolled into the lake *anywhere* along this road. Even dropped off the bridge there," he said.

"True," Ashe said and continued to examine the map.

Pat stared at Ashe. "But you're on to something else, ain't you?"

"If I were, I'd have taken your bet. No, we need to talk to these state conservation people."

"What will the possum cops know?"

"The current...ah, *currents*. You know, from one to two weeks back. This lake is tricky. Rain and drought reverses things, water temperature, all of it. I know from forty years of fishing here, and this ten-year-old map might be wrong."

"Well, here they are," Pat said, looking into the rearview mirror.

A pale-green pickup with state tags pulled up beside them. A conservation agent Ashe had met before was driving, and beside her was another, older man. They both wore tan uniform shirts and had sun-bleached ball caps. Ashe and Pat got out to greet them.

"Hey!" she said and waved. "You're Mister Ashe, right? Old cabin down the shore a ways."

"Yes, and it's just Ashe. Mister Ashe was my dad. You're... Skye, right?"

"Yes, sir." Skye released a wide and friendly grin to him. She was thin and medium height with a long blonde braid that she wore around her neck and down the front of her shirt. Small multicolored bands were tied up into the braid. Her face was tanned and a planetarium full of freckles was splayed across her face and chest. She wore green shorts and low-top hiking shoes.

Pat shook out his Metro badge and showed it to the other ranger, who had started for the office door with keys in his hand.

"I'm Keagan with Metro Homicide, and Ashe here is with Hurrt County," he said. "We need a few minutes, please."

"The body. The one found down by the park shore," the man said, not as a question. "I'm Ranger Wurts, the senior conservation agent for Minor Hills rec area and lake. I take it you know Ranger Skye Bennett."

"Yeah, we've met and yes, it's about the body," Ashe said. They all followed Wurts onto a small and very old wooden bridge that crossed a rock-lined drainage ditch to the office door.

"Hey," she said as they waited on Wurts to unlock the door. "I remember I used to see you out at the..."

"We should catch up some time," Ashe interrupted. As they walked inside, Pat elbowed him in the ribs.

"I swear to God, Chig," he said beneath his breath. "Everywhere we..."

Ashe elbowed him back.

Wurts turned on lights and almost in one motion, grabbed a coffeepot carafe and went to the bathroom sink to fill it. Skye switched on a computer at a long table. There didn't seem to be a desk anywhere, only tables with all kinds of stuff piled on them, and only a couple of chairs.

The office was small; just one open room maybe twenty-five feet square with a closet and a bathroom.

"What can I do you two for?" Wurts said as he made coffee.

Ashe looked at Pat before he spoke. "We are convinced the body of the man found near the park didn't die there. I would like to get your take on the currents at the time and maybe try to backtrack where he may have actually died."

"I'm not a cop," Wurts said. "I'm more of a boating safety and clean-water guy. Skye, here, is a law enforcement-trained ranger."

"Well, I'm not asking anyone for police help. More like, your experience and knowledge of the lake and currents," Ashe said.

"We think there's another crime scene. Well, *he* thinks there's another crime scene," Pat added.

"Hey, why couldn't the body have come off a boat? Are you sure it's a homicide?" Skye said.

Ashe nodded. "Three rifle shots from the rear…we're sure."

Wurts nodded and waited for the coffee to make just enough that he grabbed the pot out and put his finger under the filter tray to stop the coffee. He poured his mug full then quickly replaced the pot into place.

"Either of you two want a cup?" he asked and went to a table and pulled out a large map of one section of the lake.

"I'm good," Pat said.

"Never turned down a cup in my life," Ashe said.

Skye quickly grabbed a cup that Ashe assumed, by its tie-dye colors, was hers, and rinsed it in the sink.

Wurts wore thick black-rimmed glasses and had a big potbelly that seemed out of place with his narrow hips. He wore his uniform shirt over dark-green cargo pants. As he examined the map, turning it ninety degrees a couple of times, he adjusted his glasses and removed his cap, exposing his mostly bald and sunburned scalp.

He set his mug to hold the map open and nodded for Ashe and Pat to come see what he was looking at.

"Yeah, you see here? That's the service access road to the park, where that guy's body was found."

"Chuck Carter," Pat said. "His name is Charles; we called him Chuck, and we sometimes worked together."

Wurts looked at Pat then Ashe. "I see. Okay, *Mr. Carter*. Anyway, normally the current from the creek that feeds into the lake would be flowing past there, but a week or so ago, it was really dry upstream. Terrible Creek was just a fraction of itself."

Pat looked up at Ashe. "Hey, like what you said outside."

"But," Wurts continued, "the lake is fed by several underground creeks as well. So, look here." Wurts turned the large map around again and used an ink pen to point at a channel indicator on the far shore.

"Here is where Cavern Creek comes from underground and feeds very cold water into the lake."

"Yeah, I've fished near there. It must be why it's a good spot."

Wurts smiled knowingly at Ashe. "Yes, sometimes. But sometimes it runs at a much lower flow than the surface creeks. We can tell by the water temperature there, just off…this point."

Ashe leaned across the table beside Wurts, to look at the area he indicated. "What is that? Sparks Point?"

"Yes. So my deal is, we noticed coloration changes and took water temperature readings about a week or so back. If your Mr. Carter went into the lake then, and did drift in the lake for some time when Terrible Creek was low, Cavern Creek would be the main current driver."

Ashe noticed Skye was leaning across the table too, a little close to him. Ashe knew that Pat had noticed her too, by a microscopic change in his face. It took twenty-five years to learn to see it, and Ashe knew nobody else would notice.

Ashe also knew he'd get a smart-assed comment from him about Skye later.

"And you're saying if he were dumped near this Sparks place, he would drift all the way to the park?" Pat asked.

Wurts smiled. "I'm not saying anything like that. I can't see where, for seven or eight days, boaters or people fishing wouldn't have spotted him floating mid lake. I *am* saying for a floating body or even a drifting log, to wind up where your body did, *and* starting a week to ten days ago, *this* is where it would have to start."

"What if the killers put him into the water right there, at the park, near where he was found?" Pat asked.

"From the shore? No, the current outflows there. In a week, he'd be pretty far away. I'd guess, just *guess* mind you, that the only reason he was pushed ashore there had to be from boat's wakes. You get a lot of bigger boats speeding up after leaving the park's no-wake zone."

Ashe looked at the map for a minute longer and was about to ask a question, when Pat jumped in. "What if he were just dumped in the lake? From the big bridge or along Route 116?"

Wurts considered that. "Well, I'm not a big fat expert, but offhand, I'd say not. His body would have gone over to the beach at Tyler Cove in Carson County."

"Sure, sure," Pat said.

"No, not *sure* at all. Look, the whole lake system is of course, complex. Given seasonal changes, heavy rains, things temporarily move differently, like all lakes. But generally, *inevitably*, Minor Hills flows in the direction of the Hurrt River. It is the Hurrt's headwater."

"Huh," Ashe said. *I should've taken Pat's bet.* "Ranger, is this Sparks Point in Hurrt or Carson County?"

"Most of that section including Sparks Point and Cook's Inlet is still Hurrt County. All this area to the east, along the shore and by the way, up current, is McCormick County, not Carson."

Then he felt Skye lean in, presumably to look at the map, and press closer to him, looking at the map.

"So it's Hurrt County here on shore and in the water. Um…Skye, what do you think?" Ashe asked, turning his face toward hers. She had squeezed in a little too close to him.

"I think so," she said and smiled.

"Well, I think we should call Sheriff Jacobs," Ashe said, and stood up back from the table a bit.

"I'm calling Rachel," Pat said.

"I think we should take our boat and go look at the Sparks Point area," Skye said.

CHAPTER 6

Within a half hour of making calls to the HCCS staff, three of the former care workers showed up.

"I assumed someone would…" seemed to be the way they started every sentence, usually followed by, "We haven't been paid in over a…"

"Can you help out now? Come up with a schedule to get us over the next few days here and I'll ensure you're paid in the morning," Stevie said, although she was not exactly sure how.

A former employee named Judy Franks just nodded and took charge. Along with Brie, she did a head count, looked at room cleanliness, started supper and laundry, then double-checked the residents' medications.

Stevie wanted to pull Brie aside after getting things arranged to find the meeting room in the basement, but they both were sidetracked with getting the children cared for. Next thing she knew, a sheriff's cruiser arrived outside. She had met several deputies recently, but didn't know the one who walked up to the porch. He was tall, she figured about forty or so, and had his black hair combed straight up and back from his forehead.

He looked Stevie over slowly, not attempting to hide it. "So. You're the one reporting a missing person?" he said. His name tag said R.L. Dawson.

Stevie sighed and took him inside Carol's office and told him what she knew, which seemed to switch him over from staring at her to business mode. He said he was surprised no one had reported her already. He took some notes, stepped back out to the porch to use his handheld radio, then reentered Carol's office.

"See if you can find a recent picture we can have. And just to be sure, I'm going to search the facility and grounds."

Stevie nodded and then felt her phone vibrate in her pocket. Tom had texted a couple of times and tried to call. She checked the time; it was getting dark out and almost seven p.m.

Later, dude.

"Ms. Collins?" Judy called from down the hall. "All we can serve tonight is sandwiches and instant punch. We need groceries."

Stevie went to the kitchen where Judy was supervising Brie and another girl making sandwiches.

"And almost every girl here is on some form of medication. Some are out, and some don't have refills," she said, shaking prescription bottles and putting them into a cardboard organizer by each girl's name.

"Who would take care of that? And I don't mean Carol, I mean which doctor and which pharmacy?"

"Wright Street Pharmacy is on most of these bottles. The hospital pharmacy in McCormick City is on some, too."

Stevie looked out the kitchen window that overlooked the parking area and saw Deputy Dawson using a door opener on the brown Nissan, trying to get it open.

"I'll...I guess I'll call there in the morning."

"Look, I know something bad has happened. Where's family services? My husband is a reserve deputy sheriff. I think you met him last year during...all *that*, that happened then. Anyway, I'm going to get him to come sit here for security tonight," Judy said.

Stevie looked at her without speaking for a minute, at first a bit annoyed at the reference of *all that, that happened.* Judy was in her sixties at least and had the look of a life of hard work to her, but her eyes showed a glimmer of kindness. And she had, after all, agreed to stay here and help the girls.

Maybe I need to be a little less sensitive. It's probably the only way she knows me.

Stevie swallowed and said, "Your husband is Jeremy Franks? Yes, he, ah, took care of me when I was in trouble. But do you think it's necessary here?"

"These girls are scared, and Carol used to call him to come sit here sometimes. The sheriff won't mind, either."

"I'll see if the deputy knows the on-call county family services rep," Stevie said. Out the window, she saw a new model Ford truck swing into the parking lot, followed by another sheriff's car. A man in his fifties wearing jeans and a Co-Op work shirt jumped out. He and Deputy Dawson began talking, and the man was very animated. From the other patrol car, Sheriff Jacobs got out and joined the conversation.

She left Judy and Brie in the kitchen and walked to the porch just in time to hear the man shout, "Bull!" at both Sheriff Jacobs and Dawson. He spun on his heels and started for the sanctuary's porch.

"Lou!" Jacobs called out. But the man didn't stop and fixed his red-faced glare on Stevie.

"You the one in charge here?" he shouted.

Jacobs stepped up and placed himself between Lou and Stevie. Lou was solidly built, and he clenched his fists, but Jacobs was bigger.

"Lou Buckram, this is Stevie Collins. She's a...ah, kind of a lawyer around...um," Jacobs said. He kept looking at Stevie for help describing her.

"Mr. Buckram, I work for the foundation that funds this children's sanctuary and a few of the other facilities in this region. Are you Carol's...father?"

Lou ignored her question, looking past her and Jacobs toward the front door. Then he said, "*The* Foundation? You work for them? You work for that damn Durant?"

"Who? I haven't ever heard that name. My job is ensuring their funding through the...hey!"

Lou took off for the door before Jacobs could catch him. He stormed straight into Carol's office and began pulling out desk drawers, pushing aside books, and shoving files around. Jacobs and Stevie caught up, and Jacobs tried to step in front of Lou to get his attention. Deputy Dawson came in as well. Stevie tried to shrink into a corner.

"Lou, I told you, we'll find her. What are you looking for in here? We'll look at everything in here to see if we can figure out where she is," Jacobs shouted.

"Find her? Like you did that other woman last year? Dead and buried right under your nose!"

"Now you know that's not fair! This is a totally different deal. Settle down a minute and tell me, who is this Durant you're talking about."

Lou stopped his frantic searching but continued to look around the room. He seemed to size up Jacobs and Dawson then decided to focus on Stevie.

"You know what the hell I'm looking for. You know; you work for them. Where is it? And you can tell them the gig is up, and it's all Durant's fault!"

Jacobs held his palms up and wide. "Please, Lou. Who are you talking about? Does he have anything to do with your daughter?"

Lou looked at Jacobs contemptuously, like he didn't believe he didn't know who Durant was. "Hell, she knows. Michael Durant! Don't play dumb with me! And, he don't have nothing to do with my daughter anymore!"

Lou Buckram was about to say something else, but he noticed the children in the hall who had gathered to peek at what was going on, so he turned and pushed past Dawson to head outside. Over his shoulder he shouted, "You tell them, missy! Tell them the gig is up!"

Jacobs pointed to Dawson and then out the door. Dawson nodded and went after Lou. Jacobs let out a long breath and then paced around the room, seemingly trying to both calm himself and gather his words.

After a full minute, he said, "Hello, Stevie. Been a while. Hey, answer me this, how come whenever there's a *missing woman* around here, I seem to run into you?"

Stevie frowned at Jacobs and took a second before answering. "Holy cow, that was intense."

Jacobs slowly crossed his big arms and shook his head. "Talk to me, lady."

"First, I have never met this Buckram person, and secondly, I have no idea what he meant."

"He seemed to think you knew all about his daughter. And who is this Michael Durant?"

"Sheriff...Larry, I do not have any idea what's going on here."

"Is he a member of the foundation that supports this place? What did Lou mean?"

"I swear I've never heard of him before, and I've never heard of Michael..." She paused. The name rang a bell, but she couldn't place it.

"That name sounds familiar to me; he must be connected with

this place somehow," Jacobs said.

Stevie told him exactly what she did for the Foundation and how she'd wound up at the sanctuary. But she decided at the last second to leave out mentioning the men who met in a room in the basement. She wasn't completely sure why, herself.

I think maybe I want to look in there first, before deciding what to do.

Outside, she heard Buckram making more noise, so Jacobs started for the door.

"You going to be here awhile? I'm going to go handle Buckram now, but I need a full statement from you. *Tonight*," he said.

She nodded then wiped her hands across her face and pulled her hair back. For the second time in just a few hours, she felt sweaty.

As Jacobs walked out and down the front steps, Judy appeared at the door.

"I told you we need Jeremy here for security," she said.

"Judy, did you hear all that? What is he talking about?"

"Huh," she said. "I'm not letting you pull me into your drama. You best tell Lou what you know, hon. He can be pretty mean. He's a 'shiner like his daddy was."

"Judy, I have no idea..." But she had already gone back down the hall. Stevie rolled her eyes and then shook her fist at the ceiling and shouted, "Ooooo! For the freaking love of..."

"Children! Language!" she heard Judy holler from the kitchen.

. . . .

In another half hour, Jacobs had let Lou Buckram go, on the promise he'd stay away from the sanctuary. Jacobs and Dawson conducted a thorough search of the premises, inside and out, and examined and took photos of Carol's brown Nissan. Judy texted Jacobs a photo of Carol she had on her phone. As he left, Jacobs posted Dawson outside and directed Stevie to write a statement.

Judy agreed to return in the morning if someone would stay overnight, and, of course Stevie knew that meant her. Judy promised her husband would come to relieve Deputy Dawson around midnight. So Stevie called Tom to let him know. She told him about Lou Buckram's tirade and accusations.

"Wait…why you? You're not a qualified caregiver or nurse?" he asked.

"You told me to fix it, this is fixing it. Only nobody knew how bad it was. I'll be home in the morning after I figure out how to pay the employees here, and get these children's medications to them."

Tom hesitated, then, "Wait…what? Honey, look. This is not part of your job; it's just *not* your responsibility. County family services people should be there."

"They've been notified. *If* someone shows, I'll come home. If not, bring me some clothes in the morning. Oh, and my laptop…and coffee. A latte."

"This is not a good idea. You should be careful…stay upstairs by the phone."

"Hey, do you know who Michael Durant is? Is he on the Foundation board or something? Buckram seemed to think he had something to do with Carol."

"I…have never met him. It's probably not important. Look, just stay upstairs by the phone…please, babe. I love you."

They went back and forth a little more, but Stevie only half listened. Finally she cut him off and said she had to go.

It was quiet by then in the sanctuary house. Most of the children were in bed, the others upstairs reading or watching videos. Stevie left Carol's office and went to the kitchen to see if perhaps coffee were a possibility. Outside the kitchen window there, she saw Deputy Dawson in his cruiser; his face illuminated by the light of his phone he was staring at.

Some lookout. Santa Claus could walk by him and he wouldn't notice.

Then Brie appeared beside her.

"Oh shit!" Stevie said and grabbed her chest. "I mean, crap, heck, or whatever! You scared me, Brie." She went back to looking for coffee. *Tea, maybe?*

Brie put a finger to her lips and leaned closer to Stevie. "They looked, them policemen, but they didn't find that room."

Stevie stopped and looked at her. "No? I guess I'm not surprised."

Then Brie took her hand and led her around behind the stairs where the door to the basement was. She turned on a light switch by the door and they went down old wooden stairs that had no risers.

"Honey, is there any...did Carol or Judy ever make a pot of..." Stevie stopped mid-sentence.

The basement was wide and long and was under the kitchen, the upstairs hall, and Carol's office. It was filled with old boxes, a couple of shelves of cleaning supplies, hanging mops, and cartons of glass jars—like for canning vegetables.

"This is where the men met? Pretty dingy spot to hold a meeting."

Brie shook her head and led Stevie past this room to a door at the far end, and through it was the utility room. She flipped on another light switch that turned on a bare hanging light bulb.

A huge old water heater, an antique oil-burning furnace that looked inoperable, and a newer electric HVAC unit filled the much smaller utility room. There was a wide steel door to their right that had to lead to the outside. Stevie noticed it had a peep hole to look out.

Unlike the previous large room, this one was fairly dust-free. The floor was tile, and there were scrape marks on the floor where the exterior door was obviously used a good deal.

Brie pointed to a corner behind the oil furnace.

"What, Brie? What is it?"

Brie stepped forward and pulled on the huge old furnace, and it moved as if on casters away from the corner, revealing a hidden door.

"Huh," is all Stevie could think to say for a second. "The deputy, or Sheriff Jacobs? They didn't find this?"

Brie shrugged. "I don't guess."

The hidden door was steel as well and also had a peephole, to look from the other side to see who was in *this* room, it appeared. Stevie tried the door, assuming it'd be locked, but it opened inward.

Stevie could just feel, even though it was dark, that it was a big room. On the floor, just past the swing of the door and lit by the overhead bulb behind them, lay a fancy brass key ring and a set of five or six keys.

She stepped forward and picked up the keys. Engraved in the brass was the letter "C." She began to feel along the wall just inside for a light switch, but stopped, frozen by a terrible thought.

Someone, Carol probably, had been the last one to come in here. She could have dropped her keys...

Stevie squared herself off as casually as possible with the doorway to block Brie from seeing inside.

"Brie, honey, go upstairs and get my phone. *Quietly.* Don't run or make any noise."

Brie turned and initially scampered off then stopped and walked more slowly.

When she was out of sight, Stevie took her phone from a pocket and turned on its little flashlight to help find the light switch. Near the door, she found it and snapped it on.

She drew in a sharp breath as she looked around.

This was a certainly a place where men would meet. Like a lodge or clubhouse, brilliantly lit, and obviously in operation for years. Decades maybe.

She made a quick look, to see if her fears were correct, but she saw no body. No Carol.

Thank God.

Once satisfied this wasn't a homicide scene, she slowed down to really look at the heavily decorated space. The walls were paneled with real cedar, and long shelves held rows of framed photos showing men in groups. There was a bar running along one long wall and behind it, more photos, mirrors, and shelves of liquor. A pool table with a stained glass lamp hanging overhead was at one end. The floor was thickly carpeted.

She walked in and noticed the room was very still, muted even. The walls had to be soundproofed.

She next saw a refrigerator and a floor freezer. Opening them, they were well stocked with snacks, beer, sodas, and of course meats and cheeses. The freezer held steaks and other frozen foods. Everything top quality, name brand, and expensive.

"Son of a bitch," she said out loud to no one. She walked a couple of laps around to try and take it all in. Deer mounts, bass mounts, big brass-looking trophies. In one corner was a mock-up of a moonshine still, made with shiny brass coils and a big polished oak barrel.

"Oh, 'shiner!" she said. *Moonshiner. I thought Judy had said Shriner.* Looking into the barrel from the open top, there was a mirror inside where she saw herself looking down.

Kitschy.

Dozens of photos lined the walls and they were all dated. They went back as far as the 1940s. Nearer to the door, and the bar opposite it, the photos were more recent. She stepped around the bar to get a closer look, and saw here, the photos were within the last ten years or so. In each photo stood or sat ten to twelve men gathered around the mock still. Sometimes the photo was taken outdoors but mostly here in this room. In the older photos, there were as many as twenty or more people, but these recent ones showed their group's numbers had obviously shrunk.

Then she noticed something else that made her even more curious.

In each photo, the men were dressed in suit and tie. Some even wore hats. But in the center of each group was a woman, dressed in either a tiny cocktail dress, or in the more recent ones, a bikini.

Each photo was labeled "Batch Launch," followed by the year at the top. At the bottom, they had written, "Queen of the Batch," followed by her first name. Often, either sitting on the barrel or in a few cases laying across the laps of the men in the photo.

Stevie looked back over the photos and the years. The forties, the fifties, the sixties; all had a "Batch Queen" and she was always dressed like a pinup model. Sometimes, a woman would repeat as "queen" albeit in nonconsecutive years, but mostly each year showed a new girl.

In the photographs, the Batch Queen poses were never overly suggestive; more like what they called "cheesecake" than pornographic.

Stevie kept side-stepping behind the long bar to look at the photos until she bumped into something. Looking down, she saw it was a sawed-off shotgun.

By invitation only, I assume.

She took out her phone again and began taking photos of the Batch Launch pictures but also photographed the room itself. When taking shots of the most recent ones, she saw a face she knew, and it shocked her.

In a group from about ten years before, was her friend, her lawyer, and former employer, retired judge Harold Marsh. She looked back over the years; he was there in every photo, growing younger as she looked. In the early sixties, she saw a man who stood beside him in several photos that looked very much like her old boyfriend, Ashe, only taller maybe.

Must be Ashe's dad. He was close friends with the judge.

Then he dropped out about 1970 or so, although Harold Marsh continued to be a part of the batch launches until the mid-1990s. The women, she did not recognize.

She was shooting the wall and the pictures in groups then eventually stepped from behind the bar to see the most recent ones. She had a bad feeling she might see familiar faces.

Then she did.

Five years ago, was a batch launch picture, and standing in the photo was Mark Portals. He had been a powerful local attorney and had purposely taken advantage of her addiction; using her and her practice in a huge and shady property development deal. He'd ensured she'd stayed a drunk and had her sign legal papers to shield his own law practice and confuse any allegations of illegal activity.

He'd even covered up the murder of a local woman Stevie had been friends with, to protect the deal. Buckram had thrown that in Jacobs' face. Portals was waiting to go to trial, and the stain of being associated with that multimillion-dollar swindle had cost Stevie her law license and her reputation.

Mark Portals' scheme and her unwitting part in it, was what Mrs. Garrett the auditor, and also what Judy Franks, had referred to. The *all that, that* happened.

Then she saw something else. *Oh God, no!*

In a Batch Launch photo from three years ago was Portals, but standing beside him was her fiancé, Tom Fischer.

Tom had previously been an associate in Portals' law firm but was found to be completely uninvolved with the criminal activity. But, here he was in a photo in this very room. She looked at the woman; she didn't recognize her, but a couple of the men she knew. A banker, a county commissioner, a doctor, another lawyer she knew only slightly. The crème of Seacord society at the time.

We'll deal with you later, Mister Tom.

She took an extra-good photo of this picture then went to look for the most recent Batch Launch photo. It was last year. Tom was in it, but Portals wasn't of course. He had been excommunicated for screwing over half the town. But she did see a familiar face.

Sitting on the lap of a man in the middle was Carol Buckram. She was wearing a bikini; the smallest one Stevie had seen in the photos so far. The man she was sitting on was in his fifties and smiling right at her. She was smiling widely as well, but something seemed off.

In all the other photos, the Batch Queens had looked like a pinup model, or at least seemed like they were in control and enjoying themselves. Like it was an honor to model for these distinguished men in a secret society. Carol looked...different.

She looked drunk. Stevie admitted to herself she knew the look well. Carol's eyes were glazed over, and her smile was forced. Over all, to Stevie, she just looked sloppy.

I don't even know her that well, but God, this is terrible.

Looking closer, Stevie noticed the man with her had his hand on her upper thigh. Her *very* upper thigh. Inappropriately so. She guessed Carol was twenty-three or four.

Then another thought hit her. Lou Buckram. He'd been so angry and probably had found out she had been in the photo. Stevie quickly went back several years but didn't see Lou in any of the pictures.

Assuming she was right, and he was mad about *this*, how would he know unless he'd been in this room? He wasn't a member, or he'd be in the photos.

He'd yelled out about a man named Durant, and assumed she knew all about something when he heard she worked for the foundation that funded this sanctuary.

Now she knew what the *something* was that he'd meant. Was the man groping her in her queen photo, Durant? And what did Lou mean, *Tell them it's over?*

"Ah, jeez," she said out loud and tried to call the sheriff. She got no signal, so she headed to go back upstairs. Then, over the door, she saw a large and very old piece of wood she hadn't seen when she'd entered. Carved into it, in twelve-inch-high letters was apparently the group's name.

The Blockade Runners.

She turned her phone on it and took a photo, and as she did, from outside, she heard a key go into a lock, and the exterior door opened. A man stepped inside, seemed surprised the Blockade

Runner secret lodge door was open, then jumped when he saw Stevie.

Out of instinct, she took his photo.

"Who the hell are you!" he demanded.

"Nuh-uh," she said and took another photo. "Just who the hell are *you*!"

CHAPTER 7

"**W**e're about ready to head to Sparks Point," Ashe shouted into his phone.

"I'm tied up on something else. A missing woman, if you can believe it," Sheriff Jacobs said back. "But hey, keep me updated and we'll get together later."

Just as Jacobs hung up, Skye fired up the state conservation patrol boat. It was a wide and long launch that sat low in the water and was built for both lake law enforcement as well as rescue. It had flat decking across the front and rear with a textured gray, rubberized nonslip coating all around. What looked like a tall, roll-bar type lifting frame and wench, was covered with canvas and attached to the rear deck. Ashe figured this was for both towing in disabled boats, as well as dragging the bottom of the lake. He hoped neither would be required.

The twin Mercury 250 engines gave off a throaty staccato putter as they idled. Skye went about preparing to pull out and spoke with Ranger Wurts on the dock, who was staying behind.

"Pat, Jacobs isn't coming. He's got a missing woman case."

"Yeah? Hey, Chig! Rachel wants a quick word with you," Pat said and passed his phone over.

"Ashe! We're at Call's Landing," Rachel said, over a good deal of noise from activity in the background. "My team seems to think Snapper Cove is the most likely place Carter could have gone into the water. We're launching drones to fly the shoreline and look over any of the small islands, too!"

"Ok. I have different intel, but no harm covering all bases."

Rachel continued as if she hadn't heard him. "He rented a

twenty-two-foot pontoon boat with blue stripes here about eight days ago, and it hasn't been spotted since. That's probably your target."

"Good to go, I'll stay in touch."

"Uh-huh. I know," she said.

Ashe smiled. "Thanks for the big overgrown Irish tracking device!"

Pat looked at Ashe when he heard that. He had been going through the life vests looking for one big enough to fit.

"Yeah, well…you know," Rachel said, and hung up.

Skye pushed the throttle forward and began idling away from the dock through the no wake zone. Ashe pitched Pat his phone and put on his vest as well.

"They're over at Snapper Cove. Know where that is?" Pat asked Skye.

"Yeah, wrong place. Current would be wrong," she said.

"Well, they have state troopers and drones. We got you," Ashe said. "Let's get there before it gets too hot out."

Skye smiled at him. "Hang onto something."

Then she threw the throttle forward and the boat leapt up and away. The twin engines roared smoothly and were no longer firing staccato, but humming the way they were built to. In seconds, they were speeding across the lake with a great rooster tail of water flying out behind them.

As they entered the main body of the lake, still smiling broadly, Skye flipped a switch and blue, white, and red strobe lights all over the boat began flashing. She maneuvered the boat expertly, and several other craft, smaller and larger, yielded as they seemingly flew across the water.

For several minutes, they went full speed across the lake, occasionally bouncing wildly across another boat's wake so hard, Ashe had to hang on firmly to the rail near him. Pat worked his way over beside Skye, who stood as she steered, bending her knees to ride out the wakes.

"We're making a hell of a wake ourselves!" he said.

"Police business," she said, smiling even wider. It was obvious she was having fun.

"Hey," Pat said to her but looked at Ashe. "I take it you and Ashe here, know each other."

She nodded and made a small correction to miss a branch floating in the water.

"Yeah, I used to see him at the gym in the mornings a lot. He dated a friend of mine, too."

"Oh yeah," Pat said, smiling at Ashe. He was being a smart-ass. "Stevie Collins?"

"Uh-huh. She was my buddy. We used to go out every now and then. Me and her and some friends."

"Oh, wow. You know, they're not seeing each other anymore. Ashe here, well, he's single."

Ashe was not amused by all this, so he did his best to ignore them by keeping track of the numbered markers on shore. He wanted to know their position as they went, in case he had to return on his own.

Skye looked at Pat then looked around at Ashe. "Really?"

"Yeah, no kidding. He's free as a bird," Pat said.

Have your fun, buddy, Ashe thought.

"Uh, no offense, *sir*. But, he could be my *dad*!"

Pat busted out laughing, and Skye looked a little confused but smiled her way through it.

Ashe gave Pat a 65-watt glare. On any other Saturday, under different circumstances, soaring across the lake on a nice summer day would be reason to smile and joke along. But in the here and now, Ashe reminded himself of their purpose.

If things worked out the way they planned, they'd find the spot where Charles Carter was murdered.

. . . .

In twenty minutes, they arrived at Sparks Point and idled down just to the east, or right side, of its rocky point. There was nothing much to see ashore but thousands of tall trees right up to the water.

Pat clawed his way out of his life vest and unpacked some binoculars while Skye pointed the boat to the west about ten to fifteen yards off the bank before killing the engines. Ashe took a pair of binos from Pat and they began looking; Pat at the bow and Ashe at the stern. For what exactly, they hadn't discussed.

Ashe hoped it'd be obvious, but just as he began to scan the bank and the shallow water off the point, he realized they didn't know much about *what* they hoped to find.

Just anything that looks like a crime scene. Maybe Chuck's pontoon boat. Some evidence of how and where he'd met his end, Ashe figured.

Skye radioed their position to Wurts but didn't initially get him. So she went forward, past Pat, and unhinged a trolling motor, dropping it into the water. Sitting in a little pedestal seat she assembled, she worked the motor with her foot and kept them slowly tracking into the current, just enough they could hover in place where they wanted to.

After twenty minutes, Ashe said, "Hey, Skye, pull ahead some. Take us slowly around the point and in to that big inlet. Stay about this far from the bank."

"You got it," she said. She maneuvered them away from the point a few yards and into deeper water then with only the quiet hum of the trolling motor, rounded the corner and took them into Cook's Inlet.

It was a large horseshoe-shaped cove; again, lined only with trees and deadfalls and the occasional big rock. As they slowly cruised off the shore at the same distance as before, Ashe could see where fishing parties had left snagged lines and lures, suspended in the trees.

There was no sign of a road or path, nor any place open where you could walk through the woods down to the inlet. Where there weren't dense stands of trees right up to the water, with roots sticking out from the bank, there were tall thickets and brambles of weeds and vines.

After thirty minutes or more of searching, Ashe felt his stomach rumble and took a break to sit. All he had in a pocket was a protein bar, but he was happy to have it.

He noticed at some point, Skye had taken off her shoes and socks to tan her feet. She worked the trolling motor first with one foot for a while, the other propped up in the sun, then the other. She also had her ranger shirt off. She'd worn an athletic-type bathing suit top under it, and she was rubbing sunscreen on her shoulders.

They arrived after another several minutes at the base of the cove and began coasting back out toward the lake, across the horseshoe opening of the inlet. Ashe noticed there was an unusual rock formation.

What's that? Ashe saw a momentary flash. A reflection, perhaps, like off steel or glass.

"Hey. Steady. Hover us here," Ashe said.

"What'cha got?" Pat said and turned his binoculars to the same direction as Ashe's.

"Look there, something flashed in the sun, I think. Just above those rocks."

"A reflection? I don't see it," Pat said. He took off his hat and held it up with one hand to try and block the sun.

Ashe lowered his binos and using just his eyes, looked around near the rock formation and then up the hill behind it. He had seen a brief but definite reflection, about three quarters the way up and below the crest of the hill.

"Can you reverse us back, Skye, we're out of position. Pat just use your eyes, and look for it," Ashe said. "A pretty obvious reflection."

"You wanna go ashore and look?" Skye asked.

Ashe waited as they slowly backed up to before where he was sure he'd seen it.

"No. Okay, now let's go forward again just like before."

"Okay dokey," she said, and soon the trolling motor overcame the backward momentum of the boat, and they repeated their cruise up the western half of the inlet.

After several more minutes without a repeat flash, they'd reached the mouth of the inlet back out into the lake proper. Skye pulled up the trolling motor and started the main engines to idle.

"Where now?" Pat shouted over the engines.

Ashe flopped back into a seat and thought for a few seconds then looked at his watch. It was just after two p.m.

"Skye, what's over that hill? Over the hill on the west side of Cook's Inlet?"

"That's where Cavern Creek flows in. But it's underwater."

Ashe looked at Pat; Pat looked at Ashe. Both men shrugged to each other.

Skye didn't wait. She pushed forward on the throttles and angled the boat back out into the main lake channel. They didn't bother with life vests; the only person who would write them up was driving.

Ashe kept a watchful eye on the hilltop he'd spotted from Cook's Inlet, scanning for another flash. Something. Anything.

Skye drove for about three minutes and then slowed suddenly, bringing them to another rocky point and another small cove. The boat seemed to sit down and all but stop. It was not a smooth, wide semicircle like Cook's had been but a jagged, much smaller inlet that looked to Ashe exactly like where an underground creek would come out.

"See," she said after cutting the engines. "Look at the water temp."

Both the air and water temperature dropped significantly as they entered the skinny cove.

"You know this place?" Ashe asked.

"I've heard some fishing guides talk about it. Look!" she said, and pointed at a big pair of chemical light sticks, long dead, hanging from branches on either side of the twenty-foot-wide entrance.

Markers. Like if you wanted to be able to find this place again in the dark, maybe.

She dropped the trolling motor over and began to steer them up it, past trees with branches that could almost reach across the width of their narrow course. Several times, they had to duck from clawing branches, and again Ashe saw several cut fishing lines and lures hanging from trees.

Ashe stepped to the console and threw the switch to raise the big engines up out of the water. Pat was up forward close to Skye.

"What the hell can we see up in here?" he said. "It's too close. I can't see more than five or ten yards."

They went around a bend in the water where they couldn't see the lake behind them anymore. In their narrow channel, the instruments showed the inlet actually getting deeper. Suddenly, the water widened out and they entered a larger cove. A big circular area, maybe a hundred yards across.

Pat turned to look at Ashe. "Ho! Damn, I bet not too many people know about this..."

"Pat!" Ashe cut him off. Pat turned and then followed his gaze.

Ahead, at the far end of the hidden cove, was a pontoon boat, blue striped, beached against the bank.

Skye saw it too and turned them toward it.

"Careful, slow! Only come about fifteen or twenty yards to the upside of it. Don't run us right to it," Ashe said.

Pat pulled out his phone but looked at them and shook his head. No signal.

"Skye, I'll take over. You go get on your radio and get us somebody," Ashe said.

"Ah…who do we need?" she asked.

"Everybody!"

Ashe guided the boat over to a piece of the bank, pulled up the trolling motor at the last second, and beached them where it looked like he and Pat could get off.

"Chig, this is it. I mean, a hidden lagoon, or whatever this is."

"You mean like, to protect someone?"

They jumped off the boat and made their way up off wet sandy gravel to the tall grass and started toward the pontoon. Both Ashe and Pat watched where they stepped, looking for anything that might make where they stepped part of a crime scene.

One step, look 360 around where your foot is for at least a yard. Nothing? Take another step. Repeat. It made for very slow going, but at outdoor crime scenes, *especially at week-old outdoor crime scenes,* evidence and clues get blown around, buried, disintegrate, sun-bleached, eaten by animals, or…stepped on and ruined by first responders.

There'd be plenty of "help" tramping around in a few minutes, so Ashe wanted to see the raw scene first.

"I got a trooper!" Skye yelled from behind them. "I gave them our GPS coordinates! They're coming!"

"Okay. Good work," Ashe said, and waved at her as they continued walking. "Stay on the boat for now. You may need to leave us here and go out and guide them in."

He noticed that she started getting dressed in her shirt and shoes again, then Pat tapped his arm.

"There," was all Pat said.

They were still twenty feet or more from the boat, but beside and slightly behind it on the ground was a big cloud of swarming flies. Looking below and through them, another body.

Probably a man. Face down on the ground. Camouflage clothing.

Good job, Patrick. I wouldn't have noticed him without the flies.

"Let's cut left and go wide, come up on this thing from behind," Pat said. Ashe nodded and they started moving.

In another few minutes, they came up slowly behind the pontoon boat. It was only loosely beached, probably from a drop in the water level. The motor was in front of them and the bow faced out toward the entrance to the cove. An anchor line was still in the water.

From where they stood, they could see the length of the pontoon's deck. There was no one on board.

"Looks like they intentionally set up here, facing out," Ashe said.

"Lot of staining on the deck," Pat said as he carefully set one foot onto the engine mount and then stood up so he could see better without fully going aboard. "Cooler, some clothes and beach towels. Huh, a little yellow pullover, like a woman would wear."

Ashe looked over at the body in the grass. Some kind of shorty AK-style carbine was beside him, near his right hand.

"I got blood here. Lots of brass too, Chig, tons of it. Looks to be nine mil," Pat said. "No gun I can see."

"I got a pistol-length AK47 beside camo-guy." Ashe moved carefully toward the body but wasn't about to fight the tremendous swarm of hovering flies. As he got as close as he wanted to, he saw dozens of 7.62x39mm brass casings around the body, splayed about in a pattern *not* consistent with how an AK ejects when fired straight ahead. Like at the boat.

Was he an ambusher, attacking the boat? Or was he helping Chuck by shooting?

"Has to be full auto, I see probably thirty, maybe fifty rounds out here. All directions, jeez, Pat! This guy had to have shot at the pontoon, but also behind him!"

"I can see maybe twenty or so nine mil rounds rolling around on the deck, so we likely won't get a pattern. Probably more in the water. And hey! I can see what look like thirty cal ammo holes in the side panels, the pontoons themselves, hell, even in the overhead canvas!"

Ashe grabbed a bandana out of his pocket and tied it around his nose and mouth and moved closer to the body. At five feet away, he could see what he was looking for.

"Pat, rifle shot to the face. Just like Chuck, except this guy bought it face on." Ashe saw where the man's feet were tangled. He'd likely been shot then as he fell backward, turned and landed face down.

Ashe studied his position and his body configuration. If he'd pivoted about halfway around because of something behind him, continued firing, and then he was shot in the head and his body went flaccid immediately, he just flopped to the ground this way as his muscles could no longer could hold that twisted around position.

Pat hopped off the boat and came closer to Ashe but not into the fly storm.

"He was shot face on, huh?"

"I think so. Probably from *that* direction," Ashe said, and pointed back at the hill where he'd seen the reflection.

"Then he dropped like that. Yeah," Pat said, nodding.

"Losing one's brain in a nano second explosion is like a puppet having its strings cut. I think he was shooting at the pontoon then something made him twist around and…see how the brass is going all over the damn place? He turned to shoot behind him but got shot midway through turning, then, well…"

Pat nodded. "So maybe Chuck nailed him from behind? No, wait, shit. Sorry. That's a big damn hole. That's like the one that killed Chuck."

Ashe nodded. "Yeah, all this talk is just preliminary, but I think you and I agree what this stuff shows us."

"Whoever killed Chuck, killed this guy?"

"Chuck was on the pontoon, bought it by long gun, fell into the water."

"Sure. It fits for now, until forensics gets here."

Both men backed away from the body and crouched in the sun, swatting at stray flies, sitting silently for a few minutes.

Pat spoke first. "Then, Chig, help me out. If Joe Tactical Pants here wasn't with Chuck, and he didn't kill Chuck…who the *hell* is he? And why's he shooting *at* Chuck?"

Ashe shook his head. "I…don't know. I hope Rachel's on her way with help."

Pat nodded and started to check his phone again but

immediately shoved it back in his pocket. Then, as if by instinct, he patted his left breast shirt pocket.

"You want to go up to the hill and see if we can find where this rifle shooter was?"

"Pat, you quit smoking."

"I'm game to go if you are."

Ashe took off his cap and rubbed his head. "I think in this damn heat, you and I let the troopers with good knees and the flipping drones scout it out. *Then* we old farts take a look," Ashe said, and grinned. "I'm supposed to be retired."

"Hey!" Skye shouted from their boat. She was waving her arms and pointing toward them.

Pat raised a hand and waved back. "Your next girlfriend wants to tell us something. Maybe you should show her the body," Pat said.

"I think you established she's my new *daughter*. Oh, and you? Nuh-uh, you're not good enough for her, so stay away from my..."

"No! Look, there!" Skye shouted.

She pointed to the left of the boat and at its bow. Ashe walked to the water's edge, following her hand signals.

Then he saw it.

"Ah, shit, Pat, we got another body."

"Another shooter?" he asked, and carefully maneuvered around to where he could see better.

"No, I mean, I don't think so."

Clinging onto the left pontoon, concealed underneath the decking, was a woman in what looked like a yellow bikini top. She was half in and half out of the water, draped across the pontoon.

"Skye!" Ashe yelled. "Call your troopers back on the radio, and tell them we have two bodies—maybe more! Tell them this is it!"

She nodded and started talking on the radio. Pat stepped a small piece in front of Ashe to see her.

"Buddy, I think I should've stayed retired," Ashe said.

"Yeah. Hey, Chig, didn't Sheriff Jacobs say he was looking for a missing woman?"

Suddenly the canvas cover over the wench on Skye's boat let off a sudden cloud of dust and water.

Before they could say anything, from behind them, they heard the echo of a shot.

Rifle! Sniper!

Ashe and Pat jerked their guns, turned, and ran inland toward some trees, taking cover.

Ashe looked back at Skye who was standing behind the drive console with her compact Glock out. She was panicked looking, wide-eyed.

Standing still.

"Skye!" Ashe shouted. "Start your motors! Get the hell out of here!"

It took her a second to process, then Ashe watched helplessly as she fumbled with her pistol, finally pitching it onto the deck and started the boat's big engines.

The windshield in front of Skye exploded, missing her by an inch. Then a half second later the sound of second shot, even more distant.

"Skye! Go! Go!" Ashe screamed.

Pat raised up to a knee keeping behind his tree, and with his big Colt 1911 fired three shots uphill in the direction of the shots.

Ashe rolled around prone and snapped off four or five rounds from his S&W 9mm as well. He didn't expect to hit anything, but just maybe between him and Pat, they could make this shooter duck. Or at least flinch.

He didn't hear the boat. *C'mon, beat it, Skye!*

He looked back at her. She looked at him. Then she dropped the twin engines back into the water and wound them up. The powerful boat lurched backward, awkwardly, but then she turned the wheel and with a huge geyser of water, the boat swapped ends and roared away toward the mouth of the cove.

Ashe heard an angry snapping flying over their heads and through the trees; high up, maybe thirty feet. A third shot echoed across the cove, this time with a greater delay. As if still trying to hit Skye and the conservation boat as it surged out through the narrow ingress, but from farther away.

"Why is he shooting at her and not us?" Pat yelled.

"Just a guess, big guy, but I think he wanted to stop *all of us* from leaving here!"

CHAPTER 8

"**U**h…my question stands. Who the hell are you and what are you doing here in this children's sanctuary?" Stevie demanded. She put her hands on her hips and took a step toward him.

She was more than a bit nervous, especially after Lou Buckram's angry visit, but she had enough courtroom experience to keep up her bluff.

"I heard Carol had been reported missing…I'm Clarence Crawford. Oh, hey, you're Stevie Collins. You know me, Seacord Community Bank."

She looked at him. He'd lost weight since she'd last seen him and shaved his old and giant moustache. He was medium tall and mid to late fifties; all gray on the sides with speckled black and gray hair on top. He was dressed in a work suit like he'd just come from a bank committee or something.

"Oh yeah, you. You were big buddies with…"

"Now, Stevie; may I call you that? That's all just ancient history. Mark Portals will probably go to prison for what *he* did." Crawford looked around the room and tried to move past her toward the bar. She stepped back and forth a couple times, blocking him.

"You're a member here, right?" She pointed over his head at the old wood sign. "You're a Blockade Runner?"

"Why yes. We are a local and traditional social club. Goes back years," he said. Then finally walked around her.

She followed him. "I work for the group that funds this place. I had no idea it was being used as an old boys' club," she said.

"The Foundation? Oh, well, we've been meeting here since well before these kids were sheltered here. That's why we use a private outside entrance and built the hidden door. So that way, the kids wouldn't be involved."

Crawford tried to put her at ease with a smile. It must have worked for him before because it looked to Stevie to be a little too rehearsed. It was probably his, "your loan is approved" smile.

"Carol Buckram, she know about this?" Stevie pointed to the picture with her on the man's lap.

"Yes, well, no, I mean, of course but not at first." Crawford took out a handkerchief and wiped his face. "There is nothing wrong with this, we're not even all that private. We are just a select few men who enjoy the unique and precious history of Seacord and greater Hurrt County, that's all."

"That's you in the photo with her, isn't it? Who is the dude she's sitting on?"

Crawford abandoned his pretense at a conversation and began to look around the room, moving objects, looking for something.

"And the girls upstairs? You have enough food and supplies in here to support them for a month."

"That's your job, I think, not ours," he said, almost absentmindedly as he began to even more openly pull out drawers then walk around the bar to search.

Stevie joined him behind the long bar. "You're the bank president, right? I need help accessing the Foundation's funds in the HCCS account to pay bills, get meds, buy groceries. Carol's missing. I have to help these kids, Mr. Crawford."

He stopped for a minute and looked at her, calculating the answer that would get her out of his hair, it seemed. "Um…just write the checks, I'll pass them through. I'll have someone bring a signature card over Monday, okay?"

She stepped closer to him, fully realizing it made him nervous. "Why are you here? Is there a big Blockade meeting tonight?"

"No, look, I have misplaced something and I thought it might be here, that's all."

From a corner of her eye, Stevie saw Brie at the door. While Crawford searched, she made a *scram* sign with her left hand, and Brie took off.

"But you won't mind if I repurpose some of this frozen food and snacks and whatnot upstairs, will you?"

"Help yourself, I…don't give a shit."

"Clarence?" she said in her softest voice. She wanted to get him to stop looking for a second, and also make him more nervous.

He turned and looked at her, but this time, he looked her up and down. Like Deputy Dawson had. Stevie smiled very faintly and cocked her head to one side.

"What are you looking for? Maybe I can help?"

He wiped his mouth with his hand and kept staring at her. Then, "Do you have it?"

"Have what?"

"It's…a personal item."

"Clarence? That doesn't help. Is it the same thing Lou Buckram was looking for when he was here earlier?"

"Lou was here? In here? Tonight?"

That frightens him.

"Uh-huh," she lied. "Also upstairs in Carol's office. He didn't seem very happy. He told me to tell you that, 'the gig is up,' whatever *the gig* is, and that it's all Michael Durant's fault."

"Did he take something? Did he find what he was looking for?"

"No, the sheriff stopped him. So, is Durant the man she's sitting on in that photo?"

He ignored the mention of Durant. "The sheriff? Here? Damn!"

She stepped forward and physically pushed him. "Hey! Clarence! Carol is missing! Of course the sheriff's department is involved! Of course her father is angry and looking for her! She's not been seen for over a week. You get that, right? Does whatever you're looking for help find her?"

"Oh, good God…"

"Shall I call Sheriff Jacobs back? I don't think he knows about this room. Or how about Lou Buckram? I'm sure he'd have a few questions."

"Dammit, no," he said and flopped on a stool.

"Or my fiancé, Tom Fischer?"

That seemed to snap Crawford out of his anguish for a second. "Tom is your…" He stopped himself mid-sentence, but his eyes went to the area where Tom's photo was.

"What is it? Where is Carol?" Stevie said.

"I'm worried about her," he said in a low voice. "I think they ran off together. I just hope they didn't take it."

"So tell me what it is, and I'll help you look for it."

Crawford held up a hand and mimicked holding a little glass or jar. "It's just a corny ceramic souvenir jug, about six inches tall. Like, a hokey little moonshine jug."

"Moonshine jug?" she asked. Then she got it. Blockade running was an old euphemism for moonshining. "Oh, I see. This little jug, why is it so important?"

"It isn't," he said and stood abruptly. "It's what's in it!"

"I've only been here tonight, but I haven't seen it," she said.

He looked around one more time then headed for the door. "Lock up when you leave," he said as he left.

As soon as she saw he was gone, she jogged across the basement and back upstairs, pulling out her cell as she went. When she got to Carol's office and could close the door, Stevie dialed Tom.

"What the…hey, babe. What time is it?" He sounded to her like he was distracted. Still on his stupid computer, probably.

"Don't *hey babe* me. I need you to come here to the HCCS in Seacord. Tonight."

"What? That's like thirty minutes from…"

She hung up on him. By the clock on the wall, it was almost nine and fully dark. She walked out to the porch and saw Deputy Dawson still out front in his car.

She walked out and right up to the passenger side of his car. His face was illuminated by his phone as he watched some kind of video, and he had not seen her looking at him through the passenger window.

So she forcefully slapped the top of the car. He jumped and dropped his phone. After he composed himself, he rolled down the window.

"Dad gum, Stevie, you scared the crap out of me!"

"It's Ms. Collins. Did you get the tag of the car that just left?"

"Huh?"

"The man who came into the house and was walking around? He just left."

Dawson jerked open his car door and started to get out then grabbed his radio mike to call in, then decided not to and dropped it onto his passenger seat.

"Never mind, Deputy, just call Sheriff Jacobs. If he's busy, could you call your reserve deputy Ashe?" Without waiting for him to answer, she went back to the porch.

At the front door stood Brie with a child in her arms. The little one couldn't be more than four.

"What's happening?" she asked as Stevie entered.

Stevie thought hard for a second or two then said, "You're all going to have a great breakfast, lunch, and supper, that's what. Let's get this little girl back to bed."

Brie nodded and took the sleepy child and handed her to Stevie. Brie said, "She does this. She's Marie, and she's always getting up all night."

Marie immediately threw her tiny arms around Stevie's neck and burrowed her face into the space between Stevie's neck and shoulder.

"Oh, okay," was all Stevie could say. She turned and started up the stairs.

Marie felt heavy and hot, like all little kids. Her hair smelled of sweat with a hint of baby shampoo.

Just like my Nora. That thought brought a small pang of guilt. Her Nora was almost eight and lived with her ex in the city. Her ex and his new wife.

Holding the little girl as she took her up to bed, feeling her dead, exhausted weight in her arms, brought back a thousand tiny memories. She hugged Marie a little tighter.

Mommy will be better, honey, I promise. I'm just sick. She'd told Nora, but he had taken her from school and dared her to do anything about it. In return, she'd gone on a three-day drinking binge.

I have to be stronger. I have to clean up my life...for Nora.

Then she found out he was getting remarried. Her Nora was staying with them permanently.

She was so excited to be a flower girl. She was so cute in the pictures. She felt her eyes moisten. *She's going to grow up only seeing me part-time.*

Stevie shook her head. *Not now, not here. Pity Party later.* She put Marie down in a child's bed in a room with three other small girls, illuminated by little cartoon nightlights. One for each child. Marie flopped over onto her belly, thumb in mouth. Her little nightgown soaked with sweat. Behind her, Brie turned on a standing oscillating fan.

They walked quietly back downstairs. Brie yawned and said, "So…what's happening?"

Stevie nodded to herself. She could still smell Marie. "I'll tell you what. We're getting groceries and all the medications tomorrow. Then we'll get the staff paid to be back here, and I want to get everyone some new clothes. Especially you."

"We need groceries," Brie said, nodding to herself.

Stevie yawned. It'd been a long day. Then she had a thought. "Hey, do you have big shopping bags? You know the kind you reuse?" Brie nodded and she went to get them.

"C'mon, Brie, we're going shopping downstairs."

As she walked back toward the basement, she had a thought and took out her phone. She started a text message then remembered that Tom was coming. *Or he better be.*

She thought about Tom in the picture downstairs then decided to go ahead and write the text.

Ashe. I need to talk to you. It's about business and it's important. Please call me, S.

CHAPTER 9

$\bullet\ \bullet$ ———————◆——————— $\bullet\ \bullet$

Pat and Ashe took turns moving deeper into the woods, advancing from solid cover to cover. They heard no more shots. It was still plenty hot, but the sun was heading deeper into the west. By his watch, Ashe saw it was just after six p.m.

Had the shooter left? Or was he well experienced and patient. There was no way to tell, so without speaking, neither man took any chances. Ashe would lean out from cover, low, just at the height of the tall, wild grass. He'd take a look toward the hilltop then find the next solid cover. Plan a route then wait for Pat to be set. Then move. Once behind cover, he let Pat do the same thing, then they would repeat the moves. Inching forward. Eventually Ashe knew they'd have to split, to try and get at least a 45-degree angle on him.

After several of these advances, they'd made it about forty yards from the cove. Ashe checked his phone; he had one bar but couldn't get a signal to make a call.

Skye got out. She radioed the troopers and Rachel. She'll lead them back here to...

Shit.

"Pat!"

Right back to this cove.

"What?" he asked. He was ahead of Ashe by several yards, and not where he thought he was.

"Skye! I think I screwed up. She'll wait for help, then lead them here."

"Hey, yeah. But Rachel's not stupid. She'll know what to do."

Ashe waited a few more minutes then tried to text Rachel.

Maybe the one bar would allow a text to get through. As he was trying, he heard a distant, whining-type sound. Like an angry hornet, but loud and getting louder.

Above their heads and coming fast from behind them were a pair of drones, about forty or fifty feet high. One came and hovered above him, its camera and instruments looking down at him. The other drone didn't stop but flew by at incredible speed, headed straight to where Ashe had seen the reflection. In another few seconds, the first drone took off as if to circle the hill ahead and come up from the Cook's Cove side.

Ah, yeah! Good job, Skye! Good thinking, Rachel!

"Is that the calvary?" Pat shouted, a happy lilt in his voice. "I told you she was smart! She'd know what to do!"

They stood slowly but stayed behind cover. The drones flew out of sight and beyond their hearing. Then, as if on cue, came the heavy, bass beating of air by helicopter blades.

A UH-60 Black Hawk helicopter appeared, coming in tilted forward, flying low and fast. In its open doors were men in OD green with M4 carbines on either side. It flew right over Ashe and Pat toward the hilltop and began circling. After a few orbits, it turned and took off inland, as if chasing something.

That's when Ashe could hear the familiar rumbling of Skye's boat behind them.

"I think we're relieved," Ashe said.

"I think I need a drink," Pat answered.

Walking back to the cove, Ashe saw not only Skye but a pair of powerboats driven by state troopers. Another wide and low-decked boat came in behind them with Rachel on it. Altogether, Ashe counted nine officers of various agencies, converging on the beached pontoon boat Chuck had rented over a week ago.

And the dead dude in camouflage. And the dead blonde girl in the yellow bikini, draped across its left pontoon.

· · · ·

It was almost fully dark at the cove. There were more boats, another, bigger pontoon, and the state forensics lab team had arrived. Big lighting units were set up to illuminate Chuck's pontoon boat, which meant billions of flies and mosquitos flying everywhere.

On the new pontoon boat, rented by the state, were two body bags. Technicians had photographed the bullet holes in Chuck's boat and taken samples of the stains, which definitely was blood, and collected brass. Fingerprints, UV light analysis. Ashe knew the routine.

In the middle of it all was Rachel Hume, directing the activity of her growing team. She had just taken a statement from Skye and walked over to where Pat and Ashe sat.

"You need our guns, Agent Hume?" Ashe asked.

"Nah. *Detective*. You didn't hit anything," she said and closed her pad. She had his and Pat's statements already.

"That's typical, Rach. You should make a note in your report; he's always been shit for shooting," Pat said.

Ashe sighed and ignored Pat. To Rachel, he said, "Well, I know you're going to work out here all night, but I'm exhausted."

Pat shook his head up and down. "Me too. Hey, who's that Black Hawk belong to?"

"U.S. Marshals. Some big wheel is flying in Monday. They aren't taking kindly to one of their retired guys getting blown away," she said.

"I imagine not," Ashe said. The Black Hawk had made another pass an hour ago over the cove, radioed down what they'd seen, which was not much, then likely headed off to refuel.

"They saw what they thought was a small trail, like for a four-wheeler, and followed it. But they didn't find anything else. I had some troopers up on that hill, trying to find where your sniper fired from, but it got dark and they're on their way down. We'll go at it again in the morning light," Rachel said.

As both men got to their feet, Rachel said, "Uh, Ashe, Pat, good job. You found this and even with the drones, it would have been days, weeks maybe before we would have."

"Any idea on their ID's?" Pat asked.

"Not on him yet, but she had her DL in a bag we found. Carol Buckram."

"Carol Buckram," Ashe repeated. "Does the sheriff know her?"

"He said he knows the family."

"So, other than the logistics of *that guy* shooting *her*, and then *another guy* shooting *him* and Chuck, any ideas on what this is all about?" Pat asked.

Rachel shrugged. Ashe shrugged.

"I'll talk with the sheriff and poke around in town. Maybe when we know more about the young woman, we will know more about why she and Chuck were out here," Ashe said.

"Your theory, that he was protecting someone, and their boat was anchored here to meet someone secretly," she said, not a question.

"It's all I got," Ashe said. "Pat? You got any other ideas?"

"No. I mean, we don't know that there *was* a protectee yet, except that Chuck *looked* like he was on the job. That, and of course, that they ambushed him," Pat said.

"We have a shit-ton of clues, a warehouse full of evidence, and none of it yields a motive. We haven't even got a decent theory of the crime. Three dead, still nothing," Rachel said. She rubbed her temples. "I hate cases like this."

Behind her, Ashe saw Skye watching them from the boat. She looked upset, or at least wasn't smiling like before. "You done with the conservation boat and Ranger Bennett for tonight?"

Rachel nodded and jerked a thumb over her shoulder then pointed at Ashe. "Yeah, you guys can go for now. And you...*you* stay in touch, Ashe."

Pat started to reach out to her but held back. "I have court in Metro, early Monday. I'll stay in touch and bring you back whatever you need from the house," Pat said.

She leaned in toward him, and for a second, Ashe thought they were going to kiss. Instead, Pat touched her hand and she squeezed his.

The two men walked back toward Skye and her boat.

"*The house?*" Ashe said.

"Yeah, and just shut up, I'm tired," Pat said. He was vigorously scratching himself, especially his neck and ankles. "Oh, and I hate Hurrt County."

They boarded the boat and Skye started the motors without saying anything. She cut on a pair of powerful headlights and they drove slowly out of the cove through the narrow channel. Once at the main body of the lake, Ashe was about to say something to her, but she hit the throttles hard and the boat once again leapt forward and up, speeding across the water.

In a while, they were back at the conservation dock and office where they'd started hours before. Skye expertly idled in and parked; Pat jumped onto the dock with a line for the bow, pulled them in close, and tied them off. Skye killed the engines.

"Hey, Pat, gimme a minute please. I'll catch up," Ashe said. Pat turned and walked back to where his SUV was parked.

"Skye," Ashe said.

She ignored him and started stowing the vests and some line and other equipment.

"You're angry and I think I know why."

She frowned to herself but still stayed silent.

"You think I yelled for you to leave the cove because I was protecting you. Like a woman."

She didn't look at him. "I'm not a full-time cop, I know, but I could have helped," she said, almost under her breath.

"You're wrong. You're a hell of a cop. You found the crime scene. You led us there."

"Then why did..." She stopped mid-sentence and looked at Ashe.

"Skye, I know what you're feeling...well, sort of. But I wasn't telling you to get away because you're a woman. I was yelling for you to get the boat out."

Her eyes changed from anger to interested. She looked down for a second then back at him.

"See, I don't think he was shooting at *you*. I mean, I don't think he would have minded hitting you, but I don't believe you were his target."

"Shooting at the *boat*?" She turned and looked at the roll bar and wench cover. A chalk circle was drawn around the bullet hole. The lab team hadn't recovered any slugs.

"I think his target was one of the engines. The left one, I'd guess. He shot from pretty far off. Again, just guessing, but by the delay from the hit to us hearing the sound of the shot, I'd say almost eight- maybe nine-hundred yards."

"He hit the wench cover and the tow bar because..." She thought for a second. "The angle and distance he was shooting from, the wench got in the way."

"I think so. The lab techs agreed. The second shot was fired about the same time we heard the first. He must have overcorrected, or the boat had shifted some as you moved on it. Anyway, the second shot was at the other engine. It hit the windshield right in front of the right-side motor. The polymer glass windshield deflected the round to… God knows where."

"So he *wasn't* aiming at me?"

Ashe smiled. "I wouldn't take it personally."

She thought for another second or two. "So you thought this all out in that split second after he fired?"

Ashe shrugged. "Kind of. I figured he wanted to ensure we didn't leave. He could have picked off Pat or me much easier, because we were just standing there stone still. Instead, he fired on the boat."

"He wanted to strand us?"

"Like I said, I'm guessing. But a full week later, he returns out there to that cove. Assuming he's the one who shot our friend, Chuck Carter, and also the camouflaged guy, why did he come back?"

"He left something? Something that would ID him?" Pat said from the dark. He hadn't walked off after all.

"So maybe, he thought we got whatever *it* is," Skye said, her smile slowly returning. "So, he wanted to disable the boat, and get us next. That's why you sent me out of there."

"Okay, mostly. I wasn't thrilled about the idea of walking home through the woods with a sniper tracking us. But…maybe I'm also old and just incorrect."

She looked at him and wasn't mad anymore.

"Make that *definitely old* and out of time. So yes, a part was me was wanting *you* to get out, to protect you. Like you said, you could be my daughter, so for that, I'm sorry."

Then after a beat, "*Not.*"

She smiled again and they got off the boat. After the good nights and stay-in-touches were exchanged, Ashe felt his cell buzz in his pocket. *Back in the world.*

Ashe. I need to talk to you. It's about business and it's important. Please call me, S.

CHAPTER 10

Ashe climbed into Pat's dark-gray Dodge SUV, and as they drove back toward town, he went through his missed messages. There was the text from Stevie, which he ignored for the time being, but he also had two missed calls from the sheriff.

He yawned for what seemed like a full minute. He was exhausted, both physically and mentally. His head hurt a little, so he closed his eyes for a second to think.

"Pat, you said you have court Monday morning?"

"Uh-huh, early. Plus, I need to spend tomorrow going over reports and evidence. Why?"

Keeping his eyes closed and rubbing his face he said, "Ok, just drop me by the jail, I'll have a deputy take me home."

"Why? What's going on?" Pat drove down Public Avenue off the Seacord town square then stopped sideways across a couple of parking slots outside the Hurrt County Sheriff's Office.

Ashe shook his head and sat up, looking at Pat and smiling a little.

"Sheriff wants an update or something. It's okay, I won't tell your boss lady."

"Oh, you... You can just kiss my big..."

"Hey! I do not have enough years left on this earth to get all that done," Ashe said, then hopped out, quickly slamming the door.

Pat pointed a big sausage-sized finger at him through the windshield as a warning, then as usual, punched the Dodge and after an illegal U-turn, shot off back toward Metro.

Ashe walked up to the Hurrt County S.O. building that was clearly in need of replacement, and showed it. Despite recent efforts by the county and members of the community to help fix it up, you could only do what you could do with a 1960s tan brick building. The concrete sidewalk and stairs had been patched but would soon need to just be torn up and replaced. A makeshift wooden ramp that sloped down to the only handicap parking slot, had been installed as a *temporary* measure years ago, to be compliant with regulations. But it had never been updated. There was mismatched mortar between some of the bricks and missing mortar altogether between others.

Being here was about the last thing he wanted to be doing after what all had happened on the lake. Seeing that poor dead woman, slowly decomposing half out of the water. He was bone-tired and wanted a cool shower, a colder beer, and a crisp bed. Maybe a fan blowing across him.

But Ashe made himself walk up the stairs as he looked at the building. It was typical for these rural counties, and he knew this building would only be replaced, if there was a federal grant.

Or a lawsuit.

Ashe pushed through the heavy glass and steel outer doors into the lobby, which always had the feint smell of cigarettes and desperation. The tile floor had been recently haphazardly mopped, missing a part of the floor and all of the space under the chairs. Compacted into the corners were tiny and probably ancient wads of wet dust and general dirt.

Hard to find good trusty's anymore.

As Ashe entered the lobby, there were the familiar old metal-framed double chairs with plastic cushions lining one wall. A dust-covered end table held flyers for crime prevention and warnings against fentanyl and drunk driving. Signs were taped on the walls instructing visitors how to add to inmate commissary accounts, bond company numbers, court dates, and the like.

Directly ahead was a big, greenish tinted window made of thick glass that took up the whole rear wall of the lobby. Behind the glass, Ashe could barely make out the silhouette of someone, partially illuminated by the glow of computer monitors.

The dispatchers had come to know him, and whoever was on duty buzzed him through a solid door on his right and into the offices.

Inside was a hallway that led toward the back of the building, and past the walled-off dispatch station. A few feet in the door, and on the left side the hallway, a split "Dutch" door led into the dispatch office. The top half was open and Ashe knocked on the small ledge of the closed bottom half.

"Hey, Mister Ashe," said Ginny, one of the dispatchers. She rolled her office chair back and opened the rest of the door for him.

"Hi. How are you? The high sheriff has been looking for me, I believe," he said, stepping up onto the raised floor. He felt his knees go soft a little as he did.

"I'm fine, I'm here, that's about it. Hang on, I'll find him for you." She pushed with her feet and rolled back up to her console and desk just to the other side of the small room. "Hey, nice outfit. Shorts, huh?"

Ashe decided he should have brought a change, but who could have known he'd be out this long? "I was out on the lake all day," he mumbled.

As she looked through her log and some notes, over her shoulder, she said, "Hey, didn't we have a history class together in school? What was that teacher's name?"

Ashe shrugged and didn't answer her. Ginny was in her mid-fifties and often mentioned to Ashe that she had gone to school in Hurrt County with him and Tilly, but he could never place her. Then once last winter, she happened to mention the year she graduated high school, so he calculated that when he and Tilly were seniors, she would have been in sixth grade.

He never busted her out about that, but how could he have remembered her? She'd have only been a kid to him back then. Since he'd returned home, he'd been making an effort to try to get to know the people in town that had lived here all their lives, and would have known his family. She'd mentioned to him the first time they'd met; she knew that his father, Robert Ashe, had once been sheriff of Hurrt County for one term back in the sixties. But when Ashe last lived here in Seacord, as a high school senior before joining the Army, he could not have really known anyone her age.

But this seemed to be the way of small towns. Everyone sought to find a connection, no matter how flimsy, to everyone else. Ashe thought that it was human nature to seek out your tribe.

It was likely why total strangers tried to call him by his

childhood nickname, "Chig." People who could not possibly have been that familiar with him thirty years or more ago.

But not being a real people person, it was likely also why he corrected most of them.

Older ladies he didn't know spoke to him of his mother; several people talked fondly about his dad. Since he'd moved back home almost three years ago, and especially after the violent events of the past year, many more people tried to draw a line connecting themselves to him.

But lately, less so. People he couldn't have known still claimed a familiarity that didn't exist but likely not for communal reasons.

I'm that guy. The one who killed those men. Right on the town square. The guy, the retired detective from Metro, the one who dated the pretty lawyer...they said she was too young for me.

Looking at this side of the big glass window, he could see his ghostly reflection in it, illuminated by the pale TV light. Even to his eyes, he looked tired. And old.

The guy who got shot in front of Roger's Café.

Ashe wiped his face, yawned again, and decided it'd been a long day. *Hell, if Ginny's just a kid, I'm a senior citizen.*

She found what she was looking for. "The sheriff last checked out at the Hurrt County Children's Sanctuary. You know where that is?"

"Um, no. What street is it on?"

"Sixth Street just past Clark Avenue. Hang on, I'll call him."

Ashe noticed she called his cell rather than radio him. She was being discreet for some reason.

When she got him, she rolled her chair back again to hand the receiver to Ashe, and an incredibly long and twisted phone cord uncurled as she did.

"Ashe, you free from out there? Can you come by here? Shit, this is stupid! You need to see this," Sheriff Jacobs said.

Ashe agreed and hung up. He went to use the restroom before he left, then as he was passing the split dispatch door again, he saw Ginny was resting her head and arms on the door ledge.

"He ever issue you a car? I saw you got dropped off out front. Do you even *have* a car outside?"

Then it hit Ashe. *Dammit.* "Actually, no. I...could use a ride."

She smiled and rolled back across the room to her desk and

called a unit to pick him up.

"You are the new detective now, right? I heard that, you know. I mean, given our last one got fired."

Ashe wasn't sure what to say. He'd actually been instrumental in having the previous detective arrested and jailed. Jacobs had mentioned to him several people wanted that title.

Unsure what she'd heard, he said, "I'm supposed to be retired. The sheriff made me a reserve deputy last year. I don't know about this detective stuff."

She nodded slowly and seemed to be about to ask something else but looked up and over her shoulder out the long front window. "Well, your ride's here."

Ashe thanked her and went out to a waiting sheriff's cruiser.

· · · ·

Ashe rode with Deputy Ed Bell across town to the Hurrt County Children's Sanctuary. He knew Bell, and in fact, probably owed him his life for a last-minute rescue during an arrest. At six foot five or bigger, and not much, if any, fat on him, Bell was often referred to as the "Hurrt County Swat Team." Just him.

They pulled up at the Sanctuary and parked beside the sheriff's unmarked cruiser and another Hurrt County marked SUV. Ahead and on the porch was Sheriff Jacobs, a shorter man whose face Ashe couldn't see yet, and Stevie Collins.

Oh boy, he thought. Seeing her again stirred up a lot of things inside he wasn't wanting to deal with. Not after what he'd witnessed and just been through.

As he got out of the car, Jacobs noticed him and started down the steps to meet him, flicking a cigarette butt away. The man on the porch turned around to see who'd arrived. Ashe recognized him; he was Tom Fischer, Stevie's fiancé.

"Ashe, Ed, a minute first," Jacobs said. They waited in front of the car and Jacobs lit another smoke. When he got it going and the first long pull in, he said, "Tell me about what you found at the lake."

So Ashe did. When he finished describing what had happened at the cove, Jacobs was quiet. So Ashe added, "Has to be where

Chuck Carter's body floated from. And whoever shot him, shot the other armed man out there, and tried for the boat."

Jacobs shook his head. "Missed you?"

"No. He easily could have had Pat or me had he really wanted to. He wanted to stop us from leaving first. Disable the boat; take us later. At least that's what Rachel, Pat, and I are thinking."

"Because…" Bell asked.

"Well, guessing at this point, but the sniper had returned after over a week to probably try to find something he didn't get before. Search Chuck's rented pontoon boat maybe. Evidence that would ID him, or maybe something that Chuck was protecting, we just can't guess what yet. But something important enough to be worth killing us for a second chance."

"I bet that park ranger was shook up," Jacobs said between drags.

Ashe shrugged. "Skye Bennett? Sure, but she did okay, actually."

"Now…Carol Buckram," Jacobs said, and lit a fresh cigarette off the one he was finishing. "She was the administrator here at the sanctuary. You sure it's her out there?"

"Yeah, she had ID in her purse out there. I mean, at this point, it's as conclusive as you can get from that decomposed of a body."

"Did this sniper shoot her too?"

"No. The other dead guy, no ID on him yet. He was wearing hunting camo and had an AK-type automatic carbine. Looks like *he* shot Carol, but then *he* got taken out from a distance by the sniper. Wounds similar to Chuck's."

"Dadgum," Bell said. "So they weren't working together? Why'd he shoot the AK guy?"

"*That,* my friend, is a very good question," Ashe said.

"Ah rotty hell," Jacobs said and flicked his smoke away. "You know what that means."

Ashe nodded. "We have two separate shooters who were at the cove for most likely the same reason, but two opposing interests."

"Damn." Jacobs looked at the ground and kicked at some gravel for a few seconds. "I had a feeling…I told you yesterday. I knew this was going to be some complicated…stuff. Sorry, Ashe."

Ashe only nodded. "It's okay, boss. But if we're right, and we have two separate parties, both of whom wanted something badly enough to send guns out there to the cove. And someone else, I'd say a third party, got Chuck Carter involved for protection. Then...well, he got caught right damn smack in the middle."

"He didn't know," Bell said.

Ashe looked at the big man and nodded agreement. "He damn sure couldn't have expected what he got, or my friend Chuck would never have gone out there alone, in a suit, and armed with only a pistol."

Bell added, "He *had* to have been told *where* to meet one of them, or the sniper wouldn't have been in position, way out there. Carter didn't prepare for this. Probably didn't have time to plan or prep. I mean, given his witness security background."

"Yeah, that's good. Spot on, Ed," Ashe said. He liked what he was hearing from Deputy Ed Bell, and liked his thinking.

Bell then said, "So...three? We have three different groups here? The sniper and whoever or whatever his interests are; the AK camo guy who shot the girl, and whoever he represents; and then the Buckram woman and Charles Carter, for whatever reason they were there."

"Well, only the sniper is left there alive as far as we can tell," Jacobs said. "Ah, hell! Forget I said that! I'm thinking like that rookie coroner! Chuck Carter in a suit on a pontoon boat in the summer with a woman in a bikini? For what reason? He'd have dressed more like...well, *you*, Ashe."

Jacobs pointed at his shorts. "No, there surely had to be someone else on that boat. Someone who..." Jacobs' voice trailed off as a new thought ran across his face.

"Speaking of Carol Buckram, you need to notify her next of kin?" Ashe said, not really a question.

Bell exhaled sharply and he and Jacobs exchanged a hard look.

"Well, that's where Stevie comes in. Carol's father is Lou Buckram. Know him?"

"Not really, no. I think he used to run a salvage yard or something, years ago."

"Yeah. Not anymore. He's been out here tonight since Stevie reported Carol—his daughter— missing. Tearing through her office looking for something. Seemed *damned* important he find it. He kept accusing Stevie of knowing all about it. Scared the hell outta her. Me and Deputy Dawson had to brace him, threaten to arrest him if he caused any more ruckus. Of course, we didn't know at the time his daughter was dead."

"That's interesting," Ashe said. He looked back at the porch at Stevie. She caught his eye and then looked away quickly. "Does Rachel know all this?"

"Not yet. I've texted Rachel, but she'll only see it when she gets back here, like you," Jacobs said.

"So Buckram was pretty angry. Was he angry enough to kill?" Ashe asked.

Jacobs continued. "Angry? No. No, he was *pissed*! Told Stevie to tell *these men here* 'it' was over, whatever the hell that means. And, he openly threatened to kill a guy named Durant. Seemed to think that whoever Durant is, he had run off with his daughter, Carol."

Men? What men?

"Run off? Maybe as if on a pontoon boat? Who is this Durant?" Ashe asked. The name sounded very familiar, but he couldn't place it. Too tired to think too hard.

Ashe made a mental note. *Buckram angry over his daughter, she goes missing, runs off maybe with a Durant guy, and now she's dead. Where is Durant?*

Buckram was looking for something. *Something important. Which of the three groups might he be a part of?*

"Well, I think we need Rachel to hear all this. Tonight, I think you should hear the rest from Stevie. Oh, um…by the way, that's her fiancé up there," Jacobs said.

"Yeah, I know him," Ashe said as they walked toward the porch. Tom Fischer had just stepped inside the front door. "He's a lawyer and used to work with Mark Portals' law firm. Before we busted Portals."

"Uh-huh. Now he represents the…*thing* that funds this place and also…well. I'll let Stevie tell you."

As they stepped up onto the porch, Bell stayed at the foot of the steps. Stevie stood up and went straight to Ashe.

For a brief moment, they started to hug then shake hands; then they smiled and laughed at their awkwardness. Ashe leaned as if to touch her bare shoulder and kiss her cheek but caught himself and backed up. Finally, they shook hands.

"Hello, fiancé," he said, and they laughed again. "Congrats, hon…um, Stevie. Seriously, I'm happy for you."

Stevie smiled her broad, open, unembarrassed smile. "Hi, Ashe. Thank you for coming."

"You texted me. Said it was serious. Of course I would come, you know that."

"She's really dead? Murdered?"

Ashe knew she meant Carol. "Yeah, I need anything you can tell me about her."

"Nice outfit," she said, looking at his shorts. "But hey, you still got the legs to pull it off."

She had always been able to divert the conversation and avoid direct answers whenever she was uncomfortable. Before he reacted to her teasing, or could ask her anything about the night's events at the sanctuary, Tom Fischer came back outside.

Ashe stuck his hand out and was about to congratulate him, but there was a different vibration suddenly in the air. Tom squared off on Ashe, his face not as blank as he probably wanted but barely concealing anger.

"I know you," he said. "You have no business talking with my fiancé, and no business on this property!"

"Tom!" Stevie said. "Cut it out!"

Ashe saw Tom's fists were balled up and his knuckles white. He was a few inches shorter, and overall, just *smaller* than Ashe, who never considered *himself* a big guy. But Tom's jaw was twitching as he tried to stare down Ashe. He was a man in love and jealous of his woman's former lover.

Maybe mad she texted me?

They stood there, staring at each other. Ashe turned and looked at the sheriff, who looked back.

Then as one, they both busted out laughing.

Tom became obviously confused. Ashe reached out and grabbed Tom's hand and shook it.

"Congratulations, Tom. She's a hell of a woman. Best of luck to you both."

After pumping his hand a couple of times, Ashe let him go and Tom stood there stunned. Jacobs clapped him on the back, smiling. Stevie did her best to conceal her smile by putting her hand over her mouth and turning away. She caught Ashe's eye for a half second, and that made her smile again.

With the tension broken, Ashe said, "Now, somebody fill me in on tonight. Lou, Carol, the whole deal."

"And, Deputy Ashe, another man from our collective past. Clarence Crawford, of the Seacord Community Bank," Stevie said.

"Really?" Ashe said.

Portals' old crew is really coming back together, Ashe thought. He started to say it out loud but decided to not push Tom for the time being.

"Sheriff," Tom said suddenly and held up a hand as if to stop conversation. "I am the attorney of record for the Foundation that supports the HCCS. I am also going to rep...ah, *advise* Miss Collins at least for tonight, unless some conflict arises. So, I am going to consult with her now, in private, before any further questioning. Stevie?" He gestured for her to go inside with him.

Stevie was tapping something on her phone. "Yeah, one second, Tom."

When she finished, she shot Ashe a serious look as she followed Tom into Carol's office, leaving the other men outside on the porch. In his pocket, Ashe felt his phone vibrate.

"Oh, and, Sheriff? Your man downstairs, I'm going to politely ask that he leave the premises."

"There may be evidence related to a capital crime in that room," Jacobs shot back.

"Then, in as respectful a manner as I can, and with assurances we will cooperate with the state, I would request you obtain a warrant. I am sure the Foundation, and the group who lease that room downstairs from them, would not want to move forward without one," Tom said.

"Well, son of a bitch," Jacobs said.

Ashe took out his phone. Stevie had texted him just then, so he opened her text. It was two words and a photo.

Blockade Runners

What the heck did that mean? Then he looked at the photo.

It was a group of men arranged around a mock-up of a moonshine still. Twelve men and a woman in a bikini. Ashe had to zoom in with his phone to see them clearly. When he did, he recognized several of the men. A county commissioner, a couple of Seacord town officials, a doctor, and the banker Stevie had just mentioned, Clarence Crawford. He had escaped being indicted last year, along with Mark Portals. Ashe looked for Portals, but he wasn't in the photo.

But Tom Fischer was. *Who are these men and what does this mean?*

Stevie had sent this to him just *before* conferring with her fiancé. No, *her lawyer*. That meant it had to be significant. Ashe swiped around on his screen, looking at faces, then he saw a sign in the background. "The Blockade Runners, Batch Launch." The date was a little over a week ago.

He next zoomed in on the woman. A caption beside her read, "Queen of the Batch." It was Carol Buckram, and she was sitting on a man's lap. In a bikini.

A *yellow* bikini.

CHAPTER 11

Stevie entered Carol's office as Tom warned the men on the porch to stay outside and get a warrant. Since he'd arrived about fifteen minutes after the sheriff, she hadn't had the opportunity to confront him about the photos in the room downstairs.

Tom had dressed hurriedly, at least for him. Nice jeans, a French blue dress shirt, no tie, and a lightweight beige sport coat.

"Stevie, listen…" he started.

"No, *buddy*, you listen!" she shot back. She stood eye to eye to him. "You have a lot to explain and it starts with this *club*, or whatever it is downstairs!"

She opened the "Batch Launch" photo on her phone, the one with him and Carol Buckram, and stuck it in his face.

"Babe, that's nothing…look, it's a harmless men's group that's been around for maybe a hundred years. It was important to be socially active when I worked here, and they were a very influential group of local business people. But that's not important right now."

"*Not important*? That's Carol sitting on some old dude's lap. Carol. You know…the *dead* girl!"

"The Bloc…um, the *group* had nothing to do with that!"

"What? You can't even say their name? The Blockade Runners! Who is that she's all over in this photo? Is that Durant? Her father said she ran off with him! Who is he? What is it that Lou Buckram and Clarence Crawford were trying to find here? Dammit, Tom!"

Tom tried to gently take her by the arms, but she jerked away from him and stood in a corner of the room. With both hands, she brushed her hair back away from her face and pointed a finger at him.

"You better start talking to me and it better be the truth! Or I walk out there and start talking to the sheriff and…"

"Please!" he shouted, then put a finger across his lips. "Sorry, I shouldn't shout. I know, the kids."

"Tom?"

"I will explain all this to you, babe, but for right this second, I have to deal with the sheriff. First, you need to know neither I, nor the Foundation, have had anything to do with Carol's death, or any death. That she was the…model for that photo was just a silly tradition. One they will probably cancel now. I agree, it's important to explain, but I was there for political purposes only. Mark Portals and a couple of other influential men here at the time, convinced me it was a good career move. Stupid? Yeah, I agree. But we both worked with Portals in the past, and we both lived to regret it, right?"

"Who is the man she's sitting on? The dirty old man with his hands on her?"

Tom looked out the window then turned to Stevie. "For tonight, I'm going to lock this place down, and as politely as I can, make the sheriff go get a warrant to buy some time. I need you to not talk to the authorities without me being there as your attorney."

"Lou Buckram will not be so easy to put off, Tom! His daughter has been murdered! He's convinced this Durant, whoever he is, is a part of that. Tell me, that's him in the photo, right?"

Tom plopped down in Carol's chair behind her desk. He stared at it and seemed to almost absentmindedly start looking around on it. "Okay, but please do not talk to anyone. *Especially* not that Ashe."

Stevie rolled her eyes. It was a little cute he was so jealous, but had he actually thought he could fist fight with Ashe? Ashe was a cop and given all he, *they*, had been through the past year, no wonder they'd laughed at him.

"Ashe and I have been over for a long damn time. You know that. But, he is the kind of man who can help if you're in trouble somehow."

Tom shot her a firm look. She saw he hated that she trusted Ashe. After a minute, he seemed to calm himself.

"Okay, yes. *Yes*, that is Michael Durant. Lou Buckram might be right, I think, I don't know for sure. I believe Carol and he had a...*thing* going. They may have run off together, given what we know now."

"*Michael Durant*. Why does that name sound familiar, and why would they have to run off?"

"The Blockade Runners is a tight, politically active social club based off a long-standing tradition of...ah, disobedience to private distilling laws," he said.

"Moonshining. Call it what it is."

"Yeah. Moonshiners were more politely known as blockaders, from the old blockade runners in the civil war, through the Depression and Prohibition where they *distributed* their corn whiskey. Flaunting it in the face of the law. Tax laws, mostly."

"So..." Stevie held up her hands. "Durant? Carol?"

Tom held up a hand. "Please, let me finish, I don't have time for everything tonight. But this is important. You don't recognize Michael Durant's name? His face there in the photo?"

Stevie relooked at the photo then shook her head. "Nuh-uh. But, the name, though," she said.

"Michael Durant is the ex-husband of Virginia Durant. *Now* do you get it?"

"Holy shit!" she said. "*Governor* Virginia Durant."

"Yes. Divorced about eight or nine years ago. Supposedly they stayed on good terms. *And*, still in business together, although that's not commonly known."

Stevie covered her mouth with her hand, as if to hide her own words. "The governor who will be running for reelection this coming fall. Her ex is a Blockade Runner?"

"No, well, sort of. He is a big wheel with the Able Keys Foundation, you know, the Foundation you work for? His company owns about twenty- to twenty-five children's shelters, nursing homes, and are getting big into graduated care facilities. Big corporate tie-ins. Not just around here but in three states. Anyway, some of the men in the group thought it'd be good, *politically*, to invite him in. Multimillionaire ex-husband of the governor and all."

Stevie was speechless for a minute. *No wonder Tom was acting so odd.*

"Anyway, apparently, and *unbeknownst to me*, he started calling on Carol Buckram. I was as surprised as you when we got together to launch this year's batch, and he had convinced the men to have her be the 'queen' for the photo. We had never allowed the Runners' affairs to be mixed with the HCCS. We are very strict about that."

"But you knew *then* they were…screwing around?"

"I had guessed it, but yeah. It was obvious by then. None of my business, I thought. I didn't know they'd possibly run off to defy the Foundation until earlier today on that video conference. The Foundation board informed me they had another, non-Runner-associated attorney to discuss some things with Durant. But I don't know what."

"My god, this is possibly how she wound up dead, Tom. We have to talk to the sheriff and the state lady, um, Rachel Hume."

"I know, but let's not leap to conclusions. Durant isn't a shooter type, nor a murderer. We don't know he had a thing to do with what happened to her. As the attorney of record for both the HCCS and the Foundation, and, I'm going to assume for *tonight* anyway, the Blockade Runners. I have to be careful how I do that, so we have work to do."

"My God, poor Carol. How? Why?"

Tom shrugged. "Not too difficult to see, when you think about it. It's an old story. She was from a hard upbringing; you met her dad. Durant was a rich man with a Porsche. The Blockaders had decided to kick him out, and the Foundation strongly suggested to her she end it with him."

"No, I mean how did someone decide to kill her. And the two other men who are dead. Tom, you cannot schmooze this. Let me tell you as a former attorney, you must come forward with everything you know as fast as you can!"

"Yeah, you're right, babe. But first, I need to find something. Nothing much, really, but the Foundation wants me to retrieve something that may be here in the building. Then, of course I'll give everything to Agent Hume and the sheriff."

"Let me guess. A little brown jug. A miniature moonshine jug."

Tom looked at her, and a procession of thoughts and emotions ran across his face in the span of a few seconds.

Surprise, curiosity, frustration, then respect.

"Yes. Yes, exactly."

. . . .

Ashe paced around the porch of the sanctuary as Jacobs talked to someone Ashe assumed was John Price, the assistant DA for Hurrt County about a warrant. Jacobs lit another cigarette, his third in fifteen minutes and paced about as well. Deputy Bell had gone around to the back of the house to check on Deputy Dawson, who was stationed at a back door.

Jacobs made instructions to have an old but reliable reserve deputy, Jeremy Franks, come watch the front of the sanctuary. Dawson and Bell on the night shift would trade off the rear. He also gave directions for support to Agent Hume when she and the forensics team at the cove returned.

After a few minutes, Ashe stopped pacing and realized he was shivering. All the sun he'd gotten, plus all the water sprayed on him, most likely. The rush of finding the pontoon boat in the cove. And Carol Buckram. Not to mention the shots over his head. As the adrenaline dissipated, his legs felt heavy. A check of his watch showed he'd been going almost sixteen hours and had not had more than a snack to eat. He sat and felt his socks and shoes which were a little damp still.

They won't give us a search warrant tonight, he realized. *Fischer is too good a lawyer, he's probably arguing against a warrant now. Plus, if he represents these people in the photo Stevie sent me, they must be pretty big deals.*

Ashe took out his phone and studied Stevie's text photo again. He recognized Tom in the photo, and Clarence Crawford the president of Seacord Community Bank. There was the doctor he'd identified earlier, plus a couple more men he knew but couldn't name just then.

Then there was Carol Buckram sitting on a man's lap. A man he couldn't identify but sort of recognized. The man had his hands on her, in a very *familiar* way. At least in this photo, she didn't appear to mind. Her arm was draped around his neck and she was smiling, *wait, no.* The camera had caught her mid-laughter.

Her hair was blurred a bit from where she was throwing her head back and laughing out loud. The man was smiling too, as if he had maybe just said something funny. The rest of the men were standing still, posed. They smiled politely for the camera, but these two…

They were having fun. They liked each other. She let him put a hand up high on her thigh; very high, inappropriately high unless you were lovers. New lovers at that. Once you were in a more established relationship, couples tended to be less showy, a tad more private.

Looking at her picture as best he could on his phone, she looked tan, maybe even sunburned a little on the cheeks and nose. He couldn't tell if it were just the split second the camera had caught her face, but also, she looked a little drunk. That could also explain her lack of inhibition with a man that looked almost Ashe's age. A good thirty years or more older than Carol.

Stevie said her father had threatened a man named Durant.

Ashe put his phone away; his head was hurting, likely hunger and fatigue. A short bourbon, a long sandwich, a quick shower, and a good bed sounded excellent to him.

Durant. Like the governor. She was a Durant, too. At least by… Ashe didn't finish his thought. He took out his phone and looked at the photo again, zooming in on the man Carol was with.

"Well…I'll be a kiss my ass!" he said out loud. Jacobs, still on his phone, turned and cocked an eyebrow at him.

Durant all right. Governor Virginia Durant had divorced her husband…what's-his-name before she was elected.

Suddenly Tom Fischer's attention and concern began to make sense. He didn't give a shit about these kids, or likely even the men in the photo who called themselves the Blockade Runners. Stevie's text made more sense; she was showing him this, figuring maybe Fischer would block her from speaking to the sheriff. Tom was here to ensure they didn't dig into Durant's involvement.

Blockade Runners. That sounded familiar as well. Ashe looked at the photo and tried to determine where it had been taken. There wasn't much of the room in view as the men mostly took up the whole frame. There was a bar of sorts behind them. The hokey-looking moonshine still and the sign that had their name carved into it.

Jacobs punched a button on his phone harder than necessary to end his call and gave Ashe a stern look. "Dammit, Price says he'll get us a signed warrant, but not until in the morning. The judge is *out of pocket*. Says we're not to enter the place absent some exigent circumstances."

"And I think I figured out why," Ashe said. He showed Jacobs the photo. "What is the name of the governor's ex-husband? And is this him?"

"Yeah...Michael, I think. Where the hell did you...never mind, don't answer that. That could be him, yeah."

"So this photo shows he's been here, with these Blockade Runners, and knew Carol. Pretty well, I'd say."

"Uh-huh. Fits with what Lou Buckram said. He said they'd run off together. But let me finish telling you something. Before her boyfriend showed up tonight, Stevie gave me and Dawson a look inside a fancy meeting room in the basement. A club, kind of, for the group. It's where this photo is hanging on a wall."

"A room? This room, here?"

"Uh-huh. There're photos like that going back thirty or forty years. Lots of folks here in Hurrt County in them. Must have been a popular club, mostly all rich folks."

"So now I get it. Tom Fischer doesn't want us to search this place, even for evidence of Carol's murder, because these men, these Blockade Runners, are not only local bigwigs, but Durant is involved somehow."

"Ashe, it was stupid. This old place for these girls, then right under their feet, a fancy wood paneled room with a pool table, huge bar, every kind of liquor you can imagine. I got about a five minute or less look, then Stevie rushed us out before her boyfriend showed up."

Ashe thought about that. "You told me Lou Buckram knew Durant, and accused him of being with his daughter. Running off together. This photo proves they at least knew each other. So...how does that get us out to the cove, where she was shot up by our AK-carrying guy?"

Just then, Tom Fischer and Stevie opened up the front door and stepped out onto the porch. Stevie stared hard at Ashe but didn't say anything.

Tom said, "Gentlemen, with regret for any inconvenience this causes to your investigation, I'm afraid after conferring with my clients, they prefer you obtain a warrant before any further examination here at the Hurrt County Children's Sanctuary. We fully intend to cooperate, especially given the, ah, apparent homicide of the HCCS's facilitator, Carol Buckram. But, we simply need to have all the paperwork in order. Insurance, health care regulations, HIPPA, state juvenile rules, all that. By your obtaining a warrant, we have a documentation trail that protects us all. I'm sure you understand."

Ashe said, "Stevie, is this where the Blockade Runners met? When did you two know about..."

"Miss Collins works for the Lifenablers, which funds this facility. She will not be answering any questions while just standing out here on a porch," Tom cut in. He was smiling during that last part, but his eyes were shooting daggers at Ashe.

"*I'll* ask you, then, Mr. Fischer," Jacobs said. "The club calling themselves the Blockade Runners. They meet here, right?"

Tom seemed to mull that over then finally seemed to figure out it would all be exposed soon anyway. He shrugged and said, "It's no real secret. Yes, the Blockaders have met here since at least the...well, a long time. Even before the HCCS was established in this old house."

"Back door? Private entrance?" Jacobs pressed.

"Yes," Tom said and nodded.

Jacobs drew himself up to his full height. His face was red but his voice was steady. "So, Mr. Fischer, with regrets for any inconvenience it causes to your *little party group*, I'm afraid this is a capital offense we are investigating. So *I* will be leaving a deputy here out front *to protect the children*. Especially given the disturbance earlier. Family and Children's Services has been notified as to a bar operating in a facility for juveniles. I will also be posting a man on the rear, *private* clubhouse door, to not only ensure the girls' safety but *also* to see to it no evidence is *removed*."

"Sheriff, I believe that is unnecessary. The...gentlemen who meet here are absolutely no threat to the children. They've taken extraordinary measures to ensure the safety of..."

"Bull," Ashe said. "Hell, Tom, they knowingly operated what, I'll bet, is an unlicensed alcohol bar in a children's shelter."

Tom snapped out of his lawyer mode and his face boiled at Ashe for just a second. Then just as fast, he resumed his professional persona.

Ashe continued, "Carol was the administrator, the lead caretaker of the children. She's been missing a week, hell, *dead* for a week, and you and your Foundation had no clue? The *Blockaders*, as you call them, they took no action to report her missing? To call someone for the kids?"

Ashe openly smirked at Tom, almost hoping to goad him. "So, *bull*, I say."

"Sheriff, I think that…" Tom started.

"Ashe's questions stand," Jacobs said. "He's my detective now. So, what about that?"

"Detective?" Stevie asked, then shook her head with a slight smile.

Tom cut his eyes at her then said, "We are done here, tonight. Any further questions should be submitted through my office and arranged by the district attorney."

Tom took Stevie by the arm and began to turn away, but Jacobs stepped in front of them.

"Oh, we may *or may not* be done here tonight, Fischer! Since both of you are lawyers, you should know this, but let me state the obvious. I have three bodies, three *murders*. The state police are handling those dead bodies out on the lake as we speak. There is a link from the crime scene to this place *directly*. So, if I *begin* to believe, or Detective Ashe *begins* to believe that either of you, or anyone the hell else *we believe*, is concealing evidence, obscuring this investigation, or obstructing justice, then I'll haul you and the whole damn *Blockader Running* little gang's asses down to jail!"

Tom let what Jacobs said hang in the air for a beat then said, "You, do your job, Sheriff. I'll do mine."

Jacobs wasn't done. "But in the meanwhile, nothing comes, nothing goes out of your little meeting room, or the administrator's office."

Tom just nodded without speaking, then he and Stevie walked toward the front door.

"And I'm towing Carol Buckram's car!" Jacobs said.

Right as she stepped through the door back into the sanctuary, Stevie turned her head and looked hard at Ashe. He'd seen the look before. She needed to talk to him privately. Ashe knew he just had to figure how to do that.

"I see why you almost punched him," Jacobs said after the front door closed.

"I did no such thing," Ashe said. "Besides, we have someone left to talk to tonight."

"Yeah, Lou Buckram. I guess we have to go notify him about Carol."

Jacobs took out his phone and after reading a text message, showed it to Ashe.

"Rachel Hume is back. They're at the dock now. Unloading the bodies."

Ashe nodded. "Well, our new coroner is getting broken in. He's getting ten years of experience in just two days."

CHAPTER 12

◆

They drove just out of Seacord on County Route 42 to Lou Buckram's house. Pulling through a gate and up a long, graveled driveway, Ashe could see the house. It was an older home, a two story with a wraparound porch. A lone yellow security light was on a pole outside what looked to be a large shop beside the house. From what Ashe could see, the trees and bushes were trimmed, the gravel drive and turnaround were well managed and raked neatly. A few pieces of heavy farm equipment were lined up in an open shed nearby.

The house itself was dark.

Large dogs, maybe pit-bull mixes, barked and chased them up the driveway. There were three of them and a pair of smaller dogs, all barking wildly and snapping at the car; emboldened by their bigger pack mates. They crowded in and tried to jump up as Jacobs pushed his car door open to get out. Shoving the dogs back with his door created an even more furious frenzy, so Jacobs produced a small squirt bottle with a big plastic head.

"Lou Buckram! Hello!" he shouted as he began to squirt a tight stream aimed straight at the bigger dogs' snouts. Ashe could smell what he was using.

Ammonia.

He squirted it liberally all around and on them. The dogs, even more angry, reluctantly faded back away from him but still kept up their bravery by barking, sobering, and snapping even more. They did not like that this big stranger was invading their territory but were not about to rush through a cloud of ammonia.

Jacobs squirted a big semicircle on the gravel and dirt then added a squirt or two to the dogs' rear flanks. Feeling the hit, they'd turn to see what had happened and get a snoot full.

Jacobs strolled up onto Buckram's porch and began rapping on the front door. The dogs turned their attention to Ashe in the car and jumped up and tried to bite through the glass.

"Sorry. *I* didn't spray you," Ashe said to a dog.

Jacobs rapped on the doorframe again, and looked through a window. Seeing the dogs jumping all over his cruiser, he yelled, "Hey! Hey, now! Git! Get off that car!"

The dogs were confused but obeyed then proceeded to growl and circle the porch. The smaller dogs were yelping, licking at themselves, and dragging their heads on the ground to try to get the ammonia off.

Jacobs appeared to write something and stick it in the door then returned to the car. A few more streams of ammonia kept the bigger dogs busy. He got in the car, and when he started it up, they all went crazy again.

They drove away with a gauntlet of pursuing dogs on either side. The bravest followed them even out the gate and for a few yards down County Route 42.

"The whole house looks dark. I think he parks a truck in front of the shop, so I guess they aren't home. I left a note for him to call anytime day or night."

"Ammonia? Neat trick."

"Way cheaper than pepper spray," Jacobs said.

Ashe looked at his watch. It was almost midnight. "Where the heck would they be?"

Jacobs didn't answer at first but took the time to roll down his window and light a cigarette. "I had to guess? They're looking for their daughter."

"Or Durant."

Jacobs thought about that. "Either way, we better get to the park's boat dock. Rachel gets back from the cove with her army of troopers and crime lab techs, it won't take long; the town will know. Buckram might be out there now, looking for Carol."

. . . .

Ashe knew from years spent at his father's nearby cabin, the dock was usually mostly dark, with only a few overnight security lights. As Ashe and Jacobs pulled up to find Rachel, the night sky was alit with a calliope of red and blue and amber rotations, dancing off the humidity above and the lake water below. The occasional staccato of LED strobe lights penetrated the night and ricocheted against the vehicles and tin-sided buildings. And off the faces of the people working there, giving them an eerie, otherworldly appearance.

There were several state police cars, a pair of ambulances, and the converted ambulance painted neon yellow that belonged to the Hurrt County Rescue Squad. They all had everything they had turned on full blast. Of course, a small crowd of onlookers stood just close enough to see, but not so close as to be run off. Ashe looked for Rachel but didn't see her at first.

Ashe grabbed a forest-green windbreaker out of Jacobs' back seat to try and fend off his shivers; one that read "Sheriff" in tan letters. They walked over toward the action, and Ashe noted that Deputy Ed Bell and another deputy he recognized, but whose name he couldn't recall, were assisting with lifting a pair of body bags off a large flat-decked boat.

The bags were loaded into one of the waiting ambulances. Just offshore was Chuck Carter's pontoon boat being towed in by another, larger pontoon. A pair of plain-clothed stateys were aboard, and Ashe assumed they were there to ensure whatever needed to be preserved as evidence wasn't disturbed. The boat's rails, seats, and the motor were all wrapped in plastic and taped up to keep them as dry as possible.

"There's Rachel Hume," Jacobs said, and pointed to the state forensics team van.

On the floorboard where the big sliding side door opened, sat Rachel. She was watching the bodies being removed, but her eyes looked dull and unfocused.

She was mostly in the dark, but an occasional white strobe flashed her into view, then just as quickly, out. She was only there, it seemed, when illuminated.

As they walked her way Ashe kept looking at her face. He'd always thought she was attractive, in a country-girl sort of way, but just then she looked spent. Ashe guessed she was exhausted and feeling every day of her age. The reflected light from a strobe made her look pale and drawn. Every angle to her face and each corner were highlighted a ghostly white; each tiny crease, deepened into shadow.

I know the feeling, sister, Ashe thought.

As they approached, she looked at them, and a slight and weary smile appeared on her face.

"Don't take this the wrong way, Ashe, but I was really hoping not to see you until tomorrow," she said.

"It's okay," Ashe said, smiling back. "I know what you mean."

"How'd it go out there?" Jacobs asked, and lit a cigarette.

"Just…a lot to process. Sad really, that young of a girl."

"You didn't find another body, did you?" Ashe asked. He was thinking maybe Durant.

"Huh? No, no new body. We did find Carter's Glock in the lake near the boat, though. Round in the chamber, six in the magazine. He fired nine shots at somebody."

"Good for Chuck. I hope he hit who he was aiming at," Ashe said.

"And this," she said. She showed them a small plastic bag. Inside were wrinkled photocopies of photos. Ashe bent down to see. One was a blow up of Carol sitting on Durant's lap from the Blockaders Batch Launch photo. The other looked to be a printout of Chuck's driver's license photo.

"I imagine it will be too much to hope for a set of fingerprints off those," Ashe said.

Jacobs stubbed out his smoke against the heel of his boot and sat in the van beside her.

"Well, we have some news," he said.

"I thought you might," she said, and pointed at Ashe. "Or he'd be in bed by now."

Jacobs smiled. "Well, hang on." He told her everything they knew about the HCCS, the Blockade Runners, Lou Buckram, and finally, Michael Durant.

"Shit the bed," she said. "The governor's ex?" She looked at the Batch Launch photo. "I have to call my SAC right now."

Ashe checked his watch. "It's officially Sunday now. Maybe call him a little later? After some sleep."

She shook her head. "No, as of now, this is officially the biggest investigation in the state. Michael Durant! Dammit. We need to find him."

She closed her eyes tightly and seemed to try to think, to organize her thoughts, and that appeared to take a lot of her energy. Her shoulders slumped, but after a few seconds, she reached behind her for a black binder, opened up a legal pad, then flipped through a dozen or more pages to find a blank one. She started writing.

Ashe felt for her. He'd been in her shoes a couple of dozen times over the years, when he was in Metro. There were cases he'd worked when he wasn't out of his shoes for over twenty-four hours. His wife used to bring him a change of clothes and some food to the office.

He smiled to himself. She hadn't been so bad. She was probably happy to be married to a guy who was home on time every night. *Some other dude. Not like me.*

Or maybe her new hubby was retired too. And they traveled the world and danced all night around in his old house, laughing and...

Ashe shook his head. *Damn, where did all that come from? I'm worn out myself.*

Rachel yawned, finished her notes, and looked at Jacobs then Ashe. Even with his shadow blocking the lights on her face, Ashe could see she was as exhausted as he; likely more. Cops everywhere could identify with how she felt.

You can try to adopt a clinical approach to working with the violently dead, but only as long as you can mentally compartmentalize what you're doing. Doing what has to be done.

There is a stillness at the scene of an unnatural death. When first entering a place where a wild murder took place, and first seeing the victim, you can *feel* the remnants of desperation and their terror on your skin. It gets to you; you feel it on your face first, then like an icy finger, it traces a frigid line down your spine.

There is a moment, a half second or so, of confusion between the dull inanimation you observe, the absolute silence, and the dead calm of a corpse, versus how your nerves and your mind vibrate to the lingering echoes of the violence, still hanging in the air all around.

Yeah, Ashe knew what she was feeling. The pressure not to miss something, to be good enough. Smart enough.

But also knowing a sniper had just been there and might return any second. To try and take whatever it is *you* cannot miss.

Ashe looked at the other people there, working to get everything loaded, documented, inventoried. They all had varying degrees of the same, gray, tired look about them. He walked over to Rachel and put a hand on her shoulder. She looked up at him, her eyes dull and drained.

"Call your boss and tell him you're whipped. Give him the wave tops, *but*, tell him you'll call with more clarity tomorrow."

"I…I can't just…"

Jacobs added, "You're no good right now, Rachel. You'd say the same thing if you weren't done in. You need food and rest. We'll slay dragons tomorrow. Hell, I'm exhausted myself."

She took a deep, cleansing breath and stood up. "Yeah, you're right." She walked off and took out her phone.

"Okay, now, boss, same advice for you," Ashe said. "You've burned through more smokes tonight than I've seen you smoke before in a week!"

"You don't need to convince me, I'm headed in. The only thing that'll interrupt me for the next several hours is if they find another damn body. Or Buckram calls."

"It's Sunday. They won't post the bodies at the lab until Monday anyway. Let's agree to meet for a late breakfast with Rachel, and whoever else, to go over all this and plan next steps."

There was a sudden big roar and a rushing noise as one boat shoved Chuck Carter's bullet-ridden pontoon boat up onto a trailer. The troopers and the techs hooked it up, and they drove the whole rig up and off the boat ramp. They proceeded toward town with a state trooper car proceeding it, and another followed. All lights flashing and strobing, of course.

Jacobs nodded at Ashe and took out an almost-empty pack of cigarettes, seemed to think about it, then put them away. "Sounds right. How about seven thirty at Roger's?"

Ashe looked at Rachel, walking in slow circles, talking on her phone.

"Make it nine."

CHAPTER 13

Ashe arrived home at just after two a.m., after having started the day at five thirty. He decided if Pat knocked on his door again like before, he'd just shoot through the door and go back to bed.

He was still chilled despite it being sixty-eight or so outside, so he swapped his shorts and shirt for sweats, and then thought about a cup of hot coffee.

Nah, I should eat. Coffee will keep me up.

Looking through his fridge, he didn't see anything he wanted, and everything in the cupboards required cooking.

Not happening.

So to both warm up a little and help him sleep, he poured two fingers of Darkthorn Irish whiskey into a heavy bourbon glass and flopped into a big brass-buttoned leather chair in his living room. He took a long pull from the glass and breathed slowly, trying to settle.

The glass was heavy in his hand, which was something he'd always liked about bourbon glasses. Thick glass and heavy bottomed. He normally had a single round ice cube with his whiskey to roll around and bring out the smokiness, but tonight he drank it neat.

His big wood-burning fireplace sat cold and yawned at him. The old mantle clock above it hummed. Somewhere in the background, his air-conditioning cycled on. He closed his eyes.

Carol Buckram's decomposing body, draped over a pontoon. Half in the water.

He opened his eyes. *Oh, not so fast, Chig, eh?*

He thought about the guy with the AK; head all but blown off.

He'd been facing the boat, probably emerged from the brush that was close by. Hell, the grass was waist high, but he had dressed for it. He'd come to ambush Chuck and Carol, or maybe rob them of...

What's everyone wanting out there? What is everyone looking for?

Jacobs told him that Lou Buckram was angrily searching for something at the sanctuary. Stevie had told Jacobs that Clarence Crawford had been desperate to find something there at the Blockade Runners secret room.

Then out at the cove, Pat and he figured that the sniper had only returned a week later, likely to try and find something. Something damn important.

Hell, it probably irritated the tar out of him when he'd found us there, going through the scene and Chuck's boat.

Ashe shrugged to himself. The only reason they'd assumed the sniper had *not* yet retrieved what he'd returned for, was that he'd tried to disable Skye's boat. *He must have wanted to hold us in the secluded cove to see if we had it.*

Again, whatever *it* was. Otherwise, why fire and risk it? Risk being shot from those helicopters.

So, as of this minute, nobody that's looking for anything— whatever it is—has found anything.

Ashe sighed. Not knowing what *it* was didn't help. There were players in this thing that hadn't shown their hand yet. First on that list would be Michael Durant.

Also, why ambush Chuck and Carol? Was Chuck supposed to deliver something? Or was Chuck protecting someone? Carol?

They weren't expecting trouble.

Ashe swallowed the rest of the expensive whiskey. It was getting rarer and hard to find in the states since young urbanites had discovered it. He rested his eyes again and thought about going to bed. But the chair sucked him in deeper, and it was warm and comfortable where he was.

Carol Buckram opened her eyes. "I'm sorry," she said, though her mouth didn't move. Ashe stood there at the cove and he started to wade out to help her.

"Why are you sorry?" he asked her.

Behind him and from his left, he heard what he knew was the

AK guy standing up. His decaying body, in the sun for a week, was pulling apart from the ground as he stood. Weeds and dirt were ripping away from his clothing and flesh. Like Velcro separating.

Right then, a loud rifle shot rang out from the hilltop behind them. He saw Skye take the hit in her throat and tumble overboard.

Ashe jumped as if shocked and opened his eyes.

He let the empty glass fall to the floor and stood up. After a couple of breaths, he switched off the lamp beside him and started for the bedroom.

As he got to the door, he stopped and without turning around, pointed a finger at nothing behind him and said out loud, "Any of *you* that want to rattle chains or moan tonight, keep it amongst yourselves! I'm too damn tired."

. . . .

Ashe arrived a little early the next morning at Roger's Café on the Seacord town square. He'd dressed better this morning, hoping to stay off the lake. He wore a white nylon polo untucked over khaki chinos, and a pair of tan and burgundy summer trail-running shoes. The forecast was for 90 degrees.

He'd eaten at this place since high school. Every old booth with worn lumpy seats and oil-stained and scarred wood banisters, held a memory for him. Roger himself still ran the place, although he had to be eighty. Roger saw Ashe enter and waved then pointed to the rear corner where Sheriff Jacobs sat.

"Chig, you doing okay today," Roger said, and led him back through the small breakfast crowd toward Jacobs.

"Not bad. I do need coffee, though. The good stuff, not the crap you give the sheriff."

Roger laughed at that and turned to wave at a waitress then went to the kitchen. Ashe took the chair beside Jacobs so that both of their backs would be to the wall.

The round table actually only had one "blind" seat out of five. The windows were on the opposite side of the café, and in all but that one seat, you could see the front door. An emergency fire door that led to the alley behind the place was just ahead and to their right.

In other words, Ashe knew, the perfect cop spot. *Last one here has to sit with their back to the whole restaurant.*

"You sleep okay?" Jacobs asked.

Ashe recalled his brief dream. "After a bad start, I slept fair, I guess." Ashe looked up as a waitress approached with a coffeepot.

"I hear you. It must have been pretty bad out there for both you and Rachel to be…" Jacobs paused as the waitress arrived.

She poured Ashe a cup, refilled Jacobs' cup, then sat the pot on the bare wood table and took out her pad. "Anybody else coming this morning?"

"One or two, but if they're late, we'll go ahead and order soon. Say, where's Tilly?" Ashe asked.

The waitress tucked away her pad, picked up the pot, and frowned. "Something she said she had to do is all." Then she turned and walked off as Roger came over.

"Sheriff, Chig, what are y'all up to on a Sunday?" He grabbed the blind chair and turned it around to sit on it backward and smiled at them.

Roger Clancy was short and a little heavy, but Ashe knew he'd been an Army boxer in his younger days. He didn't look his age until you stared into his eyes. Rumors had gone around for years that he'd punched a couple of men half to death who'd once tried to hold him up.

He'd talked Ashe into joining the Army straight out of high school, and was one of the few true locals who'd known Ashe back then. So, his using the nickname "Chig" seemed normal.

Roger also was one of the first to run outside last year, when Ashe was shot and bleeding on the sidewalk. He'd pinned one of Ashe's assailants to the ground until help arrived.

"Today?" Jacobs said. "Breakfast with a couple of friends is all. Rachel Hume should be here in a minute."

"Oh yeah, the state trooper lady. Hey, Sheriff, I don't mean to pry, but I hear everything here. All them, uh, you know, that you brought off the lake last night…they related to the one you found at the park? I mean, have to be, am I right?"

Jacobs looked at Ashe, who lifted his coffee cup and took an intentionally lengthy swallow. He held the cup to his mouth until Jacobs scoffed and turned back to Roger.

"I'm not saying anything yet, Roger, but I think the state or the

ADA's office will have something out on the radio later today or tomorrow. People shouldn't worry. This isn't random," Jacobs said, then picked up his cup.

Ashe saw Rachel enter and lifted his arm high so she could see them at the table.

Roger stood and turned the chair back around. "Sheriff, three or more dead people. All shot, I hear. Just a suggestion, but I think you better release something soon," he said with a wink. He then roughly clapped Ashe on the back and went back toward the kitchen.

Jacobs turned to glare at Ashe, who quickly lifted his coffee cup to his mouth again.

"Well you're a big fat help," Jacobs said.

'Hey, I'm not on salary, and I'm off on Sundays," Ashe said with a wink.

Rachel smiled at the two of them, and grabbed a chair; not the blind one.

"Yeah, boss," Ashe continued. "Roger has a point. I'm surprised the big news trucks from Metro aren't here yet."

Rachel said, "Good morning, I overheard you. The press haven't gotten the story yet. My boss has put a lid on this for as long as it'll hold, or we get Michael Durant into protective custody."

Ashe set his cup down. "That's a neat trick. And *Durant* needs protective custody?"

"The big deal from the US Marshals I told you was coming? He's here, and has talked with my SAC. They believe Carter was hired privately to protect Michael Durant."

Ashe and Jacobs both stayed quiet a second, taking that in. Then Ashe said, "So...Durant could have been on the pontoon boat with his girlfriend Carol, and Chuck as protection."

Rachel nodded then waved at the waitress who started back over with the coffeepot.

"That's a guess, but a solid one," Rachel said. "The Marshal's guy, his name is James Wynn, says even though Carter was retired, he'd apparently recently hit up some of his old friends at the federal courthouse for any intel as to threats against Durant."

Ashe smiled to himself then looked at Rachel. "So, I get why Durant would warrant security on him now, but before, about a week or so ago, why did Durant think he needed protection?"

"We'd only be guessing, but, hey, his instinct was right. He just underestimated the threat against him."

"It sounds like you didn't get much sleep last night," Jacobs said.

She shook her head. "Did you? Or you, Ashe? You think Pat did after what all you two went through, and what we found out there?"

"So, not sleeping, you dug into Durant," Ashe said.

She yawned and it caught her off guard; she belatedly covered her mouth.

"I did. He is a busy guy. He has invested a lot of money into senior and special needs health care facilities through the Able Keys Foundation that he, his ex, and a few less well-known friends started ten years ago. It's the foundation that provides the life blood for the local 'Lifenablers' funding group, and twenty other such facilities. From children's shelters, like the one here, to senior living homes, all the way up to large graduated care facilities. They operate in several states."

"Huh," Jacobs said. "So, Ashe, your girlfriend works for him, indirectly, or course."

Ashe smirked at that. "Not my girlfriend, Sheriff, but that does mean that Stevie and her fiancé, Tom Fischer, work for Durant and company, *indirectly*." He cut his eyes at Jacobs with that last word. Jacobs winked.

"It took me most of the night to work all this up, but the rest I need will take subpoenas. And we have nothing to even start asking for them yet," she said.

"Anybody we could talk to? Any of his friends?" Ashe asked.

Jacobs jumped in. "And how about the governor? Could she spread some light on why Durant needed protection in the first place? I mean, like you said in hindsight, I see that he *did* need it."

"All good topics, but we're getting ahead of ourselves," Ashe said. He paused as the waitress filled cups and took their order. It was then Ashe realized he was famished as he hadn't eaten much yesterday.

When she walked away with the coffeepot and their orders, Ashe began again.

"First, if Durant *was* out there at the cove, he's either dead or in danger. I assume that's why his former employer and your special agent coordinator want him in protective custody."

"That, and he's the governor's ex." Rachel took a second to sip at her coffee. "She never remarried and I've heard they are at least on speaking terms. Meaning, I suppose she doesn't want him shot to death."

Jacobs nodded. "I doubt he's around here. He's too big a deal to be hiding near here."

"Secondly, everyone seems to be looking for *something* since they heard Carol went missing. And so far, nobody seems to have found it," Ashe said.

"A guess, that last part," Rachel said.

"Well, yeah. So here's another one. Whatever *it* is, it's with Durant, wherever *he* is."

Jacobs said, "So we need to know what it is, then maybe that'll help figure out what in the holy hell is going on."

"We need to start with the Blockade Runner room," Ashe said.

"We need to find Michael Durant. Alive or dead," Rachel added.

"If he was at that cove with Chuck? He's dead, I expect. Plus, from what you've told me, Sheriff, I think Lou Buckram would have liked to…" Ashe didn't finish his sentence. Something was suddenly different. The hair on the back of his neck seemed to itch.

At the front left side of the restaurant near the front door, Ashe saw a man was staring intently at him. Black male, probably six foot to six two, well built, short hair. As soon as Ashe noticed him, he immediately *un-noticed* Ashe.

"I think Lou would like to get his hands on him. I don't know, maybe if he knew Carol was dead, he could kill," Jacobs said. "But a week or so ago? Would Lou kill him? Maybe. I'll head back out there here in a little bit and see if I can't find him to notify him about his daughter."

"I'll look into the Blockaders. I have an idea of someone who will know more about them," Ashe said.

The man at the front of the café began talking normally to another man seated with him. A dark-haired white guy, who had his back to Ashe. They seemed to be carrying on a regular, normal conversation.

But then he blew it. Across more than twenty other people in the café, the guy looked directly back at Ashe.

Bingo, you're had, pal.

"We have an audience," Ashe said with his coffee in front of his mouth. He'd done enough surveillance to know.

"Where?" said Jacobs, who, to his credit, didn't start looking around.

"Ignore it," said Rachel.

"What?" Ashe asked in a low tone. *How did she know about them?*

"Front left. Black male and a white male at a booth?" Jacobs asked.

"That's them," Ashe said.

"Wait...*inside* the café?" Rachel said. Without being obvious, she found them. "No, that's not what I'm talking about."

Jacobs then looked at Rachel. "Yeah, what the hell *are* you talking about?"

"Be right back, I need to wash up before breakfast gets here," said Ashe. He stood and walked through the café toward the restrooms.

As he walked, he made a special effort to not look right at that front booth but didn't avoid the whole area. He didn't want it to be obvious he *wasn't* looking at them, which would be as bad as staring at them. He did look behind them and at the front door; then using only his peripheral vision, he saw the man watching him as he walked.

He stopped near the cash register and looked out the front door and waved to an imaginary friend outside. Then turned and walked past the cash register to smile at Roger standing there. All in full view of the booth with the two men.

Could it be innocent? I'm sitting with the sheriff; people know him and who I am in town.

But the man in the booth looked intense. He wasn't local. He was dressed decently but also so as not to attract attention.

Ashe had a bad feeling. This guy had *the look*. If you knew what you were looking for, you couldn't help but notice it. *That look*, the look of a pro. Surveillance is tough, and it depends on either you not being noticed at all, or if you do get noticed by the person you're watching, they don't know what to look for when they see it.

Ashe knew what to look for. However you tried to describe *that*, this guy had it.

So, his attention on Ashe and the others wasn't simple curiosity. *This is a pro. Pro military, pro intelligence, pro…hit man?*

Ashe entered the restroom. He washed his hands and dried them then waited about three minutes. The hairs that itched on his neck before, seemed to crawl. Ashe took out his phone as if on a phone call, and stepped out. This time, as the man and his friend would be straight in front of him, he made no effort to avoid looking at them. Instead, he pretended to be focused intently on his "call," and his eyes just naturally went to their table.

The booth guy had shifted in his seat and had his left leg up on it, casually turned so his back was to the window, and he could see the restrooms without turning his head. As Ashe stepped out, he looked right at Ashe then casually looked away.

Bingo again.

Ashe ducked his head and covered his other ear as if the background sounds of the café made it harder to hear. He paused and stood just past Roger and the register. *Don't rush. I'm on a call, no hurry to get back to my table.* Then he pantomimed hanging up and walked to the table.

"What the heck was that all about?" Jacobs asked. Their breakfast had arrived, so Ashe sat down and began to eat.

"You were right. That guy is seriously interested in us, particularly you, Ashe," Rachel said.

Ashe nodded and smiled. All casual and normal. Between bites, he said, "So by 'ignore it,' I take it you've had someone outside?"

Rachel sighed. "I put an asset down here undercover when I found out a former US Marshal was *sniped* to death. Then after the cove last night, I alerted him to go active."

Jacobs sighed in disgust. "Dammit, Rachel. You didn't tell me anything about…"

"It's my case, Sheriff. You and your…*detective* here, are coordinating with me. Plus, hell, Larry, when have we had time to talk?"

"Okay, that's fair. Let's go introduce ourselves to this gent, then," Jacobs suggested, and started to stand up.

"Whoops, he's leaving," Ashe said. He started to get up. Maybe Jacobs was right.

"Never mind, I have a better idea," Rachel said. She took out her phone and texted someone.

"Your...asset? Outside?"

She finished her text. "Uh-huh. I just told him to follow the black and white males, just now walking out. And you'll appreciate who our man is."

Ashe kept eating but wiped his mouth and said, "Oh?"

"Yeah. We hired Dan Breslin away from Metro. He's with us now."

"Sergeant Dan Breslin, from Metro Homicide?" Jacobs said, not actually a question.

That made Ashe smile. "You slick little cherry picker, you. I bet that pissed Pat off."

Danny Breslin had been Pat Keagan's partner for the past couple of years and was a seasoned investigator. Ashe met him last year and they worked together on the Portals case. He knew Breslin to be serious, smart, and tough, having come up to Metro Homicide from Vice and SWAT.

"He's a good man," Ashe said. "And good at what you have him doing today."

"We should finish here and go to the office. More privacy," Jacobs said.

"Yep, we just got made by the visiting team," Rachel said.

Ashe nodded. "Uh-huh. But unless I'm wrong, we just made their quarterback."

CHAPTER 14

Stevie awoke on a couch in the sanctuary's dayroom. After Tom had spent the majority of the night looking through Carol's files and searching the whole place for the little jug, she had organized the children's medication and doctor appointment files.

After one a.m., she'd calculated what she'd need to pay the staff and get more groceries, hoping Crawford lived up to his promise to honor any check she wrote.

Bastards. They had what would be, to these kids, a couple of weeks' worth of food down there. By emptying the shelves and freezer in their club, she wouldn't need to spend near as much as she'd first thought.

Tom at one point started to object to her coming into the Blockaders private room and carting off food, but she shot him a look, and he held all further objections to himself.

Satisfied she'd done what she could, she'd found this couch and a blanket. Tom had appeared at the door, but she turned over to face away from him. *He's one of them.*

Fully awake, she could hear a TV somewhere in the house and smelled...*could it be?*

She got up, tossed her hair with her fingers some, then slid into her shorts and padded barefoot down the hall to the kitchen; one eye open. There, Brie and Judy Franks were making a big pot of oatmeal and cooking bacon in the oven.

But it was the fresh coffee that got her attention.

"Your man went to get cleaned up and get you your fancy coffee," Judy said. "Said he'd be back in an hour to take you home."

"I prefer what you have here," Stevie said, grabbing a plastic mug off a shelf. In three more minutes, she felt human and considerably more awake.

"Where did all this food come from? You couldn't have bought it last night," Judy asked.

Stevie paused between sips. "It was donated. I'll show you when you get a minute."

"It's Sunday. I'm all that will be here today, but you can go home, dear," Judy said. "Brie and I can handle things. My husband will be in here later. He's been on the porch all night."

Stevie frowned. She thought about why there had been a deputy outside. "There was another officer, a young man…"

"He's gone on as well. I saw him about seven when I came in. He said to call the sheriff's office if we needed anything."

Stevie looked at her phone. It was Sunday, almost nine.

She said, "I have your check ready based off Carol's books, and added in some for your showing up yesterday. There are checks for the other staff's back pay as well."

Judy tilted her head to one side and made a thoughtful pout. "Oh, okay. Good."

"And, I got the meds and appointments organized and on the calendar in the office. I'll get everything refilled when I can, but I've made an arrangement at the bank."

"Oh, no. You go on, I'll have Jeremy get the scripts we need."

Stevie didn't argue. "Okay. I'll sign the checks for that, just keep the receipts and the amounts for each check."

Judy frowned. "We can do that?"

"Oh, *hell* yeah. I think if you needed a pool table, I know where we could get one."

Judy laughed at that, but Stevie added, "I'm totally serious."

Stevie went back to the dayroom with her coffee and put on her shoes. She saw a note near where she'd slept, from Tom.

Love you, please remember that. We will talk as long as you want today.

"Huh," she said out loud to no one.

She went to the closest bathroom and washed her face then using a brush from her purse, tried to get her hair under control. As she did, she had a thought.

They will soon come take everything. These Blockaders, they might try to hide their connection with Carol before the sheriff gets his warrant.

So Stevie walked back downstairs, sipping her coffee, across the basement to the room with the old furnace that concealed the meeting place.

There was a new hasp and large padlock installed.

Stevie didn't hesitate. She looked around, and back in the basement, she found a shovel. She wedged the tip of the shovel head underneath the hasp where it was screwed in and began to pry. Shaking the head of the shovel back and forth, the screws loosened. One by one, they fell out and the hasp and lock flopped uselessly.

Sent a lawyer to do a carpenter's job, she thought with a smile. Tom was many things, but he was a lousy handy man.

Opening the concealed door and turning on the lights, she found herself completely surprised. Her fiancé had indeed been busy last night. From what she saw, she doubted he'd slept at all.

All of the alcohol was gone, and there had been a lot of it. Empty bottles of very expensive scotch and bourbon, along with rare brands of tequila, were stacked into boxes by the door to be thrown out. He'd poured it all out. The smell of it all was everywhere, and it was for a second hypnotic to her.

In another life, he wouldn't have had to dump so much; she'd have drunk what she could.

Parts of wall molding and even some of the paneling had been pried off and lay in piles on the floor. In the huge antique case of drawers behind the bar, every drawer was pulled out. Every small cubby door, open.

There were tools scattered across the bar. A small cat's paw pry bar, screwdrivers, a Sheetrock hammer.

He's still looking for that damn little jug.

Then she noticed large black trash bags crammed full, also staged to be thrown out. Opening a couple, she saw he had tossed all the club's party games and gambling paraphernalia. There were decks of cards, dice, a disassembled roulette wheel, dart board, and darts.

One box she stumbled over held paper records and books. There were meeting notes and receipts of dues paid; who'd won what, and who had contributed to the group. The box wasn't with the trash, and he likely meant to come save these documents. There was one document that caught her eye.

It was a stack of papers in a file folder that had Lou Buckram's name on it.

Looking at the file, there were receipts for payments made to him. Thousands of dollars' worth, where the club had paid for his supplies and hardware. Large amounts of glassware from a chemical company and sacks of corn and barley from the farm supply store.

Lou Buckram? The guy who said to tell the Blockaders, "It's all over?" The man who seemed like he wanted to tear Michael Durant limb from limb.

She took out her phone to start taking photos then thought again. Instead, she lifted the heavy box and carried it out to the basement.

Lou had asked about "it" and assumed she'd known about what it was. Then it dawned on her. *Lou was looking for the same little mock moonshine jug as Clarence Crawford.*

And so was Tom!

She came back in and looked around once more. She noticed the photographs were mostly still up on the wall, except the most recent ones. All the older photographs, going back decades, had been left in place, but the photos for the past ten years were gone.

Oh, Tom. Dammit.

She grabbed a screwdriver and went out into the basement then as best she could, reattached the lock and hasp. It didn't look too good but held enough that maybe they wouldn't notice. Then she grabbed the box with the files and ran back upstairs.

· · · ·

It was almost lunchtime before Stevie got back to her apartment. Tom wasn't there, but he'd left another note.

Baby, if I missed you there or here, call me.

"Huh," she said out loud. "Later, dude."

She dropped the box on the bedroom floor and went and showered. She'd grabbed a sub to eat and when she'd dried her hair and felt human again, she scarfed half of it down.

She flopped on the bed and thought about a nap but decided to look at the box she'd brought from the sanctuary instead. Tom's box.

Again, she found documents and ledgers with membership lists, banking statements, and the records of money spent for Lou Buckram. Finally, she found a letter to Michael Durant from the Blockaders, asking his financial advice on how to invest the group's money.

I need to know more about Durant, and...more about Tom and his involvement with these people.

She thought about that. She picked up a framed picture of him she had on her side of the bed and looked at him. Her heart told her Tom was a good man. She set the photo back down. This series of revelations lately had shook her faith in him. From the photo, he looked at her and smiled. It was a pretty recent photo, taken after he'd cut his hair shorter.

Like in another recent photo.

She turned the bedside picture away from her and decided she needed to find out as much as she could before talking with him too much more. In the meanwhile, she was going to take these documents to a place she knew and have them all copied.

As she lifted the box, her phone buzzed. She didn't immediately recognize the number but answered anyway.

A man's voice said, "Stevie Collins? This is Clarence Crawford, at the Seacord Bank. I'd like to talk with you, if you'd be willing to. I think I should explain some things that might seem all very...ah, *confusing* to you."

"Mr. Crawford. I..."

"Please, call me Clarence. Can I still call you Stevie?"

She was intrigued. Why was he calling? Maybe afraid she'd been talking to the sheriff? And why did he care what she thought? Then, she had an idea.

This may be a way in. To find out what I want to know.

"Yes, of course. What do you want, Clarence?"

"I thought we could get together and go over any...misconceptions, on both our sides, of course! Just talk."

"We can talk now."

There was a momentary pause. She thought it sounded like maybe he had held his hand over the phone. Then he returned.

"I was thinking...oh, are you alone? I only ask because I've seen where your fiancé, Tom, has started exercising some...ah, legal *oversight* at the HCCS, and perhaps for the...um. For the..."

"Blockade Runners?" She smiled to herself. *Why did these men have such a hard time saying it?*

"Oh. Yes. But, you see, that representation has not yet been decided. Now, I'm sure he is acting within his principles, of course, and in our best interests. Anyway, I was thinking as he is such a *conscientious* young lawyer, well...there's really no reason to involve him in a...casual conversation, between friends."

"I see," she said. *Why don't they want me talking to him?*

"I mean, we did a good deal of business together in the past, your old firm and the bank. I think, and I know many others here in Seacord that believe we will see you back here. Reinstated fully again in the near future."

She sat on the bed. *Does he think I'm that easy? That dumb?*

"What do you have in mind, Clarence?" Stevie said, then regretted she didn't have a recorder available.

"Well, we should sit down, have a...some, ah, coffee or something."

"Sure, tomorrow." *Wait, what's the most expensive place around here?* "Say lunch at the Fireside restaurant? On you?"

"Actually, I was hoping tonight. About six. At the...Blockade Runner's meeting...*venue*."

Tonight. Stevie thought about it. They wouldn't dare do anything stupid with her, knowing her fiancé was a lawyer, and her ex was the detective who brought down both Roger and CJ Portals.

What was it they thought she might know?

"Okay, Clarence. I'll see you there. I assume I should come to the *private* entrance? You guys have a code? Or a secret knock?"

Clarence actually laughed out loud at that. "That's funny, no. No secret knock. But sure, come to the side entrance. I'll be there with a couple of the other members and we'll have a drink and talk."

Stevie hung up and thought about that. A drink?

Guess he hasn't seen the reduction in their inventory yet.

CHAPTER 15

At the sheriff's office, Rachel spread her notebook open on a conference table in Jacobs' office. Ashe sat across from her with a zippered brown leather pad portfolio he'd been using since his days as head of the MCU.

"The deputy attorney general for the state and Mr. Wynn from the Marshals will be here tomorrow morning," she said. "The county Assistant DA, John Price, will want me to have some sort of overview done so we can brief them."

"The sheriff made a good point earlier, Rachel. We should interview not only those members of the Blockaders we know of but anyone associated with them."

"Might be half the damn town. Shit!" Jacobs said.

"And, we need to be prepared to possibly interview the governor. She may be able to shed more light on Durant and his business dealings," Ashe said.

Rachel set down her pen and seemed to mull that over for a few seconds. "I think the DAG, Rollin Ashad, will want to make that decision. But I don't disagree."

"I need to find Lou Buckram and notify him about Carol. I've had dispatchers trying to call him and deputies looking, but no luck," Jacobs added, then walked out of his office and back toward the on-duty dispatcher. As he left, he patted his shirt pocket and dug out his cigarettes.

Rachel's phone buzzed and she immediately took the call, standing to walk around.

Ashe noted that little had changed in the office. Jacobs still had his desk in a corner with a pair of chairs facing it. Several file cabinets lined a wall, and finally the short conference table where he sat with four chairs around it, filled the rest of the room. He had several training certificates and an official, oversized "Hurrt County Sheriff's Office" calendar on the walls.

One of the training certs was from a company called "Tactical Analysis Group." Ashe smiled to himself.

TAG, huh? Well then, he's a shooter.

Near the desk was a door that led to another, much smaller office where the previous detective had worked. Ashe assumed it was cleaned out and empty.

Rachel hung up her phone and returned to the table. "I have more searchers and crime lab personnel at the boat dock. They're preparing to head back out to the cove."

"You need to go?"

"Here in a bit, I guess. I mean, I feel like I should be out there if they find Durant."

Ashe nodded. "Let's do this, and hear me out. Put out a BOLO on Michael Durant. Not wanted, just missing. Contact HCSO or the state troopers if seen."

She made a note. "Done. You think he's alive?"

"I don't know. But if we're right, and the man we saw at the café this morning *is* the trouble we think he is, then he *has* to still be here because he hasn't finished his work."

"You mean killing Durant. Out at the cove?" she asked.

"He made a point of finding us at the café. I think he's doing what I might do. Instead of searching endlessly, he's decided the fastest thing is to tag onto us. Let *us* lead him to Durant, or the thing that everybody else is looking for. Or both. Like us, maybe he's guessing Durant has it."

"It, *it*!" Rachel sighed forcibly and flopped in a chair. "I'm not… I get what you're saying but…"

"I know. You're tired. Let me run down a hypothesis and you shoot at it," Ashe said.

Jacobs returned to the office, fresh cigarette odor on him, and said, "Yeah, I want to hear this. By the way, no search warrant for the HCCS yet. ADA Price says he's putting on as much pressure as he can."

"Do I need to get my people involved?" Rachel asked.

Jacobs shrugged. "I don't know, maybe, let's give Price a little longer. I still have a man there to be sure nothing vanishes."

They all agreed, so Ashe opened his portfolio, flipped the pad of notes to a clean page, and wrote as he talked.

"Okay, we originally thought the first event was when Carol went missing. What was that, nine days ago now? But that's not the real first important event."

"Uh-huh," she said. "I agree."

"The first item on our timeline is whenever Carol had that photo taken with Michael Durant and the Blockade Runners. I have to assume their affair was kind of a recent thing, then."

Jacobs said, "Yeah, that would be about a month. She looked like she had some sun on her face, so it couldn't be too long before that."

"Okay, second is somehow Buckram finds out about Durant and Carol. Then it gets dicey; he claims he's going to 'kill' Durant and blames the Blockaders, *but*, only goes to her office to threaten them once Stevie reports her missing."

"There's a possible gap there," Rachel said, and made a note. "Unless he only found out she was missing that same day. Hell, that evening!"

Jacobs frowned. "No, I don't buy that. She'd been gone from the sanctuary a week by then. From what he said out there yesterday, he knew about what was going on in the basement of the place. In fact, he wanted something from her office. He was ransacking the place! He even accused Stevie of knowing about *it*."

"You think, then, maybe he knew what happened at the cove, before that night? So he went to search her office, but found you and Stevie there," Ashe said.

"Yeah. When he heard Stevie worked for 'the Foundation' or whatever, he basically thought she was in on everything. So he knows that the Foundation runs the sanctuary," Jacobs said.

"Then his outrage was a show? To throw suspicion off himself," Rachel said. "You think he might have had something to do with the shootings on the lake?"

"Let's not get too far down the road on that," Ashe said. "We know third, Chuck rented a large pontoon boat and went to that cove. On board, minimally, was Carol and him. But we assume someone else, and I think that someone was likely Durant."

"Then where did the camouflaged man with the AK come in? Why was he there and how did he know to be there?" Jacobs asked.

"And...how did our sniper know when and where to set up to kill them all?" Rachel said.

Ashe tapped his pencil against his pad. "No. Yes. Maybe. Shit! This doesn't add up."

They were quiet for a few seconds. Then Rachel said, "Well, the shooter with the AK shot Carol, so Lou wasn't involved with *that*. If he was the sniper on the hill, then why kill Chuck?"

"And who is the man in the café this morning?" Jacobs asked. Not a real question.

Ashe nodded. "Hence, why we need to get our hands on Michael Durant. Dead *or* alive."

"I'm going to find Lou Buckram to notify him then bring him here. He needs to talk to us," Jacobs said.

"Yeah, that makes sense. Afterward, we go and get Clarence Crawford," Ashe said. Then, to Rachel he said, "I assume you want to interview Stevie as well. Officially."

"But not today. I have to go back out to the cove. Plus, we need to devise a way to separate her from her lawyer fiancé."

"Yeah. Maybe she won't invoke, and we can learn what she knows," Ashe said.

Just then, there was commotion out in the lobby. Jacobs turned to listen then walked back up the hall toward the front. Ashe got up and walked behind him with Rachel.

"Sheriff!" the dispatcher said, and pointed to the lobby door.

Ashe could hear a man yelling and cussing loudly, and what sounded like a deputy trying to calm him.

I'll just bet that *is Mr. Buckram.*

Jacobs opened the lobby door and immediately Lou Buckram turned toward him. "Dammit, Larry, get this kid off me!" Then with a powerful heave, Lou shoved a uniformed deputy back against a wall. The deputy lost his footing, fell, and started clawing at his belt for his Taser.

"Hey!" Jacobs shouted. They all rushed Lou and got him pinned against a wall. Jacobs and Ashe got control of his arms, as Rachel took Jacobs' handcuffs off his belt and locked Lou down.

"Quit! Damn you, sons a bitches!" he yelled, but some of the steam was going out of Lou. He was breathing hard and his face was beet red.

"Lou, settle down, now!" Then Jacobs turned to his deputy. "Jim, what the hell was this all about?"

"He came in demanding to talk to somebody. They brought me in off the road, said he was acting crazy. I didn't know who he was. He tried to shove past me!" Deputy Jim said. "I was gonna arrest him for assaulting me."

Ashe thought he remembered him from last year. Young guy, early twenties, skinny. He was related to another local sheriff named Minor.

After a few seconds to let Lou breathe, Ashe said, "Take the cuffs off. Lou Buckram, I'm Ashe. Please, let's go sit down and talk about this."

"Arresting me? Me? Good..." He gave a momentary surge to try and fight the handcuffs but gave up. He continued to breathe shallow and fast.

"C'mon, Lou, hell!" Jacobs said. "I've been trying to find you since last night to talk."

Buckram suddenly collapsed to the floor, his big meaty arms behind him. "Damn you, Larry, I used to do business with you." But he was out of gas. The fight was over.

"Let's help you up. Let's uncuff you and go talk," Ashe repeated.

Lou looked at Jacobs hard then looked at Rachel and Ashe. "You're an Ashe? You kin to Robert Ashe?"

"My dad. Let's talk. We want to hear everything you have to say."

Jacobs waved the deputy over who looked like he'd gotten the worst of it from Lou Buckram. He passed Jacobs a handcuff key. After Lou was uncuffed, he rubbed his wrists where he'd been straining against them.

"I come down here to find out who you done brought in off the lake last night, and a little kid tries to manhandle me! Who you hiring these days, Larry?"

"You need help? You hurt at all, Mr. Buckram? Can I call for a medic?" Rachel asked.

"Naw. Hell, I'm okay."

Good, Ashe thought. *If we're going to try to get a statement, him refusing medical attention is a good start. Although this deputy getting into it with a man who probably knows his daughter has just been found dead, isn't.*

Jacobs led them back to his office. The deputy entered the hall but stayed up with the dispatcher.

Rachel brought him a glass of water and they sat at Jacobs' table. "Sir, I am Rachel Hume, a criminal investigator with the state patrol."

"Yeah, I heard a lady agent was in town." Then Lou turned to Jacobs. "You brought some bodies off the lake late last night."

Jacobs nodded slowly. "Yes, actually Ashe here and Agent Hume."

"You find Michael Durant?"

Ashe sat back in his chair slowly. *Huh. Not, did we find Carol?*

Rachel caught that too, as her face registered a half a degree change. If he wasn't looking, he'd have missed it, Ashe realized.

"Uh, no, Lou, but we found who we have good reason to believe, is your daughter Carol. I'm very sorry."

Lou nodded and looked at the floor. He took a long drink of water and his hand was shaking. He carefully set the water down and looked at each of them. Ashe braced himself. This man was unpredictable.

Then Lou shook all over and burst out crying. Hot tears came and he wiped at his face with his fingers. Rachel stood and found some paper towels from the bathroom.

"I...I figured that. Somebody told me there was a girl body." He got up abruptly and walked around Jacobs' office. They all stood and waited for him. "Michael damn Durant. Thirty-five years older than my Carol! Now who the hell wants to date a girl thirty-some-odd years younger than him? Tell me why?"

After several minutes, Lou seemed to grow calmer, then he would suddenly stop to sob. He wiped his face and went into the bathroom out in the hall.

Jacobs, Rachel, and Ashe looked at each other. They didn't say anything; they didn't have to. Rachel held up her pad and showed it to them. It read, *Ask if he will tell us about the Blockaders and Durant?*

"You did business with him?" Ashe asked.

"Damn, Ashe, I ran the farm supply for years before running for sheriff. I did business with almost everybody here."

Lou came back out and seemed to think about leaving. Instead, he came back into the office and sat in a chair.

"Lou, I really am very sorry. Do you feel up to talking to us about Durant?" Jacobs asked.

Lou shook his head once left and once right. "My baby is dead, and I have to go tell her momma. Where is she?"

"She's been taken to Metro for an autopsy. I'm sorry, I tried to find you to tell you. We'll let you know when they release her. You want me to go with you?" Jacobs offered. "Call somebody for you?"

"No. Durant? Where is he?"

"Do *you* know anything about where he might be? Do you know if he's alive?" Rachel asked.

"What? How the hell should I know? You think I would know? I hope he is dead! Them damn Blockaders, they invited him in! Him a big rich guy with big connections, they said."

"Are you a member of the…" Rachel started.

"What? No! I'm not a bigwig around here. I have only one thing they want."

"What's that?" Jacobs asked.

Lou abruptly stood then faced away from them, and said, "Damn you, Larry. Damn Michael Durant, and damn them Blockade Runners!"

With that, he walked out.

"Larry?" Rachel asked, and pointed after Lou. "Are you going to arrest him?"

"I could hold him for assault, but hell, Rachel…" Larry said.

"A grieving father, distraught," Ashe added. "Better if we can approach him later. Have him speak to us voluntarily. But at least we know some things. He has a connection with the Blockade Runners. And, he was first concerned with Durant. And for the same reason we are, I'll bet."

"Huh," Jacobs said. "Good for one thing, he said."

Then Rachel said, "Anybody else notice he never asked us *how* Carol died?"

CHAPTER 16

After another twenty minutes of frustrating discussion on what they didn't know, Rachel and Ashe decided the best use of their Sunday was to locate Michael Durant. Sheriff Jacobs got on the phone with ADA Price about his search warrant request for the HCCS facility.

Ashe took lead with the Durant hunt as Rachel also had to coordinate with the troopers and forensics team that were coming and going from the cove. They had shifted their efforts from crime scene analysis, to finding where the sniper had operated, in hopes of finding anything that would ID him or...her.

But the main effort at the S.O. was Durant. After four hours of trying everything they could think of to find him, including phones, texts, emails, airline reservations, passport usage, even having state troopers knock on his home and office doors in Metro, it was apparent Durant was not around.

There were no highway or Metro ticket cameras that had pinged his car tag. His social media was ten days stale. He wasn't listed as the subject nor the suspect in any police or sheriff's department reports. He wasn't wanted anywhere, nor did he have any civil process listed for or against him. There were no court dates of any kind that listed him as even a witness.

Rachel requested a FINCEN report from the Treasury Department, which would take at least until Monday afternoon. In the meanwhile, borrowing Rachel's login credentials, Ashe ran a credit check which showed no withdrawal of funds or movement of money from any of the three banks he commonly used. There was no credit card usage in over ten days, nor any new cards, either. The FINCEN would give them any financial dealings they weren't aware of.

Durant had two vehicles registered to him. One was at his home just outside Metro proper, the other at his office address in the city. Ashe punted to Rachel to have the state look for vehicles registered to the Foundation he worked for, or leased to anybody where he was named as a driver.

They checked Uber and Lyft records, taxis, car rental agencies, and a couple of Metro-local ride-hailing services. Ashe even checked the records of bus and train lines. Nada, nothing.

Finally, erring on the side of caution, he ran it all over again but using Carol's name. She only had a debit card, and considerably less access to money in which to run, but if Durant paired his cash with her lower profile, well…Carol could be a man's name.

Still nothing. Everything he checked on Carol's life, both real and virtual, also ended abruptly ten days ago. That was to be expected.

"Uh-oh," said Ashe. He took off his reading glasses and wiped his eyes.

"I know," Rachel agreed.

Durant just might be found floating out at that cove, yet.

"Anything new out there?" Ashe asked.

"I know what you mean, but no. No new bodies."

"Your people find the sniper's hide?"

"Maybe. I have state police SWAT snipers out there, using the latest tech to try and determine exactly where the shots were fired from based on the GPS coordinates we took from the boat he hit. Whoever he…or she is, they're good."

"Hmm."

"'Hmm' is right. Okay, I'm done gathering data. Time to ruin other people's Sunday," she said.

Rachel first interrupted the Sunday of her special agent coordinator, who was golfing. Next, she contacted one of her colleagues to get a regional "Be On the Lookout"—or BOLO—for Michael Durant, on the wire to every law enforcement agency. He would not be listed as "wanted" for any crime but as possibly "endangered." She used photos from his driver's license and Linked-In account. It read there was an urgent need to locate and make contact with the state police, or Hurrt County S.O. as soon as possible.

Knowing everyone would recognize his name on the BOLO, she also had her SAC notify the state attorney general's office, and she gave a heads-up to the trooper in charge of the governor's protective detail.

By the time Ashe and Rachel finished what they could on a Sunday, it was well after lunch.

Jacobs was at his desk and hung up his office phone. "Damn, now Clarence Crawford isn't home, and he wasn't at his church this morning."

"Interesting. Other than Durant, I think I want to have a talk with him the most," Ashe said.

"Well, Price says to hold off on picking anyone else up for now. But, you'll get your chance."

Rachel stood and arched her back, rubbing her neck and shoulders. She heaved a big sigh. "I have to at least go check in at the cove, you guys. I'll be out of range except by radio."

"When you get back, we'll let you know if anything's broke open. And, we'll radio if we get Durant," Jacobs said.

"You might have hung onto Lou Buckram," she said, almost absentmindedly. "I know, I know. Charging him would have looked bad, but maybe after sitting in the jail for a while…"

Jacobs shook his head. "Nope. Lou would just get stubborner."

Rachel packed up her stuff, and as she left, she playfully punched Ashe on the shoulder. "Good work today," she said.

"You too. Keep your head down and let me know if Mikey D. floats to the surface out there."

Rachel grinned and left then Jacobs came over to the conference table and sat across from Ashe. "Your grim humor aside, anything at all we're not doing?"

Ashe shrugged. "All kinds of stuff. I think we should probably start running the financials on the HCCS itself, to find out if Carol ran off empty-handed or not. Maybe she looted the place?"

Jacobs scratched out a note as Ashe talked. "We should question Stevie, or I should say, *you and Rachel*, should interview her, about how the Foundation funds the sanctuary. I think we need to know way more about that. And of course, I have to assume these Blockade Runners have money, accounts, business dealings. Knowing everything about that might be illuminating and open some leads. Hell, maybe Durant looted them at the same time Carol looted the…"

Ashe stopped, and he and Jacobs looked at each other.

"Surely it ain't that simple," Jacobs said.

"Surely. But I think we need to know."

"I'll call Price back. We need subpoenas for this stuff, I imagine," Jacobs said and went to his desk.

"Sheriff, remember, the first subpoena to any financial institution should require them to provide an overview and written description of all financial relationships. Open or closed accounts. Arranged by type and account number. Then we start subpoenaing the details of each account we need."

"Got it."

"And, I know you know this, but these people will have accounts in every bank and credit union around. We'll need Rachel to fire up a FINCEN report to find them all. Maybe they even have offshore accounts."

Jacobs walked back to his desk and started dialing his office phone then looked up at Ashe. "Didn't you say last night you might know somebody who might know something?"

Ashe smiled. "It's actually sad I understand that. Yeah, maybe I do." He stood, stretched his back, and added, "I'm going to see a man about a dog."

"Do that, but keep your phone handy!" Jacobs shouted after Ashe as he left the office.

. . . .

Ashe knew who he needed to see. He only had to drive around the town square and up Fifth, until he found Burlwood Avenue. It was a short street that connected Fourth and Fifth, but it had most of the old historic homes in the county. Classic, stately wood, and all at least two stories with big, wide porches. Some even had stone or brick tastefully styled around the corners and windows to accent how important its occupants were. While there were more expensive and modern houses on the lakeshore, Burlwood was old money.

Halfway down, on the left, sitting on an oversized lot as

compared with any of the others, was number nineteen. Retired circuit judge Harold Marsh's residence.

Ashe parked on the street behind another car; a convertible with a set of golf bags in the back seat. It was a hot afternoon everywhere else in the county, but here underneath a canopy of hundred-year-old plus trees that lined Burlwood, it was ten degrees cooler. As he walked up through a waist-high iron gate, he saw an old Asian man wearing a broad cotton hat, on his knees, working in the small garden beside the porch steps.

"Hello, is the judge home?"

The man looked at Ashe as if he owed him money then shook his head and went back to work.

Is that a no, he's not home? Or a no, I don't know?

Ashe stepped onto the porch and rang the bell. As a child, he'd played on this porch more than a few times. Old Judge Marsh and his dad has been close friends, and for a few years, even business partners.

A woman, likely in her seventies and dressed as a housekeeper, came to the door. Ashe introduced himself then added, "I'm an old friend of the judge. I need just a few minutes of his time."

"He's on a call, and he has another visitor. You may need to wait," she said.

Ashe stepped in and waited in the front hall while the housekeeper went to inform Marsh. Ashe looked around. Not much had changed in forty years, even the pictures on the walls were the same. A dull-green runner covered the dark polished wood floor that creaked and popped beneath his feet. Somewhere deeper in the house, an old clock rang the half hour.

The housekeeper returned, and with her was a tallish, blonde woman, maybe late forties, dressed for golf, or tennis. She was tan, very fit looking, and to Ashe, she was somehow familiar. She wore a visor to keep her hair off her face, and a mint-green top over white shorts.

"Mister Ashe, isn't it? You're a detective out of Metro, right?"

"Yes," he said as they shook hands. "Well, I'm retired from Metro, but sometimes help out down here. I was raised here."

She smiled broadly and they walked into a sitting room. The furniture there was newer than he remembered, perhaps recently updated. Still, like everything in this house, it was designed to make a statement.

That statement being, *I have the power. You don't.*

"You don't remember me, do you?" she said as they sat in chairs facing each other.

Ashe looked at her and was about to give up, when it came to him. "Ah, you're an attorney from Carson County! I'm sorry…Lisa?"

"Linda. Linda Ingles. Yes, you were there at the Carson County jail to question one of my clients. Tracy Davis."

He remembered Linda. Smart, professional. He of course remembered the Tracy Davis case. Linda worked Davis a plea arrangement that was far better than she deserved.

"That jail was stifling," he said.

"God, I know! I was sweating like a horse and took off everything I could, *and* maintain *some* decorum. Ten more minutes and I'd have lost that!"

"Yeah, that was a miserable day," he said, not knowing what else he could say.

"You look much better," she said, pointing to the left side of his head.

He instinctively touched his head, just beside his left ear.

"So. You here to lock up old Harold?" she said, still smiling.

Ashe laughed. "Not today, although I'll wager he likely deserves it. What brings you to Seacord?"

"Well, since you put Mark Portals out of business, *for now*, I have partnered with Harold to build a new team to do some crim work over here in Hurrt County. If fact, I was playing golf and got his call to come discuss a case. I know, it's a Sunday, but hey! Now here you are. You working today, too? How is your head? That was some nasty business last year. Your ear does look better."

Ashe nodded slowly as she spoke, trying to keep up. "I'm not sure which of all that I should answer first, so I'll just say, yes, better, and thanks."

She laughed. "Sorry. I'm all jacked up on energy drinks and protein water from the club. I thought I was going to be out for eighteen. You golf?"

"Meh, badly." Ashe leaned forward in his chair. "Must be *something* important for the judge to call you over here on a Sunday?"

She held her smile but didn't answer. Red Bull or no.

"May I ask *you* something? You can refuse to answer if you want." She leaned in close and Ashe could smell her body wash or shampoo. Lilacs. Powder.

"Of course." He immediately worried what he smelled like to her. *Coffee, more coffee, and Jacobs' cigarettes.*

"You going to arrest Lou Buckram?"

"Hey, I asked first. But me? No. I don't figure I'll be arresting Lou today. He's a man in extreme pain right now. I can't imagine losing a daughter."

"I agree. It is awful. You found her on the lake?"

"Yeah," he said, while thinking, *She just jumped off Lou Buckram to his daughter.* "Me and a couple of others. And yes, it was as awful as you might think."

She shook her shoulders in a mock shudder. "Ooo. Any leads as to who killed her? You guys getting anywhere with that man who washed up here a few days ago?"

"Yes. Several leads. In fact, I'm here to interrogate my lead suspect," he said, smiling, and pointed to a large photo of Harold Marsh.

Linda laughed. "Seriously, what *can* you say?"

"Why did you ask me about Lou?"

She dropped half her smile and most of her flirtatious banter. "Harold told me you were good."

"I'll let the high sheriff make any statements on this case. Or Special Agent Rachel Hume."

Linda looked at her watch. "Damn, as much as I hate to, I have to go, Mister Ashe. Or is it…*Chig*? The judge calls you that."

Ashe gave her a 75-watt smile. "You two were discussing little ol' me?"

"Of course!" she said. Then slapping her knees, she jumped up and gathered her clutch purse, phone, and keys, then handed Ashe a business card.

"It's been nice seeing you again. Now that you work over here, maybe we can have lunch sometime," Ashe said as he stood, and they shook hands again.

"I'd like that, Chig." She smiled and headed out. She looked back at him as she left the room. Ashe stepped where he could watch her walk to the convertible.

Somehow, her using his nickname didn't bother him like it did from most new people.

After she'd left, while waiting on Marsh, Ashe strolled around the sitting room, looking at old photographs. One in particular surprised him. On a table by a window, there were a dozen or more framed photos, and standing behind most of them was one of the Blockade Runners.

It was a "Batch Launch" photo and had to be twenty years old or more. Ashe picked it up and blew the dust off it. There sat Harold Marsh among about twenty other men. There was the same mock moonshine still, placed in the center of the group, and the same sign above their heads. Exactly as in the photo Stevie had texted him, although decades apart.

A woman Ashe didn't recognize was queen that year, and she wore a short, flirty cocktail dress. A tall man was standing in the back, his face partially concealed behind another man, but Ashe knew who he was.

Dad. Damn.

He set the photo on the table and was about to take out his phone to get a shot of it, when Harold Marsh walked in.

"Robert?" Marsh said, then quickly corrected himself, "No, I mean, Chig. Hello."

Ashe went and shook his hand. Retired Judge Harold Marsh was what people used to call "stately" when they meant old. He was on the high side of eighty, and wore his snow-white hair in a big pompadour, combed straight back to where it added a couple of inches to his height.

Normally he wore a formal suit and tie, even when he didn't have to, but Ashe noticed he wore his sky-blue shirt open collared under a white V-neck sweater. A pair of tan chinos and white sneakers completed the look of a sporty and well-heeled bachelor. Albeit, fifty years in the past.

"I have been waiting on you to come see me," he said, and sat where Linda had. As he did, the housekeeper brought in a service of iced tea and water, set it on an end table, then left, closing the door behind her.

"Judge, I need to talk to you about Michael Durant."

"You saw the photo there, of the Blockaders, I don't know why I keep it. I think only a couple of us are still alive."

"I've seen another of their photos, a very recent one. One with Durant in it. And Carol Buckram."

"She the young girl that went missing?"

"She's the young girl who's *dead*. Michael Durant is missing." Ashe described the scene at the lake cove, and how this all started with Chuck Carter washing up at the park.

"I see." That was all he said for a couple of minutes. Ashe thought he'd maybe fall asleep soon.

But he didn't. "Chig, the Blockade Runners is almost a hundred-year-old club. Your father and grandfather were members, as was I. But you know that. It was nothing scandalous, heck, it was even *desirable* for men of business or political ambition to be associated with the Blockaders. At least, that's what it *was*."

"Was," Ashe said, trying to keep him going.

"Yes, well, our old friend Mark Portals and his banker, Crawford, took it over. They were using the group as a way to get investors in on their real estate dealings. You know, all that trouble last year."

"Yeah, I know. But...Michael Durant?"

"They recruited, heck, *courted* Mr. Durant into the group because of his connections and money. I've been long gone from that club for years, but I've heard everything went south when Portals was arrested by the state. Recently, I also heard the club had all but fallen apart. Then that girl, the Buckram girl, who worked at that children's sanctuary? She supposedly had an affair with Durant, then they both went missing. Or took off."

Ashe knew most of this, but sat through it anyway. "Any idea why?"

The old judge thought about that for a beat then just shrugged. "Who can tell?"

"Did Durant have access to any of the group's money?"

Marsh was surprised by that. "Money? *Money.* No, no money I wouldn't think. Durant was pretty wealthy on his own. I wouldn't go looking at that for a reason."

"You have any idea where he might be? Any way you know of to contact him?" Ashe asked.

Marsh paused again, gathering his words. "Michael Durant was brought into the Blockade Runners well after I was no longer associated with them," he said.

Not an answer, you crafty old hawk.

So Ashe took another tack. "Your new associate, Linda Ingles, asked me if I were going to arrest Lou Buckram. Is he a client?"

Marsh smiled. "No, but let me say this. You do need to talk with him. Don't approach him officially at first, just talk. He's a straight-ahead kind of guy. Let him calm down, then just talk with him."

Ashe nodded then spread his hands wide. "Judge, what don't I know that I need to know? Three people are dead, maybe four; shot to death. One of them was a man I knew and worked with in the past. I'm going to find out why he's dead. I'm going to find out why another man shot and killed Carol Buckram, who worked right where the Blockade Runners had their headquarters!"

"I expect no less from you. You proved your mettle last year, and you're Robert's son."

"This is going to get big and it's going to get loud. Starting tomorrow probably. I have US Marshals, the state AG's office, and God knows who all else arriving. Hell, the national media will be here soon."

"I see," Marsh said.

Ashe stood and paced around the room. "If you can help me, now is the time. I'm not interested in tearing this town apart, so please, if you know anyone who knows how to contact Durant, we really need to get his story. What the hell happened at the Blockade Runners? Why'd he and Carol run away? Why is there a damn sniper out there looking for someone or something still? And, what the holy hell happened out at that cove?"

Ashe returned to his chair and flopped in it.

Marsh straightened up. "You're like your father, I swear." Marsh thought for a minute then said, "Give me an hour or so. I'll see what I can find out."

Ashe stood again; the old judge remained seated. "An hour? Of course. I'll just see myself out."

He walked back toward the front of the house and felt his phone buzzing in his pocket. It was a text from Jacobs.

Warrant here. Meet at HCCS

"Ha," he said out loud as he reached the front door. "About damn time."

"Chig?" Marsh called out from behind him, so Ashe waited at

the door. Marsh came shuffling up to him and put a hand on his shoulder.

"One thing, son. Stevie. I think our girl may be getting into trouble." Ashe frowned. His old girlfriend had worked for the judge in the past, and he had grown very fond of her.

"Stevie? She works for the company or group, or whatever, that funds the HCCS. Where the Blockaders meet." Ashe left out she'd put him onto the Blockaders to begin with.

But Marsh warned Ashe again. "Maybe trouble her fiancé won't be able to get her out of. Tom Fischer might be personally and professionally conflicted."

CHAPTER 17

Stevie lifted the box of files from the Blockade Runners and locked it up in the storage cage they had in the basement of the apartment complex. Returning to the apartment, she dressed in nice jeans, boots, and a lightweight summer sweater for her meeting with Crawford. As she started to put on some makeup, her reflection in the bathroom mirror caught her eye.

Clean. Decent. *Like I'm going to the grocery store.*

The one thing she knew about Crawford was while he had ogled her before, he was also intimidated a little by her. He was trying to get something, wanting to meet her "to talk." There was *something* he wanted, so until she knew more, she decided to ensure she had every advantage she could.

She changed into a short black silk skirt and a dark-gray silky-looking tank. She wanted to look nice, and a bit spicy, and put Crawford off his game like before. So she put her hair up, added a pair of bright-red high heels, and did her makeup for an evening out. She took an extra few minutes and gave her eyes the full "smoky" treatment. A thin red blazer completed her look.

She checked herself in the mirror again.

This is even better than when I wanted to get Tom's attention.

That thought, though, brought a small pang of guilt. Was she being overly hard on Tom? She decided she couldn't know that until she knew more. So she grabbed a small red-and-black clutch and found her small digital recorder, when Tom came home.

He stopped just in the door, keys still in his hands, and wide-eyed, looked her up and down.

"Uh, wow. Hey," he said.

"I'm going out to meet someone, it's work related," she said, and started to walk out.

"Dressed like that? Damn, I thought we would talk tonight?"

"Talk? Well, where have you been all last night and today?" she asked, even though she'd seen some of his efforts at the sanctuary basement. And had a box of it hidden in their cage.

"Stevie, please. I had some damage control to do. I'm their attorney. I left messages for you to call me."

"You're *whose* attorney? Huh? Okay, I'm doing damage control too."

Tom held up his hands as if surrendering. "Honey, are we in jeopardy? I mean, *us*?"

There's so much I don't know, she thought.

"I'm...not sure yet. I want to think before talking. One way or the other, we'll get through this."

Tom was about to say something more, but she turned and walked out.

. . . .

Stevie drove toward the sanctuary but when almost there, she got a text from Crawford.

HCCS is still off-limits. New place out at the lake

Then he dropped her a pin with an address. This made her more than a little nervous. At the HCCS, she could go upstairs if need be. There'd be people there, the kids, and a cop outside. But this new place; she just wasn't sure.

But I want to know. She linked the address to her dash GPS and drove toward the lake.

She arrived at a nice home on Minor Hills Drive that overlooked the lake. There were a couple of cars outside, so she drove past the place, then came back and parked facing outward near the street, so she wouldn't get blocked in.

She stepped carefully in her heels up an uneven cobblestone walk to the front door, but before she could ring the bell, the door flew open.

Crawford stood there, smiling, with a mixed drink in his hand.

"Stevie, thank you for coming! He extended his hand, so she took it and stepped into the house. From the corner of her eye, she saw he was looking her over as she passed. He closed the door behind her and she thought she heard it lock.

Oh lordy, I hope I don't regret this.

Crawford escorted her to a sunken living room with tall, wall-to-wall windows that granted a spectacular view of the lake. Outside was a veranda, and as she entered the room, two men stepped inside through a glass door. One was a county commissioner and real estate agent she knew, named Jasper. The other man was a local doctor. They waved her over to a chair and the men sat close around her.

Crawford looked at the other gentlemen first then nodded and spoke. "We asked you here because we want to clear the air. About our organization and the terrible things that have happened."

"We want you to know, we find what has happened to Carol Buckram and those other men at the lake…just awful," Jasper said. He was late forty-ish and balding. "We are fully cooperating with the sheriff and the state police."

Funny way of cooperating. Tom locked the place down and wouldn't let them look for evidence. Then tried to empty it out. Assuming he's with you.

"And we want to assure you that neither us here, nor the Blockade Runners, had anything whatsoever to do with that poor girl's death," Crawford said.

Stevie made sure she sat upright and a little forward on the cushioned chair. "Why are you concerned what I think?"

"You work for the Lifenablers, which draws its funding from the Able Keys Foundation. Your fiancé, Tom, represents the foundation," said the doctor, whose name she didn't recall.

"So?"

Crawford said, "So, you need to understand something. The Blockaders have been around for a very, very long time. It's not really a secret organization, just private. Business leaders in town and so forth," Crawford said. "We have, very privately, helped fund all sorts of charitable causes. Like, ah, that family of the deputy who was killed a while back. We took care of his family, and there was the improvement project at the elementary school, we donated quite a lot to see to it those kids…"

"Just not the kids at the sanctuary," she interrupted. "You guys had your posh, well-provisioned club house downstairs, while the disadvantaged children upstairs were left to fend for themselves!"

The men sat back. She noticed they all had mixed drinks in their hands.

"Well," Jasper started, but Stevie held up a finger.

"When I went there the other afternoon, it was because of the Foundation and a state audit of Lifenablers. They discovered there were funds provided to the sanctuary but unused. I called for Carol Buckram, and instead got a teenage girl, who was doing her best to feed and care for the other ten children there. They had very few groceries on hand and needed prescription refills. In another few days or less, they would have been in crisis! So, gentlemen, I don't think you do yourselves any good to brag about how wonderful your moonshine club is."

"By the way, I'm Dr. Gregory, we've never met." Gregory was mid-fifties, handsome with a full beard and salt-and-pepper hair. "You make some excellent points, Ms. Collins; mistakes were made, big ones. But we're committed to correcting all that. That's why we're here tonight."

She drew in a breath and let it out slowly. *Getting pissy with them won't find out what you want to know.*

"Stevie, let me assure you, as I did, the second I discovered Carol was missing, anything they need there at the sanctuary, you just write a check. The bank will stand good for it."

"I'm not the administrator of the place, but..." She paused as she had a thought that hadn't occurred to her before. *Administrator. Gives me full access to all the accounts, all the records. Plus, I could help Brie and the kids.*

"I have already issued checks for the staff's salaries, and the groceries and medications," she said. "Nearly five thousand dollars."

"Not an issue. I'll get with you at the bank tomorrow and we'll go over the amounts, vice what funding they've received to date. We could...ah, maybe even approach the Foundation for any additional monies needed to fix up the place?"

Crawford stood and dropped a huge single, round ice cube into a bourbon glass then poured a clear liquor from a crystal decanter over it. He finished off the drink with a splash of Mountain Dew.

Jasper added, "Yeah, buy some new...well, whatever they need. Doc, maybe you could go look them over; check them kids out."

Crawford set the drink beside Stevie with a napkin wrapped around it. "Try this," he said.

"No, no thank you," she said. But it smelled wonderful.

Dr. Gregory finished his drink and gave the other two men a hard look. "I'm a cardiologist, not a pediatrician. But, I can put in a word with whomever currently is overseeing their care."

"See?" Crawford said. "We just want what's best. For them, and, Stevie, for *you* as well. You shouldn't be working for that Life-whatsit place. You should be back here. Practicing law again. Try the drink, Stevie."

No! You've worked too hard on sobriety these past years. That's got to be moonshine.

"We can start that ball rolling," Jasper added.

She picked up the drink and held it on her lap but didn't sip it. "Well, until we can change the mind of the state bar, perhaps I can continue to assist at the sanctuary there, part-time, until the HCCS hires a new administrator. By the way, who does that?" Stevie said. She wanted to offer the idea to get an official nod.

"Well, Clarence?" Gregory asked.

Crawford said, "Um, actually the Hurrt County Children's Sanctuary is managed by a local board, us included, but it is owned by…"

"Michael Durant's company," Gregory finished. "His LLC runs multiple shelters and senior care facilities."

"So…not the Foundation?" she asked, knowing better. *Ah-ha.*

"I know you had some difficulty a while back, but hey…this is high-quality, handmade, stuff. Just try it," Crawford said.

"Michael's on the board of the Foundation as well. Or was, or maybe still is," Jasper said.

"Oh," Stevie said, and crossed her legs the other way. *If I don't at least try their stupid stuff, they won't fully trust me. I can handle one drink.*

Stevie took a timid taste of the drink. She made sure they all saw her try it. She'd never tried moonshine before; she'd always been a vodka or expensive-kind-of-tequila girl. But this was good.

The moonshine was strong but didn't burn. It was smooth and warmed her throat and chest from the inside as it went down. Just that tiny amount. Before she thought about it, she took another drink. More than before.

Damn. That is every bit as good as he said it was.

Crawford gave Jasper a look. "It's not like it sounds, Stevie.

Michael was a very engaged man in several different business ventures," Crawford said.

"Let's hope he still is," said Gregory.

Stevie smiled. "I see. It's *not* like a man who sits on a Foundation board and votes money to a children's home he owns." She shook her drink in a small circle to stir it.

Dr. Gregory smiled back. "You'd be surprised, Ms. Collins, how common such things occur in business. Or then again, from what I know about *your* recent past, perhaps you wouldn't be."

She took another swallow. The conversation was getting offtrack. "Gentlemen, may I ask a personal question?"

"Of course," Crawford said, and leaned forward. She could smell the liquor on his breath.

"What has Tom Fischer to do with this?"

The men eyed each other then Crawford said, "You're worried about your fiancé. Of course, Tom was introduced by Mark Portals, your old associate, to the group and we voted him in. He's not been an active member since all *that*, last year. Oh, and we of course have voted Mark out."

"Does Tom serve as council for the Blockade Runners? Or the HCCS?"

The men looked at each other without answering, and the hesitation became awkward.

"Gents, he…doesn't know I'm here," she added.

"I see. That's discreet of you," Crawford said. Then he paused another few seconds while seeming to formulate his words. "He does *not* represent either organization. I thank him for his initial instinct, and his swift actions to try and protect us. But, well, we are an open book as far as the investigation into Carol's tragic death. If we need council, we can hire someone *not* connected to the Able Keys Foundation."

Damn, he lied to me. So there's some space between the two. Stevie had wondered if the Blockaders were somehow tied to the Foundation. Now she knew they weren't.

"He stopped the sheriff from conducting a logical investigative inspection of Carol's office, and of course your meeting room downstairs, where her picture hung on the wall as one of your batch queens. I think the sheriff and the ADA are pursuing a search warrant, though," she said.

She went to take another sip, but her glass was nearly empty. She set it on the table. *Enough.*

"He has good reflexes, but I assure you, and you can tell your old boyfriend, Ashe, this from me, we will cooperate," said Crawford.

Stevie had learned something big. Tom was on the outs with the Blockaders. At their sanctuary room, destroying liquor and boxing up records; he wasn't covering for the Blockade Runners. His "damage control" and the cleaning up of the place, it all had to be for the benefit of the Foundation. He'd been gathering evidence and searching for that little jug, just like Crawford and Lou Buckram.

Why? Why did that small jug mean so much to the Blockaders and to the Foundation?

Jasper stood and mixed himself a fresh drink and also took Stevie's glass. "I'll call the sheriff tonight as a commissioner and tell him to go do whatever he wants." Then he raised her glass to her. "You want one the same as before?"

"No, um, not so sweet," she said. *No! Yes! Wait, I have to keep them talking.*

"You can't do that, Bill. You nor the county own the place," Gregory said. Jasper offered him a refill as well, but Gregory waved him off.

Jasper handed her the drink with much less Mountain Dew in it. She smiled and let it sit on her lap just below the hem of her skirt. Every few seconds, Crawford was looking right there.

Stevie decided to ask the obvious. "Did you ever find your little jug? What on earth is in it that's so important to so many people?"

They all looked at each other. Finally Crawford said, "Well, no, we haven't actually. You haven't found it, while you were there all night, have you? Or maybe…Tom?"

She took a drink. *Yes, it's stronger but doesn't bite.* She felt the warmth and by it, felt more confident.

She said, "No, but I wasn't looking. I was taking care of the children. I don't think Tom found anything either. Why?"

"It's important, that's all," Jasper said. Crawford shot him a look.

She asked, "Did it have anything to do with what happened out on the lake? With Carol?"

That drew quick looks at her.

"I'm just asking. If *I* wonder that, what do you bet the state police are wondering it, too?"

Crawford shook his head. "Gentlemen, if we are to have Stevie here help us at the sanctuary, and one day be a trusted legal advisor again, we need to show her some trust now."

Stevie took another long pull from her drink. Her chest and shoulders felt warm so she took off her blazer.

Crawford paused, probably trying for dramatic effect, and looked Stevie directly in the eyes.

"It contains a small handwritten copy, very old actually, of the one-hundred-year-old recipe for this delicious homemade whiskey you're enjoying, Stevie," Crawford said. "So you see why we want to find it."

Bullshit.

"And Lou? Is this what he was also looking for?" She took another long drink.

Damn. I could get used to this.

She knew this was trouble; she knew because she suddenly thought of Ashe. Of kissing him, holding him. Somehow being a little inebriated brought making love to him into her mind, and she felt her face and chest flush with the thought.

"Lou Buckram is our distiller," Gregory said. He reached over and took Stevie's empty glass from her and set it on a table behind him. Out of her reach.

Buckram, huh. The "gig is up," he said. Now that makes sense.

"We were at that house for years before Michael and company bought it to set up the sanctuary. We didn't like it, so we set a firm rule to never mix the two," Jasper said.

"Michael Durant broke that rule and also our trust, when he became infatuated with Carol. His influence and his business dealings overwhelmed some of the members, and they allowed her to be our queen a month or so ago. The three of us, of course, voted against that," Gregory said.

"Anyway, when we found out she was missing, later dead, we were horrified," Jasper said.

Crawford looked at his watch. "So, to set things right as we can, we will cooperate with the sheriff. We will donate heavily to the sanctuary; we will move out of that house as soon as we can. And, as Mr. Jasper, the doctor, and I are on the local board, work to appoint a new acting administrator."

"And *Durant?*" Stevie asked. She realized she slurred Durant's name. *Uh-oh.*

"When he reappears, he can of course have his input. But like you've said, things need to be done there. I think we are in agreement? Gentlemen?"

They nodded. She noticed Gregory kept an eye on her.

Crawford said, "Then, Miss Collins, you are as of now, the official administrator of the Hurrt County Children's Sanctuary."

Gregory stood, reached over, and shook her hand, saying, "Congratulations." Then he said goodbye to the other men and walked out.

His leaving seemed to have caught the other two men by surprise. They exchanged a couple of looks, trying for an unspoken conversation of sorts.

So Stevie stood. *Whoa.* The moonshine made by Buckram was stronger than she'd realized, but she kept her balance. "Bathroom, please?"

Crawford showed her where it was. When she came back into the room, the two men who'd remained were engaged in deep, quiet conversation. She wanted to stay standing, but was worried she'd appear drunk, so she sat and crossed her legs. Her skirt rode a little high, showing more than she intended, so she tugged at it and tried to twist it down a bit, discreetly. It had the opposite effect; they both watched her wiggling in her chair.

"You want another drink, Stevie?" Jasper asked. He was having one. Straight, no Dew color.

"No, um, coffee," she said.

"I'll drive you home, Stevie. Look, that stuff takes a little getting used to. Hey, you're out of training too, eh?" Crawford said. He reached over and patted her on her bare leg.

I need to try one more thing, she decided.

"If I had to guess, Durant...he probably has your jug, and whatever is so important that's *really* in it," she said. "Or Carol did, and it's at the bottom of the lake."

The men looked at each other. Jasper looked very concerned; Crawford looked angry.

Bingo, she thought. *Recipe, hell.*

"You know this, how?" Jasper said, then Crawford immediately hushed him.

"I'll make us some coffee," Crawford said. "We *all* need it."

He glared at Jasper as he went toward the kitchen.

Jasper drained his drink, leaned close to her, and lowered his voice. "You are friends with that Ashe still, right? I imagine Larry Jacobs too? Have you shared your thoughts about our little jug with them? Have they found it? At the lake, maybe?"

She lowered her voice to match his. "No. But really, I dunno. Did you boys even ask Durant?"

Jasper looked back toward the kitchen then turned to her. He reached over and put a hand on her leg above her knee. "We first thought it was just hidden. Then we figured *they* had it. So we tried calling him and her. Left messages, even sent a guy to go make him an offer. Two hundred thousand for that stupid little jug."

"Holy shit, that's a lot of cash for a recipe!"

"No, not the frigging recipe. Anyway, Michael set the location. Things must 'a got all out of hand. Not our fault," Jasper said.

"Out on the lake?" she asked. She let him keep his hand there.

"Must've. We never heard back from our guy, or Michael or Carol, either. Then the state and sheriff and everybody was out there. I never even *heard* of such. Not here, not in Seacord," Jasper said.

She figured he was drunker than she was, but she was an experienced-enough drunk to know she too was headed down and out herself soon.

"A lot of money. What's that kind of money buy?"

"Maybe something important, maybe. Maybe too, you're working with the sheriff," Jasper said. He let his hand drop off her leg.

"You men got me all wrong," she said.

"How's that?" Crawford asked as he returned with the coffee. She took a mug from him and drank some as he sat beside her.

"I want to help. But you've got to quit bullshitting me," she said. She realized it sounded like she'd said, *bullshishtering.*

"Stevie, we will sit down at the bank to catch up the sanctuary's accounts tomorrow…ah, say around lunch?"

She drank a good deal more of the coffee, but something was wrong.

"Sure. Hey, Clarence, are you Irish?"

"No, I don't think so," he said. "Why?"

"Because this fucking coffee sure is," she said and laughed. The floor moved. Her feet were suddenly hot, so she kicked off her shoes.

"Just easing you off your little high, girl. A bit of the hair of the dog, so to speak."

"You know, you boys... you need a new batch queen."

Crawford put his arm around Stevie's shoulder and pulled her close. "That is an excellent idea. Now let's get you home. Keys?"

She handed him her car keys and saw that Jasper had his eyes closed and was slumped in his chair. She finished her coffee; she no longer cared it was spiked. She wanted to call Ashe.

Come and pick me up.

Then two men she didn't know entered through the front door. Young men, she thought, but she was having trouble focusing. Crawford pitched one of them her keys. The other man bent down and effortlessly scooped her up in his arms to carry her to her car. She put her arms around his neck and tried to hold her head up. Her hair had come undone some and fell into her face and on her shoulders.

Her eyes were closed but she could still hear them.

"Is she about to have...sir, do you want her to have an..."

Crawford interrupted him. "No! Take my car and hers, get her up to her apartment. Tell her fiancé, Tom Fischer, to come see me," Crawford said. "Be sure he sees her like this. I want him to get the damn message."

The man carried her out the door into the night air, where she passed out.

CHAPTER 18

Ashe sat in an office-type chair and pitched an empty beer can at a trash bag and missed, sending it rattling across the tile. The Blockade Runner's room in the basement of the HCCS had been looted, ripped up, emptied out. Even the very thick carpet had been pulled up in places, and nice cedar paneling pulled off the walls.

There wasn't a drop of alcohol left in the place. Large black garbage bags were full of beer cans and liquor bottles. Boxes also lined one wall with trash and empty bottles. Some of the Batch Launch photos had been taken down and packed into boxes.

Jacobs was furious. The Assistant DA for Hurrt County, John Price was listening to him rant.

"Dammit, John, this was the nicest place you'd ever seen! I saw it. All this *after* we were here, and that weasel Tom, Tom Fischer, must have done all this. I had a peek in here just last night, it was set up like something out of the flippin' playboy mansion! And all this done while we were waiting on the damn judge to make up his damn mind on my damn warrant!"

Ashe looked at his phone. Six thirty p.m. It'd been well over the hour requested, and Harold Marsh hadn't called. Ashe had tried him twice but had to just leave messages.

Price was sympathetic to the sheriff but also not surprised. "Larry, at best, you would have found something like records, somehow showing the connection between this group and the girl that worked directly upstairs. Maybe a 'someone' down here, knew something about her murder."

"John, don't start...you saw the photo of her with these men!"

"No, I get it. I do. It's the logical move. You have a dead girl with no apparent motive, you search her home and office looking for clues as to *why*. But none of the men in that photo you showed me is a criminal. You have someone over at her apartment, I assume?"

"Yeah, Ashe and I will head over there to check on things. Dammit! Something needs to be done about Fischer!"

"What exactly?" Ashe asked. He was pissed off too, but he'd had a hundred or so dry holes before in his career. This was one of Jacobs' first.

Ashe continued. "I mean, seriously. I think we know who killed her; the guy with the AK at the cove. We don't know why, of course. But Fisher? We could maybe go for some sort of interference or obstruction into a felony investigation, but I don't think something like that would stick, would it? He was under no direct suspicion of anything. We wanted motive and a connection, and we didn't know for sure it was here. As far as we can prove now, all he did was dump out the liquor in a children's sanctuary. Bully for him."

Jacobs scowled at Ashe. His face said he was in no mood for that. He tried to get a cigarette out of his shirt pocket, but the pack was empty. Jacobs ripped it out, wadded it up in his big paws, and threw on the floor with the rest of the debris.

Price looked at his watch. "You find out Tom removed something critical to establishing a case of conspiracy, an accomplice in her murder, or identifying your sniper, you give me a call. I promise things will be speedier, Larry. But Ashe is right, your sniper killed the man who killed the Buckram girl. I don't see the urgency here. I recommend you go find that sniper," Price said.

"By the way, which judge?" Ashe asked Price.

"Demarest, why?"

Ashe poked through a box and held up a Batch Launch photo from about ten years ago. Demarest was in it.

"Are you suggesting the judge intentionally held up this warrant until these men could clean out this room?" Price said, obviously annoyed. Well, good night." And John Price left.

"Huh!" Jacobs said loudly out the door behind Price.

"Sheriff?" Deputy Minor asked. He'd been watching the back door from outside. "Nobody took nothing out that door, I swear."

Jacobs drew in a long breath then sighed and patted Minor on the back. "Okay, son. You can go 10-8. Oh, hey, Jim, do you have a smoke?"

Minor shrugged and shook his head. As he walked out, he said, "I get why that man poured out all the booze before family services saw it here, but why tear up the dang walls and carpet?"

Ashe rocked back and forth in his new favorite office chair. "I have a theory on that."

"Yeah. Fischer was tearing this place to pieces, looking for the *it*," Jacobs said.

"We're forgetting something. Or actually, *someone*."

"Oh yeah, Stevie Collins was here too," Jacobs said.

"Stevie Collins was here too," Ashe said.

"Let's go see if they found anything at Carol's apartment."

"Actually, Sheriff, if you can handle that, I need to go re-see that man with the dog. He promised to come through, and he hasn't."

Jacobs frowned again. "Okay, I'm running out of stuff to do. It's late on a Sunday and I'm going upstairs to talk to the ladies up there. Then we'll get our subpoenas like we discussed in the a.m. You going to be around for that?"

"I'll see you later tonight, if *you're* around."

Jacobs smiled but not in a good way. He walked out, kicking a beer can in front of him as he did. Ashe swiveled and leaned back a few more times in the fancy chair then went to see the old judge.

He drove up to Burlwood and parked as before, grabbing his old brown leather portfolio off the seat beside him. This time as he stepped onto the porch, there was no gardener glowering at him, and the front door opened without his having to ring.

"He's expecting you," the housekeeper said. She led him down the hall past the sitting room and to a thick solid wood door. She knocked and Ashe heard a woman from inside say to come in. The housekeeper opened the door for him and closed it firmly behind him.

Ashe entered what was a library or home office. The walls on one side had floor-to-ceiling shelves with hardback books, and the others had diplomas, and maps, and family paintings.

A desk sat on one side and Harold Marsh sat behind it, still dressed as before. A huge modern set of computer monitors took up half the desk. In front of him was a big leather desk blotter and on it a pad where he'd been taking a lot of notes.

But most surprising to Ashe was that sitting in a green leather high-back chair was Linda Ingles again. She wasn't in golf clothes anymore. She wore a beige pantsuit and heels and had a pad on her lap. She'd been taking pages of notes herself.

"Chig," Marsh said. "You are just in time. I have someone I want you to meet."

"Ms. Ingles and I have already met today, Harold. Hello again, Linda."

"Hello, Chig," she said.

"I'm sorry but you misunderstand." Marsh leaned forward and swiveled one of the big 42" monitors around so Ashe could see, as he took a seat across from the judge.

There was a man on the screen, obviously on the other end of their video conference call. He was lean-faced, maybe late fifties, and seated against a blank plaster wall. Sunlight from a window beside him shone across one side of his face.

"I think you should meet Mr. Michael Durant."

"Good evening, Detective Ashe," Durant said. His voice came surprisingly loud and clear over speakers somewhere in the room. "Or I hear you prefer, Chig."

Ashe took a second before responding. *This is unexpected.*

"I think Detective Ashe works best here, Mr. Durant. A lot of people sure want to talk to you."

"Then aren't you the lucky one," he said and smiled.

Marsh said, "Chig, let me be clear. I'm representing Mr. Durant here, and Linda is sitting in. He wants to give the authorities a statement but doesn't know who to trust. I've vouched for you; that you could get his information into the right hands."

Ashe rubbed his face. "This is damn odd, Harold. Why don't we meet face-to-face?"

"You'd have a twelve-hour flight ahead of you," Durant said over the speakers.

"Before I ask you anything, I should read you your, well, hell, are you even in the U.S.?"

Marsh raised a pen up. "He will not answer that. He is not wanted, so his travel plans are irrelevant. You may advise him anyway, but I am here as his council."

"I've never questioned someone by video chat," Ashe said and opened his portfolio on his lap.

"I've never been questioned about a murder," Durant said.

Ashe thought about trying to text Rachel, the sheriff, or even Price, but didn't want to complicate or delay things just yet. *Let's see what the man has to say first.*

Ashe advised Durant of his Miranda rights. Marsh answered for him, "Waived; understanding we may stop at any time."

"Yes, Harold, but again this is pretty unique. If I have follow-on questions, or say the state investigator in charge wants to speak with him, how do we…"

"The Blockade Runners tried to have me killed, Detective Ashe," Durant said. "And I think the Able Keys Foundation, or at least Searl, is still trying."

Ashe sat back. He looked at Linda for a second and she raised an eyebrow. "I see," he said.

"Before you ask anything, I want to make a statement. But you should know, these unusual circumstances are in place to protect me. I had to leave the area to protect myself."

Ashe stared at his face on the monitor and then realized he didn't know if Durant could even see him. "Okay, Mr. Durant. Start at the beginning."

Durant looked down, probably at some notes, and cleared his throat.

"I had some business dealings with an attorney named Mark Portals through my office in the city. He eventually invited me to Hurrt County to the Blockade Runners and recruited me as a member." Durant shifted some paper off camera, but Ashe could hear it.

"He wanted my help with my ex-wife, the governor, in his projects involving the Doorbella corporation. Particularly in building a new highway loop to service a new distribution center he hoped to build, and with the idea of privatizing some state land along the Minor Hills Dam area. He wanted to open up more lakeshore property."

"You and your ex-wife were on such terms you could approach her with this?" Ashe asked.

Durant paused and touched his chin. Marsh answered for him. "Yes."

"So I drove to Seacord a couple of times a month, to meet with

Portals and his investors, and of course, to enjoy the Blockaders hospitality. Then, quite by chance, I met Carol Buckram. She was admiring my Porsche. We, over time, became involved."

"Involved how?"

A small smile came to Durant. "We became friends, very close friends."

"You were lovers?"

"I sometimes didn't want to drive back to my place in Metro at night, especially after drinking at the club."

Ashe returned his small smile. "You were lovers, and you stayed at her apartment."

Durant sighed. "Yes. We *very gradually* became romantically involved. Not at first! No, I was very hesitant; but she was a very special person."

Ashe made himself a side note. *Durant's DNA in Carol's apartment.*

"In any event, we kept it a secret for a time, but both my associates with the Foundation, which I started by the way, and a few of the Blockaders told me to end it. Conflict of interest, they said. I tried, really, but Carol was very much in love with me and I was certainly falling for her. We began to make plans together, you see. Simple things at first, like a vacation together, then maybe I could help her finish her college."

"But?" Ashe said.

"But, see, before I met her, I bought the house where the Blockaders met, because the previous owner had died. Then, when I established the children's sanctuary for Hurrt County, which was badly needed, I used that house as a temporary facility. Later, I wanted the Foundation to work on building a proper facility down the road. When they discovered, and I blame Mark Portals for this, that I was involved with Carol, the sanctuary administrator, well *that* was off the table."

"They didn't want to build it anymore?"

"They even asked me to resign from my seat on the Foundation. My ex-wife even joined in the vote!"

Marsh and Linda both reacted to that, Linda holding up her hand to Ashe.

"Wait, the governor, *our state governor*, is on the Able Keys Foundation board?" Ashe asked.

"That's for another time," Marsh interrupted. "No questions about her, or I'll have to end this."

Better let Rachel know. Crap! We could be in over our heads.

Ashe started to press the issue but didn't want to miss the opportunity to find out what had happened to Chuck, to Carol. So he made a few notes then asked, "So let's get to the part where these entities all want you dead."

Durant looked at his papers. "Yes, well, Carol and I decided to leave together. I'd gotten her named as the club's Queen of the Batch which she really wanted. Then they voted me off the island, so to speak. I was out of the Foundation, *that I started*, and out of the Blockaders, that they *begged* me to join!"

"You decided to leave?" Ashe said, trying to keep him talking.

"Yeah, but I guess Carol decided, *on her own*, that she wanted something more than just a goodbye and a reference when she left. You see, she had access to their financial records and their banking. She knew how the Foundation funded the sanctuary through a shell company called Lifenablers. *Somehow*, she found out more than she should about the financials of the Foundation itself. Like, how they invested their money, like their connection to other international companies. *That* was her mistake."

Carol *found out, bull! Durant used her to get his revenge.*

Ashe shrugged, and hoped Durant could see him. "The financials of a charitable foundation? Doesn't sound so terrible." Ashe had an idea of where Durant was going with this.

"She also managed to discover the Blockaders were snooping into my foundation, to try and get something on me. They wanted the sanctuary gone, and wanted the building for themselves. It had belonged to a former member after all, and since they'd excommunicated me, they wanted me to sell."

"*Carol* discovered all this?" Ashe looked at Marsh and Linda. Their faces were blank.

"There was much more to it all. But suffice it to say, the clever girl in the process of trying to get a golden parachute for herself as we left together, may have accidentally stumbled across some issues with how the Foundation money was being raised and spent."

"So, she left with this information? And you. You would know how to leverage that information," Ashe said.

"A tiny thing. I didn't know they came that small. A little button of a USB drive. Almost a terabyte's worth of data, spilled from the computers at the bank and the Blockaders own accounts."

Ashe made another note. *Subpoenas now a priority.*

"She put it in a little clay jug her father kept his moonshine recipe in. Carol wanted to take both the financials and the recipe. Sort of a symbolic 'screw you' to everyone."

"Mr. Durant. You hired a bodyguard? Charles Carter?"

"Yes, Chuck. He came highly recommended. I...hate that I seriously underestimated how angry the Blockaders were. I knew that certain members of the Blockaders could play a little rough. You know that yourself from last year. When I found out what Carol had done, I immediately contacted Mr. Crawford at the bank. He's the current president of the club. I never asked for money, he said they'd pay our expenses for the jug's return, *with all* its contents."

"So you set a meeting."

"Carol did. Again, this was to be a simple exchange. A token amount of money and we'd turn over the item. I suppose I surprised Chuck when I said we had to meet at that cove. Carol had shown it to me before. We went out there that day to make a simple exchange. Simple..."

His voice trailed off then he got up and walked off camera.

Everyone waited, assuming he'd return. Ashe had a lot of questions once he was done with his horseshit story. While waiting, he went over his notes.

He lays everything off on his dead girlfriend. At best, there's extorsion, but hard to prove as even with that he says Crawford offered money. And again, Carol is doing the masterminding here?

As discreetly as he could, Ashe took out his phone and sent Rachel a text.

When you get this, find me fast. Re: Durant

Then almost on cue, Durant returned. His eyes red as if from crying. Ashe kept his face neutral while thinking he had probably scratched them himself. Durant signaled he was ready to resume.

"The lake. The cove. You survived."

"Yeah, this is the hard part. We were there early, but not early enough. I got a call on my phone to have Carol toss the little data drive onto shore near a tree. When we got back to our cars, the money would be there. She refused. She yelled she'd swallow the drive or throw it into the lake."

Liar, Ashe thought. *There's no cell signal out at that cove.*

"You weren't alone out there," Linda said. That surprised Ashe. *Had she not heard all this?*

"No, a man dressed in all camouflage stood up. Surprised the hell out of us, especially Chuck who saw him first. I guess he was to retrieve the item after we left. Anyhow, he pointed a rifle at us, Chuck of course drew his gun, and yelled at me to pull away. I was driving the boat."

"And things got loud," Ashe said.

"Yes, that stupid man fired off some rifle shots! I think he was aiming for our engine, but they came close to me and Carol. One shot must have bounced off something and hit her. Oh God, this is so tough to tell!"

"Yeah, I'm sure it is. Try to buck up and continue," Ashe said. Out of the corner of his eye, he saw Linda give a slight smile.

"Well, this man and Chuck exchanged fire. I think Chuck hit him, but before he did, the man let go a rapid sequence of, what do you call it? A burst? I don't know, I just jumped off the boat. But that man from the Blockaders shot and killed Carol."

"You jumped? You jumped off the pontoon boat?" Ashe asked. *He left Carol there, in a bikini, facing a man armed with an AK-47.*

"I know by the sound of your voice what you think of me, but I knew Carol was dead. Too many bullets in her. My God, I knew these men could be a little tough, but I never, and...and Chuck didn't either. *He* was the professional."

Ashe let out a breath as quietly as he could. "Okay, Michael. Something else happened out there. Maybe after you were in the water."

"Yeah. Someone else fired a rifle. From far away. Shot Chuck several times."

"Why Chuck?" Ashe asked, but he knew. *One professional recognized the other. Had to take him.*

"I don't know, but then whoever it was also shot the Blockader's man, the man who killed Carol."

"You saw this man, this far-away shooter?"

"No. I jumped into the water where he couldn't see me, I guess. Maybe he thought I was shot. So I tried to swim as quietly as possible to the far side of the cove and hide. I hid for an hour maybe. I didn't hear anyone come down there, so I got out and I made my way to a road. A man and his wife gave me a ride."

"You ran?"

"As fast and as far as I could. Where I am now, no one will find me. And until I can know I'm safe, here I stay!"

"You didn't try to contact anyone? Your ex-wife could help, maybe. She's the governor, after all."

"Uh, excuse me. Enough of that," Marsh said.

"God, hiding out there in that cove, crawling through that brush to the road; I put two and two together! The damn Blockaders sent that idiot with the automatic rifle, and the Foundation, or Searl, or *maybe my ex-wife*, sent that…that sniper!"

"I'm sorry, Chig. But as I warned, we are not going to reference the governor in this forum."

"So, all this evidence on the flash drive. The jug, the recipe. Where is it? In the lake?"

Durant didn't answer but touched his chin again.

"And it's evidence of what? Misappropriations of charity money? What is there that's worth killing all these people over?" Ashe asked. "Who the hell is Searl?"

Marsh said, "Thank you, Michael." And the video call ended.

"Wait, damn, Harold! I had more questions!"

"Well, as I do not know where he is or how to contact him, I suppose we'll both have to wait," Marsh said. Then he handed over a copy of a set of spreadsheets. "He did send this in an encrypted email, to give to the authorities. That's you, and so I have completed my agreement with him. Anything further he will need to seek other council."

Ashe took the stack of printouts and flipped through them. Twenty, maybe thirty pages front and back. "You know I can't do anything with something like this, not being able to establish its source."

"Now you know how we feel," Linda said.

"I'm very tired, Chig, please, go do what you must. But tell your fellow officers I do not have any way to re-establish contact with Michael Durant. If he contacts me again, I'll notify you or our sheriff. Good night. Linda, please?"

On cue, the housekeeper entered the room, and she and Linda

helped Marsh up, and then they helped him walk out of the room, holding on to her arm.

Ashe stood when he did, out of respect, then when he was gone, looked at Linda.

"You know more than you did," she said and picked up her papers and stuffed them in a large leather messenger bag. "And as much as I do. Good night, Chig."

Ashe stood in the room as she walked out. There was something in the way she left that said, *I have nothing more to say* without her having to say it.

So he took out his phone. Rachel was off the lake and had returned his text, asking "WTF," and asking where to meet.

WTF indeed. He tucked the spreadsheet file into his portfolio and went to find Rachel.

CHAPTER 19

Ashe left Marsh's home about seven forty-five or so and walked to his Jeep to head for the sheriff's office, assuming that's where Rachel would want to rally up. He started his old Cherokee and rolled down his driver's side window until the AC got running then opened his portfolio to scan through the printouts, and finish a couple of notes before meeting with her and the sheriff. It was still light out, but the sun was all but down. In another month, it'd be full light out past nine.

That's when he saw them.

Looking in his driver's side rearview mirror, he saw an older blue Dodge truck about three houses down and on the other side of the street from him. It fired up its engine; a diesel by the sound of it. Two men in the front seat being unduly observant of him.

Very un-Burlwood, unless they were workers. They were also parked on the wrong side of the street to be facing the rear of his Jeep. Unless they had just delivered a big freezer or a chandelier or something.

Warning bells rang in his head. *Maybe it's that I'm only a couple days from being shot at out in the cove. Maybe not.*

Ashe pulled away from in front of Marsh's house and drove toward the square. The Dodge truck followed.

Another car, a very nondescript Ford pulled alongside it, and the Dodge boys just couldn't help but look at its driver and nod. The man driving the Ford did not acknowledge them but paused.

Black male, dark shades. He probably expected Ashe to go straight to the jail or maybe the courthouse.

Ashe grabbed his phone. He didn't have Bluetooth in an '03

Jeep Cherokee, so he had to dial while steering around the square.

"Judge Marsh's residence," the housekeeper said.

"Ma'am, listen. This is Detective Ashe; I was just there. Do as I say right now! Drop this phone and go lock all your doors! The judge might be in danger!"

He hung up and tossed his phone onto the passenger seat then circled the square fully again. He'd wanted to draw the truck and the Ford away from the judge's house, and in a few seconds, he saw the truck. It was pulled over in front of the hardware store.

Are you over reacting just a bit? That's just where a work truck would stop on the square.

So Ashe stopped in front of the bank. Through some trees and across the square, he saw that they were just sitting there, looking around. *Let's make sure before we make a fool out of ourselves, Chig.*

Ashe sat at the bank and tried to look casual, while trying to keep the truck in his rearview.

Me sitting here changed something, forcing them to reveal their hand. Well, let's find out.

He took off out Century Avenue and out of town toward Old Martin Road; the route to his house. They would be very conspicuous if they followed him this far out of town. After clearing the last stop sign in town and veering right onto Old Martin, the houses became sparser then none at all. Ashe slowed some and reached for his phone again. There were only woods and the occasional hayfield on both sides of the road, as the name dropped to just County 429.

No traffic. No Dodge and no Ford.

Then about a quarter mile behind him on a straightaway, he saw the Dodge truck. He punched it, or at least as much as his twenty-year-old plus Jeep would punch, and headed for his house while thumbing the sheriff's phone number.

"Hey, Ashe! Where are you? We're here with Rachel's team at the S.O. What's this you texted her about Durant?"

"Larry, listen! Get someone up to Judge Marsh's house on Burlwood. I have a blue Dodge diesel pickup with two men tailing me, and possibly a burgundy Ford sedan with our guy from the café. I'm on 429 headed to my house."

Ashe could hear Jacobs shouting orders to someone with his

hand over his phone then to Ashe he said, "I got Minor and a trooper headed up to the judge's. You—turn onto Turkey Trace Road if you can and circle back toward town. We'll come to you."

Ashe saw the turnoff for Turkey Trace Road, so he slowed and used his turn signal; he didn't want to lose them. As he made the left turn, he saw the Dodge truck slowing a couple of hundred yards behind him. But no Ford sedan.

Crap! Where did he go?

. . . .

"You don't have to carry me," Stevie said to the young man who had driven her home. She walked as best as she could to her apartment door and took out her keys. She tried a couple of times to get the key in the lock, but finally he took them from her and opened the door.

"Thanks, you may go now, whoever you are," she said as she stepped inside. She was still drunk and had only come to when he'd pulled her out of the back seat of her car and into the still-warm night air.

He smiled. He was late twenties, and from what she could see through the haze over her eyes, he was handsome. When he'd picked her up, she could feel he was muscular as well.

"I'm supposed to give your fiancé a message first," he said.

She stumbled in, bouncing off both walls of the foyer before reaching the kitchen counter to lean on for support.

"Where…where are my shoes?" she asked.

"I don't know, where is Mr. Fischer?"

"Stevie!" she heard Tom call out from his office.

"He's in there," she said. "Hey, those are Christian Louboutin. You better find them."

Then she went and fell on her bed. After snoozing for how long she didn't know, she felt someone sit on the bed.

"Stevie, who was that guy? And why were you talking to Clarence Craw…oh my God, you're drunk!" Tom said.

"What's worse? I lost my damn shoes," she said and lifted her head off the pillow.

"Who was that man? Is *that* who you went to see tonight?"

"No, Tom, he's nobody. Or, I dunno, maybe he's a good guy. He just drove me home. Very tall, did you talk to him? I bet he could carry you too."

Tom shook his head. "Okay, forget that. Why does Clarence Crawford want to talk to me?"

She put her head back down on her pillow. "You've been acting very mystery-e-ous-ly lately, buddy. I saw what you did at your little boys' club. You cleaned it all up."

Tom looked at her, his brow furrowed. "Okay, sleep this off. But we talk first thing."

She looked at Tom with one eye open. "Did that dude leave my shoes?"

"No, babe. No shoes. Maybe they're out in your car."

Then she smiled and laughed to herself. "Hey, Tom. Babe. Are you Irish?"

"What?"

She giggled some more at her own joke, and then went to sleep.

Hours later, she sat up. Tom was asleep in bed beside her. It was still the middle of the night. She still felt woozy but had to use the bathroom, so she carefully padded in there. When she was done, she stripped off her skirt, top, and underwear she was still wearing, and pulled on clean panties and a robe.

Something still bothered her. *Not the damn shoes, what?* She walked out into the kitchen to get some water when she saw her small clutch purse on the counter. Red and Black. Fake alligator.

Then it hit her. She opened it up quickly, and there on top was her small digital recorder. Eighteen hours plus of battery life. She took it out and forced herself to focus on its little screen.

It's still recording. I got it.

She turned the recorder off, gave it a kiss, and put it in her robe pocket, before going back to bed.

I'll see you at noon, Mister Crawford.

· · · ·

Ashe drove the exaggerated circular route on dark country roads until he was back on CR 429. The Dodge truck must have figured out what was happening; they accelerated and came up directly behind Ashe as he turned toward Seacord.

They pulled up even with his left rear quarter panel; Ashe figured they were trying for a pit maneuver. So he smacked his brakes on hard one second then off. The truck surged past him as immediately he stomped on his gas. As they were still braking, he flew by them.

It was a neat trick but not likely to work twice. The truck more aggressively this time drove up behind him. The passenger had some type of long arm.

Oh, it's that way, is it?

Ashe didn't try for his gun. *You either drive or shoot, not both.* He waited a second or two until he was at the narrowest length of road. When they lined up on his left rear quarter panel again, he tromped his brakes. This time, they thought they were ready and only slowed without much braking. So once Ashe brought his old Cherokee to a stop, as they were still rolling forward, he dropped it into reverse and floored the gas pedal.

As he reached what he figured was more than thirty-five miles an hour, and saw the truck was just then braking hard, he spun his steering wheel as fast as he could, let off the gas, and stayed off the brake, then slapped the shift lever into whatever forward gear was there. Letting the steering wheel spin back through his fingers, he mashed the gas again and with a lot of noisy old Jeep Cherokee complaints, he came out of the bootleg turn facing away from the truck, and sped off in the other direction.

"Yeah!" he shouted out loud and pumped a fist in the air. "Try that in a fat damn long-assed diesel truck!"

He pulled ahead nearly a mile on them but was headed away from town. He grabbed his phone and called Jacobs. "Hey, you coming? I'm running out of tricks and they know that I know."

"I have Ed Bell on Turkey Trace now, and me and another man have to be about up to you."

"Okay, but look out! They're armed, and tried to pit me!" he shouted, and tossed the phone onto the passenger seat again. Ashe braked again and rolled to a stop. He heard a couple of noises from his Jeep that he didn't recognize.

"Not now, baby, just a few more minutes."

The truck came around a corner about a hundred yards behind him at warp speed. They slammed on their brakes, but the big truck couldn't stop that fast. Even on dry pavement, their rear end started to come around, so Ashe hit his gas and took off fast as he could to avoid being rear-ended.

They got it under control, and both vehicles came to a stop about thirty yards apart. The truck passenger took off his seat belt and brought an M4-looking carbine up.

Ashe dropped his Jeep into reverse and floored his gas pedal, sending his rear end into the grill and bumper of the truck. Their air bags exploded in their faces.

Ashe tried to go forward, but his engine had died. He laid down across the front seat and pushed himself toward the passenger door. There was a ditch out there. He took a quick peek before trying to get out.

The truck passenger was out of the truck; his nose was bloody. He was reaching back into it, probably for his M4, when the driver drove forward and shoved Ashe's Jeep into the ditch, back end first, crushing his right rear fender. The passenger had to jog forward, yelling at the driver.

Ashe got out, or fell out, and felt his left hip and knee take a hard bump against something. Using what was left of his vehicle for protection, he pulled his Smith and Wesson 9mm, and limped to get behind the engine block. He knew cars were poor cover, but he had no option.

The truck guys started yelling and sounded like they were about to get their show together, when Ashe saw blue and red flashing lights approaching.

Jacob's unmarked but well-illuminated cruiser arrived, and a very familiar dark-gray Dodge SUV pulled up beside him, blocking both lanes. From the other direction, a Hurrt County Explorer and a state police cruiser with all kinds of lights flashing arrived.

The Dodge boys were smarter than they had previously demonstrated; they immediately gave up. Jacobs was out of his car, 1911 pistol in hand, and from the gray SUV came Pat Keagan.

Ed Bell jogged up from behind him, his gun in hand and aimed at the suspects. "You okay, Mister Ashe?"

"Yeah, watch those guys," he said, and tried to get out of the ditch without leaning on his old Jeep. He'd bruised something and it hurt like hell. "Aggravated assault, armed criminal action." He looked at his Jeep in the ditch and sighed. He'd had it since it was new.

"And add...reckless damn driving."

The trooper and Deputy Bell got the two guys in custody, and Pat walked over to Ashe, who was limping.

"What the hell's the matter with you? You injured?"

"No, I just...I think there was a rock, maybe. I thought *you* had a big court case in the morning?"

"I guess there's a plea. Anyway, I came to drive Rachel home since she's beat, you know."

"What is this all about, Ashe?" Jacobs asked.

"They picked me up leaving Harold Marsh's house. Chased me and pulled a rifle at one point. Tried to pit me into the ditch twice. Is Harold okay? Did anybody see our guy from the café?"

"What guy at what café?" Pat asked.

Jacobs said, "Harold's okay. I heard from Minor who said Harold was upstairs and his new law partner stayed with him. But someone broke into the house by a side window. Housekeeper ran upstairs after talking to you. They stole his computer and ransacked his desk then left. My deputy got there in less than two minutes, but whoever it was, he was gone."

Then Ashe realized something. Something that made him feel like an idiot. "Crap!"

"What?" Jacobs asked.

"These men in this truck. Probably just local 'talent' from the city, not real pros. He just wanted to know where I was, to give him more time at Marsh's."

"*He*? He who? That man from the café?" Jacobs asked.

"What man? And what...ah hell!" Pat said. He took Ashe by the arm and led him to his Dodge SUV.

"Yeah, him, Sheriff. He must have put these two to work. I bet they've been tracking the comings and goings at the cove, too. Our stranger had them watching the judge; saw me go there twice today and wanted to find out why. Or...maybe figured out Marsh was in contact with Durant. Anyway, these two were just amateur enough to let me see them, then they *had* to keep me busy. Stupid."

"So, this man you're talking about, you think he's also the sniper from the cove?" Pat asked.

"I dunno, but it's a good bet," Ashe said. "And had these men been cooler, and just watched me, he'd have had more time for searching Marsh's place. They went all cowboy, so he had to hurry."

"And again, looking for whatever the hell everyone else is looking for," Jacobs said.

"Only now, I know what it is. According to Durant, it's a thumb drive. Containing financial information on the Foundation."

"So that's it. Where the hell is it?" Jacobs asked.

"You mean, he says all that at the cove, all that killing. And Chuck, too. All because of some damn money records?" Pat said. "Damn, Chuck."

Jacobs looked Ashe up and down. "You're beat up, go home. We're meeting in the morning with Price, the deputy AG, and a US Marshal. We need to lay all this out for them, and get Rachel up to speed."

Ashe didn't argue, so Jacobs went to his car to answer his radio and Ashe heard him mention tow trucks. Pat stepped closer to Ashe and pounded on his shoulder.

"Hey, Chig, it's okay. What else could you have done?" Pat said. "Like you said, what you did actually cut into this guy's time at Marsh's house. Maybe saved his life."

Ashe looked at the two men, in two separate patrol cars. One looked a little nervous, the other defiant. He limped over to Ed Bell's cruiser where the defiant man was, and jerked open the back door.

"Why were you chasing me?" he asked the suspect inside.

"Kiss my ass," the driver of the Dodge boys said.

"Ashe! C'mon, that's not the way to do this," Pat said, and tried to pull him back.

Ashe shook off Pat's arm and leaned slightly farther into the caged back seat. Pat turned around and put his back to the open car door, blocking the view of anyone who might look over. To his credit, Ashe noticed Deputy Bell came over and did the same thing.

The driver in the back seat noticed this. "What? You going to beat it out of me?" he said.

"No, I just want you to think on something. The man who hired you isn't here. He won't face charges yet. He's probably not even local. I'm betting you are. Here's the deal, the first rule of hiring local, expendable people like you, is once you're done with them, you get *rid* of them."

The driver stared at Ashe.

"So whatever you do, you lie, you say whatever you want. But now he'll know you've been in custody. He'll not want you to talk about him. *Ever.* So stew on that."

Ashe slammed the door before he could say anything. Then, with Pat's help, he limped over to the state trooper's car and opened the back door on the second suspect.

"Hey, your friend is going to talk with us about the guy who hired you. He's going to try to nail him so you two don't get killed in your sleep six months from now."

"I...he...shouldn't you read me my rights?"

Ashe looked at Pat. Pat shrugged. Ashe advised him of his Miranda rights, then when he agreed to talk, asked, "Okay, you're Drew. Drew, what was your job tonight?"

"Get you, and as many cops as possible out of the way."

"Out of who's way?" Pat asked.

"I don't know his real name. English kind of man, black. But he wanted to get in that house and he didn't want any of you around. We were supposed to get you to chase us, like the Bandit in that Burt Reynolds movie? But you took off."

"You were going to run me in a ditch, and then shoot me? That part of the plan?"

"No, just pit you and then throw a scare into you," Drew said.

"Do I look scared? Did I drive like I was scared?"

Drew shook his head, so Ashe took a breath. Then asked, "Okay. Why me?"

"He said to keep anyone busy and away from that house; but he especially didn't want *you* around. That man, the Englishman? He had a photo of you." He thought for a minute, then, "Why would he want to kill us?"

"You're just like a used paper cup to him. Drain you, then trash you."

"Bobby's really going to cooperate?"

Pat and Ashe looked back over at Bell's cruiser. Bobby the driver was yelling something and throwing himself around in the back seat. He could see them talking to his partner, and he did not look happy to Ashe. Ed Bell slammed a hand on top of his car and pointed a finger at him.

Jacobs walked over, so Ashe closed the back door on Drew.

"What's this about?" he asked, but had a small smile on his face.

"I think you should question these two right away, Sheriff. Starting with this Drew, who's waived his rights already," Pat said.

Jacobs nodded and looked in the back seat at Drew. "Okay, but I told you to go home, Ashe," Jacobs said. "Pat, can you meet me at the jail after you drop him off?"

"Sure. I'm waiting on Rachel," he said.

Jacobs whistled to everyone and made a circle in the air with a finger. "Let's go! I'll wait on the wreckers!"

Everyone jogged back to their cars; they'd been looking at Ashe's Jeep and the blue Dodge. Ashe shrugged. "My Jeep is trash," he said, and hobbled over to it. He found his phone on the floorboard and retrieved his portfolio from inside.

"Be late before I can get Rachel home in Metro, then right back here in the a.m.," Pat said. "She'll likely get a motel room for the night. Me, I'm staying with you. Hey, where are you going?"

Ashe walked as best he could over to the blue Dodge truck. The trooper had looked through it and recovered the M4 carbine and a handgun. Ashe grabbed a handle on the front pillar column and pulled himself up into the passenger seat. Sweeping the deployed airbag out of his way, he checked the glove box and center console then flipped the sun visor down.

Into his lap dropped a full-sized sheet of copy paper, folded. Printed like off an inkjet printer, was a cropped picture of him. Ashe stared at it; it was from maybe a year or so ago, a photo of him and Stevie, but she had been cropped out before printing.

Where the hell would he get a photo like this?

He handed the photo to Pat, then said, "You both can stay at my place, or whatever you want to do. Anyway, I'm low on coffee, so whoever comes, bring your own coffee grounds."

Ashe climbed down and then wobbled over into Pat's SUV and closed the door. They'd need his statement and a report, but the sheriff could hold them until morning. Pat got in.

"They tried to pit you, eh? Why that big a damn pickup? Sure sticks out," Pat said.

"Not around here it doesn't. Maybe because they figured it gave them a weight and power advantage."

Ashe looked back at his wrecked Jeep Cherokee.

I should have stayed on our stranger from the café. I won't make that mistake again.

CHAPTER 20

Ashe didn't sleep well. Even though he'd turned in fairly early, his hip and knee bothered him enough that he took two ibuprofen and finger of Darkthorn before bed. At just before six, he got up to make coffee, but from the smell down the hall, Pat had beat him to it.

He heard Pat in the guest bathroom as he walked past, still limping a little, and when he got to the kitchen, there was Rachel. She was dressed and ready for the day in a white oxford shirt and a fire blue pant suit, and had the spreadsheets from Judge Marsh spread out on the kitchen bar.

Somewhere under all that, he knew she had a Glock 9mm concealed.

Ashe was in a T-shirt and old gym shorts. "Excuse me, but I live here. Alone mostly," he said. She nodded without looking, engrossed in the papers.

He went around the counter and looked at the coffeepot; Pat must have made it. Pulling out the filter basket, he saw it was crammed to the rim with grounds. So he dumped all that in the trash. He took a mug, filled it with Pat's thick coffee in case he wanted more, then dumped the rest of the pot down the drain.

"Thank you," she said without looking up.

Ashe then made a fresh pot with what he thought was a normal, human, amount of grounds and stood there waiting on it. After a minute, he said, "Did you...I don't care but, I don't remember you..."

"I just got here a while ago," she said, then looked up at Ashe as if confused. "It was you who let me in." She looked back at the door then at Ashe. "I...it was you. Looked like you. You had a different shirt on though."

"Um, I just got up. Probably Pat."

"No, it wasn't Pat," she said, and resumed staring at the spreadsheets.

"Yeah. I must have still been asleep." *Best leave that alone,* he decided to himself.

When enough of the coffee was done, he quickly swapped his mug for the carafe and filled it, then swapped them back, and went to get cleaned up.

When Ashe was showered, he dressed in a white cotton shirt, navy slacks, cordovan shoes, and a light-gray blazer, with a blue-and-burgundy tie. He looked in the mirror. *Professional, not too dressy, though.*

Pat was wearing what he had on yesterday; a medium-brown suit, yellow shirt, and a dark-copper tie. They stood in the kitchen a minute while Rachel made some final notes on a pad. It was six forty-five.

"So, Pat, what did Bobby and Drew give up last night?"

"Nothing new, really. Like you said, local guys from over in Mac City in McCormick County. Hired through an online chat site and paid in cash. Bobby clammed up, but Drew gave us a statement."

"Huh," Ashe said, then suddenly turned and went to his home office then returned with his checkbook in his hand.

"What's that for?" Pat asked.

"You reminded me, I guess I have to buy a car today," Ashe said.

Rachel set down her pen. "Ashe, tell me about this video call with Durant, and how you came to be there," she said.

"I knew if there was a private gentlemen's club that catered to the Seacord upper class, old Judge Harold Marsh would at least know about it. So, after you and I searched through the internet for Durant, and we came to a dead end, I went and asked him about the Blockade Runners. He knew all about them. Hell, both he and my dad at one time were members."

Pat heated the mug of mud Ashe had saved for him in the microwave. "Okay, Chig, so how did that tie into Durant?"

Ashe told them how Portals and company had recruited Durant

for help with the governor's office, and how Durant blamed Carol for digitally raiding both the Blockaders and the Foundation's financial records. The cove was supposed to be a meet to exchange the data for cash.

"So, this little thumb drive is what everyone's been looking for," Pat said. "He has it, and he was extorting them all, but it went south."

"Well, according to *him*, and him alone. Notice how everything is Carol's plan, not his," Ashe said. "Convenient, eh? Since she's dead."

"As far as these spreadsheets, there are, what I'm assuming to be, intentional gaps. This is incomplete information," Rachel said.

"I'm no forensic accountant, and I've not really had any time to look them over, but I assume this is a tease. He gave those to Harold Marsh to give to us," Ashe said. "Durant has to want something for the rest."

"Like what?" Pat asked.

"Like we don't know yet. He never said. I'd guess he wants the government to protect him so he can have his revenge by testifying against them," Ashe said.

"Great. He wants to try and make some kind of deal with us," she said.

"Damn, Chuck," Pat said, almost under his breath. Then he rapped his big knuckles on the counter loudly. "Poor bastard. He had no idea what he was walking into."

"You knew him better, but the Chuck I remember was a pro. Had he known all this…this shit that Durant was setting up, he'd have been better prepared," Ashe said.

"Typical of rich folks. Hire a bodyguard mostly for the look of it then hold back information that is actually important to protecting them!" Pat said.

Rachel looked at Pat then Ashe, and quickly moved on. "According to this, the Blockaders, as you call them, were syphoning Foundation money off the children's sanctuary. Tens of thousands at a time, and regularly. Just what I see here? It could total a half a million over the past year and a half," Rachel said.

"No wonder the place looks like it does. Half maintained, poorly equipped," Ashe said. "Stevie should have caught that. She was supposed to be managing the funds for the sanctuary."

"Actually I think the inappropriate and probably illegal transfer of funds occurred *after* she had loaded funds into the HCCS expenditure account. So, as long as they executed the funds, *in this case*, she's in the clear," Rachel said.

Ashe drank his coffee. "Neat how Durant has everything set up, huh?"

"Then these other printouts show completely different accounts where the Foundation was kicking charitably donated money out to some offshore account. But then, boom! Nothing else," she added. "Just enough to make me want to get more."

"You see any mention of a person named 'Searl,' or maybe a 'Searl' company?"

Rachel shook her head. "Not so far, but maybe it's one of these numbered accounts. Who is it?"

"Something Durant mentioned. But we may not need Durant; we can get subpoenas. You have enough justification even without these printouts. They're useless in court anyway, given how we received them," Ashe said.

"And both Judge Marsh and Durant would know that," Rachel said.

"Huh," Pat said. "You know, it'd be just like a privileged prick like Durant to have been caught pitting these people against the other? I mean, for *all* the data. Especially the stuff we don't have; like a bidding war. Whoever won, has a throat hold on the other."

They all thought about that for a second. Then Ashe said, "Whatever we *don't* have must be very valuable to them, and damaging. Worth killing over."

"That's good, Pat. That might be just the reason both sides decided *not* to leave the two of them walking around," Rachel said.

Ashe nodded. "That makes more sense than anything I've heard. Plus, it explains why he's sent this to us and why he hired Chuck, both as insurance. And…why he's in hiding somewhere overseas," he said. "They showed they weren't going to deal out at the cove, so now he's got nowhere to turn. He's casting bait at us because he doesn't want to run the rest of his life."

Rachel picked up her phone and made a call. From this end, all they heard her say was, "Find Seacord Bank's president, Clarence Crawford. Keep 'eyes on' until we're ready."

Ashe and Pat smiled at each other. "If that's our Danny Breslin, that's the kind of job he gets out of bed for," Ashe said.

Pat turned his head and mumbled back, "Oh, I bet he's got a diamond cutter right about now."

Rachel next called what sounded like ADA Price.

Ashe lowered his voice. "Pat, that idea you had about Durant pitting the Blockaders against the Able Keys Foundation? Did you steal that from Rachel?"

"Huh?"

"I ask because generally, you're too slow to come up with an actual helpful insight," Ashe said.

Pat slowly shook his head. "I thought you'd grown up, Chig. You keep that up, I'll bruise your other leg," he said.

"I don't think so. You're pretty slow."

"Yes, but you're older, and a gimp now. I could catch you," Pat said.

Rachel hung up and, pretending she hadn't heard them, looked like she was trying hard not to smile.

"So, Rachel. I'm guessing the guy at the cove with the AK, probably belongs to the Blockaders. They sent him out to make the deal, but according to Durant, it went south," Ashe said.

She nodded. "Anderton. His name was…something Anderton. He's from McCormick County also, so what you're saying makes sense. He's local."

"And the sniper, your stranger from the café? I'm assuming he's more money and harder to connect with. This Able Keys Foundation might have sent him," Pat added.

"And," Ashe said. "They *didn't* want to make a deal."

. . . .

Sheriff Jacobs met them at the courthouse, and juggling a large set of keys in one hand, a newspaper, and a big to-go cup of coffee in the other, he unlocked the main entrance for them. No one else was at work there yet. They walked to the second floor and into a large deposition room. They all set their papers and notebooks down on a long table with ten or so chairs. A small end table in a corner held a well-stained coffeepot, but no coffee was in sight.

Jacobs dropped the newspapers he had in his hand on the table.

There was the morning Metro paper and the local, once-a-week Hurrt County/Seacord Review.

Mass Murder on Minor Hills Lake and **Multiple Gunshot Victims According to Coroner.**

Ashe sighed. *Damn. The morning, noon, and night TV news will be all over this.*

"Speaking of shit, anybody want me to try working that?" Jacobs asked, shaking the dry, stained, carafe.

"No, I'm good," Pat said, and Rachel shook her head as well.

Rachel looked at her phone. "ADA Price and the team from the capitol will be here in forty minutes or so," she said. "You guys have time to grab a quick bite if you want."

"I just ate," Jacobs said. "But, Ashe, why don't you and I walk across to Roger's?"

"I'm good," Pat said, although he hadn't been asked.

Before he left the room, Ashe said, "Hey, I think until we know more about the Foundation and the Blockaders, as far as who all is involved with them, I think we need to go easy on mentioning the governor."

Rachel pondered this. "I've already told my SAC, and the head of her protective detail. Minus what you told me this morning."

"Just a recommendation, but let's leave it at this level for now."

"You're afraid they'll shut us down? Or lock us out of the financials we need to see?" Rachel said.

"Both, maybe," Ashe said, then left with the sheriff.

Jacobs and Ashe walked out and across the square toward the café in a light drizzle that had just started. "You still got a limp," Jacobs said, starting at Ashe's left side.

"It's sore is all, I think I hit something on the ground in that ditch. Bruise, maybe."

Jacobs dug a receipt from his pocket. "Oh, huh. By the way, here's your Jeep's tow ticket."

"I don't suppose the county would…"

"Nope. I never authorized you to go tearing ass around the countryside in a twenty-some-odd-year-old Jeep," Jacobs said.

Inside the café, it was a little slow for a Monday. The people there turned to look at them and stopped talking as Ashe and Jacobs came in. Several of the patrons had the newspapers spread out on their tables.

Ashe saw his old friend, Tilly, wave them over to her section. "Morning, Till," he said after he slid into a booth. She didn't bother to offer either of them a menu.

"Coffee for one? You need a refill, Sheriff?" she asked.

"No, I'm coffee'd out."

"I'll have…"

"I know, Chig," was all she said as she left.

No cutesy banter? No smart-aleck comments? Something is up with Ms. Tilly.

"Okay, *detective*, you need to fill your boss in," Jacobs said. So Ashe did.

When he was done, including the video call with Durant and Rachel's quick look at the spreadsheets, breakfast arrived for Ashe. He dug in. "I don't remember when I ate last, Till," he said.

"Enjoy," was all she said. She refilled his coffee and without another word, left.

"So that's it, boss. Is Harold okay?" Ashe asked once Tilly was out of range of their conversation.

"Yeah, and that other lady lawyer, Linda something-or-other. She asked the same thing about you! 'Is *Chig* okay?' Anyway, the old judge probably slept through it. His housekeeper got a good scare, though," Jacobs said.

"Ingles. Linda Ingles," Ashe said. He was glad she had been there for Marsh and was okay.

"So Durant's out of reach as far as we know, but listen, there's still Lou Buckram."

"I would assume our next move would be to pick up Clarence Crawford, and possibly Stevie, this morning after our meeting," Ashe said.

"Well, you may be right, but I just have a sneaking suspicion against Lou. He has more motive than anyone to hate them Blockaders and especially Durant."

"Lou Buckram," Ashe said to himself.

"Yeah," Jacobs said, also mostly to himself.

Ashe drained his cup, wiped his mouth, dropped enough cash on the table to pay the bill, and left Tilly an oversized tip. "Let's go find out!" he said.

As they left the restaurant, Ashe saw Tilly watching him from behind the counter. Her eyes looked just a bit out of focus to him.

It was like she saw him, but maybe in another place or time.

"Hey, Till! I haven't forgotten you wanted to tell me something. I'll be back as soon as I can."

Her eyes came back into the here and now for a second. She just slightly raised her chin in acknowledgement, and then went back to work.

Okay, it's something. There's something for sure going on with her.

But Ashe turned and, still limping some, went out the door after Jacobs.

. . . .

Stevie sat in her car across the square in the early morning hour and watched Ashe through a light rain on her windshield as he walked out of the café.

Why is he limping? My God, he's hurt again?

She knew better than to have driven here alone. Despite getting a few hours' sleep, she knew she was likely still legally drunk. But she was thinking clearer and had a loose plan.

She knew she very much wanted to help the children at the sanctuary. In her heart, she felt like she owed them a chance at a real life.

Then, and only if possible, somehow help Tom. She was very afraid he was running scared, acting outside of established standards of practice for a lawyer, and she, more than anyone, knew what that could mean for him. He'd already lied to her, and given what she suspected, he was in danger. Both professionally and also, with his life.

Especially since these people he was covering for were involved in murder.

Does he know that? Would he even admit it to me if he did?

Beside her on the passenger seat of her car sat the box of papers and files Tom had packed up from the Blockade Runners. Just from what she'd seen, it was evidence. Evidence enough that he'd wanted to hide it from the sheriff. When she'd removed the box, there technically wasn't a search warrant in play yet. But, tampering, concealing, destroying evidence in a capital case, is a felony itself.

Stevie sighed. She knew she had only one play left. Turn this box over to the state investigator, or at least the sheriff.

All she'd had to do was roll down her window and shout, but as the sheriff and Ashe disappeared into the courthouse, she just sat quiet and still in her car.

No matter what I do, Tom will see it as a betrayal of him. No matter how much I explain it to him; point out that he'd lied and hidden his involvement. Tell him that we can both forgive each other and move on, he won't hear me.

He'll just... hate me.

She took out her phone and thumbed through her contacts. At the top of the list, alphabetically, was Ashe.

Lord, if I go to Ashe, Tom will really be done with me, then. He'll not only be furious, he'll leave me.

But Ashe was always on her side. She knew he was probably a bit blind that way, always trusting her. Always caring, even when she was wrong. *Especially* when she was wrong.

And even when I don't deserve it.

And, she decided, he was the best way to get the box into the right hands.

Then there's this little digital recorder. Two hundred thousand reasons for those men to kill Carol and Durant.

She wanted coffee. She needed food. Roger's was all that was open, but that meant walking in there and putting up with Tilly. She knew Tilly hated her for her past relationship with Ashe. She'd made it clear enough through snide and openly hateful remarks toward her. Tilly and Ashe had been high school lovers, but never since.

We both, at different times and different ways, loved the same man. Now neither of us are with him, and both of us are with different men. Why?

She and I still carry a little torch for him, knowing it would never work out for either of us.

Then a thought entered her mind. A wild thought, that led to a dangerous plan.

CHAPTER 21

$\cdot\cdot$ ——————◆—————— $\cdot\cdot$

In the deposition room, in chairs along the back wall, sat Rachel, Pat, Ashe, Jacobs, and ADA Price. On the other side of the long table sat Rachel's SAC, then a man Ashe hadn't met, and finally the Deputy Attorney General for the state, Rollin Ashad.

Ashe had known Ashad since they'd both worked in Metro and Ashad was an assistant district attorney. Ashad was plucked out of Metro's DA office when the new governor and new attorney general were elected, and his career had done nothing but rise like a firecracker since.

Plus, he's tight with the governor, and allegedly she's on the board of the Foundation. Need to tread carefully here.

"To benefit Mr. Wynn of the US Marshals, let's all introduce ourselves to get started," Price said. "I'm John Price, and I'm the assistant DA here in Hurrt County."

"Rachel Hume, Special Agent with the State Police Criminal Investigation Bureau. I'm the point on this investigation."

"Lieutenant Pat Keagan, Metro PD, Major Crimes. I'm here at the request of Agent Hume as there are ties to the city by some of the suspects, and at least one of the victims."

Ashad cut in, "I assume your Captain Speakes knows you're working with us here."

"Yes, sir. He is aware and concurs," Pat said.

Ashe sighed to himself as Pat had to sit there quietly. Ashad could be an arrogant ass.

You just had to gut-check Pat; showing off that you know Pat's boss, who just happens to be a buddy of yours, Rollin. You'll work golf into the conversation today, somehow.

Ashad turned to Wynn. "Captain Speakes is the head of criminal investigation for Metro, and a good man to know. We'll have you out for a round of golf and you can get to know him," he said.

Ashe smiled to himself.

"I'm Sheriff Larry Jacobs, Hurrt County," Jacobs suddenly boomed. Knowing Jacobs, Ashe figured he was as unimpressed with Rollin Ashad's boasting as he was. Jacobs fondled his shirt pocket but then seemed to remember there was no smoking in the courthouse.

It was Ashe's turn, so he introduced himself then said, "I'm the, ah...*new detective* for Hurrt County." He gave Rachel a side-eyed glance, but she didn't seem to react.

Then Rachel's SAC introduced himself, followed by Ashad.

"You all know me. The AG and the governor's office are concerned by the sudden rise in violent deaths here, especially in such a short span of time," he said. Then, "Hello, again, Ashe."

"Hello, Rollin," Ashe said, using his first name on purpose.

"Ashe? You were with Metro before, right?" said the man Ashe assumed was the US Marshal.

"Yes, sir. I was head of the MCU, but I was born and raised down here. Now I'm...well, I *was* retired here."

The man smiled at him. "Well, I'm Jack Wynn, and I'm the Chief Deputy US Marshal for this judicial district. I'm here because Charles, or Chuck, Carter was a damn good deputy marshal and a friend of mine. I want to offer whatever assistance is needed, and provide any information we have to solve this case."

Rachel started to speak, but Ashad pointed at the newspapers on the table and spoke first. "Tell me what you're doing about this," he said to Price.

"Um, we will release a statement today to the local press, let them have it first. Something like, 'we are working with state investigators, these are not random killings, lots of clues, closing in on a suspect, no danger to the public.' I'll write something up for Larry to announce, and add a quote of my own," Price said.

"Good. Get some of the county and town officials to concur with you, and stay off the TV news if you can," Ashad said. "Now, what do you *actually* have so far?"

Price pulled out a file folder and opened it. "This started with the body of former Deputy Marshal Carter washing ashore on Minor Hills Lake near the county park. It became obvious even before he was identified, that based on the equipment he was wearing, this was a law enforcement officer, or some kind of protective service agent."

"Okay," Ashad said, and steepled his fingers.

"Body was posted in Metro. He died of multiple gunshot wounds to the chest and one to the head. High caliber precision rifle. Body had been in the water about a week. We ran his personal financials to determine who would profit from his death; nothing unusual there. Then Agent Hume checked with your department for any known enemies, former protectees, et cetera."

"Meanwhile, Mister, ah, *Detective* Ashe and Lt. Keagan, with the assist of state park rangers, backtracked where the current would have brought his body from, and they discovered the scene at the cove," Rachel said.

"And that's where you found the body of the second man, and the caretaker girl from the shelter?" Ashad said, and leaned over and whispered something to Wynn.

Rachel said, "Yes, and post-mortem has estimated they died out there, about the same time as Mr. Carter. Sensing a potential connection, the sheriff looked into the Hurrt County Children's Sanctuary, or HCCS, and later discovered the local men's group called the Blockade Runners met there. Understand sir, the sanctuary is funded by charitable donations from the Able Keys Foundation. A member of both groups, Mr. Michael Durant, went missing at the same time as the shooting at the cove."

Wynn looked at Ashad. "*The* Michael Durant?"

"Yeah," Ashad said. "But there's no clear evidence the Foundation has anything directly to do with these Blockaders. I mean, other than supporting these children, is there?"

Price looked at Rachel who frowned. "Well, yes. At least through Durant. He was both an original board member of the Foundation, as well as a recruited member of the Blockaders."

"Ah. But, you've never found Durant to interview him, right?"

"Wrong," Ashe said.

That seemed to startle Ashad. Everyone turned their attention to Ashe.

"I was contacted by a local attorney and retired circuit judge who had been personally contacted by Durant. A video call was arranged and I had a limited amount of time to talk to Durant, who claimed he was out of the country for fear of his life."

"Go on, Ashe," Ashad said. Then to Wynn he said, "This is new to me."

"Durant claims he had a romantic affair with Carol Buckram, the administrator of the HCCS, or just 'the sanctuary' as it's called here, while he was a member of both the Foundation *and* the Blockade Runners. This conflict of interest, both financially and personally, caused him to be excommunicated—his words—from the Blockaders. His seat on the board of the Able Keys Foundation was, according to him, also in jeopardy," Ashe said.

Price jumped in. "Ah, it's important to note, the Children's Sanctuary is owned by an LLC that Durant started. We have confirmed that he personally owns the actual building where the sanctuary operates and the Blockaders met. That LLC, called Lifenablers, funds more than one such facility, and also several senior care homes."

Where Stevie works. Dammit, girl.

"We discussed this on the way over here, Rollin. You said he was on the board of the Able Keys Foundation, right? And they funded this Life…Ablers LLC," Wynn said to Ashad.

That is interesting, Ashe noted, but tried to keep a poker face. *So Mister Ashad knows more that he's letting on.*

"To further complicate matters," Price said. "The sanctuary is locally managed by a board. A board that is made up entirely of alleged members of the Blockaders."

"Anyway," Jacobs said. "Durant and the girl ran off together."

"And, he also claims that Ms. Buckram stole some financial records and stored them on a flash drive. Records that allegedly indict both the Foundation and the Blockaders," Ashe said. "And that this action is the reason for the killings at the cove, and for his being in fear for his life."

"Now let's not get ahead of ourselves!" Ashad said. Ashe figured he'd spoken more forcefully than he'd meant to, as he opened his palms to everyone and closed his eyes a second to calm down. "You have no evidence the Foundation has been contacted, nor is involved in any way, whatsoever, with any of these deaths."

"Well, that's true, but we do have some documents provided by

Durant that show the Foundation transferring charitable funds to an off shore account," Rachel said, and laid out the spreadsheet copies from Durant on the table.

Ashad ignored them. "What records? What documents, and how do we know they're legit? C'mon, people! You had better get your evidentiary game on better than this?" Ashad said. He punctuated his words by jabbing his finger into the table. Jacobs picked up his coffee cup as the vibration was making it walk on the table. "Nothing like that is admissible in court, John!"

Ashe noticed that Rachel's SAC hadn't spoken at all but had been monitoring the conversation closely.

"Mister Deputy Attorney General," Price said. "We do not have a prosecution, nor even an indictment here yet. You asked us to brief you on the current status of this investigation, and to include Chief Deputy Wynn."

Ashad nodded. "Yes of course, John, excuse me. Chief Wynn? You have anything to add?"

Wynn nodded to Ashad and then opened a folder of his own.

"Agent Hume and her boss here asked me for any cases Chuck had worked, or any intelligence I could offer," he said.

Wynn took out several five-by-seven photographs, and spread them across the table so Rachel, Ashe, Pat, and Jacobs could see.

"Anyone here look familiar?" he asked.

Ashe and Rachel stood and leaned over the table to examine the photos. They were color, official looking, and posed. Like identification card or passport pictures. Pat looked them over as well and shook his head. But Jacobs noticed one.

"This is one of the guys at the café the other morning," he said. "He was sitting with…"

"This guy," Ashe said. He stuck his finger beside the photo of a black male. Military looking, short hair. Even through the photograph, Ashe could feel the intensity in his eyes.

"I thought so," Wynn said. "Mr. Ashe, that's Arthur North. He's ex-British intelligence and works with a group we've been monitoring. He left Great Britain years ago to work in central Europe then Canada. He's reported to be based in Canada now, or sometimes in the Dominican Republic."

Pat and Jacobs took a better look at him, and the rest of the photos.

"The man you recognized, Sheriff, is a known accomplice of North. He's Enrique Garza from the Dominican Republic."

"What are they to Chuck Carter?" Ashe asked.

"Nothing we know of, except the organization North works with has popped up when we do threat assessments for special protection witnesses, and other protectees."

"None of these are your Dodge boys," Jacobs said. "You're probably right, they were local contractors."

"Dodge boys?" Price asked. Jacobs just held up a finger, as if to say, *later*.

Wynn continued. "North is a surveillance and intel gathering specialist, but he's known internationally to have done targeted assassination jobs. He's sniper trained by the Brits, and the FBI wants him for questioning on a data theft from a US embassy. Homeland has him on a no-fly list, and the group he works with is on the Terrorist Watch List," Wynn said. "If he's here, if he was the man who shot Chuck, there's a bigger reason than what you've told me so far."

Ashe let out a deep breath. *The old judge was lucky.*

Ashe explained how he'd seen North in Seacord near Marsh's house the day before, and how the blue Dodge truck had been staked out to watch it.

"Why is this caliber a guy even here? Assuming he's the talent that killed your friend and mine, as well as another man out at the cove, *and* took a couple of shots at Ashe and me…why? Like you said, it must be bigger than the Blockade Runners screwing the Foundation, or a poor local girl and her rich boyfriend trying to screw both of them over," Pat said.

"That's a good question, and one that we will continue to investigate," Price said, staring at Ashad.

"Wait, he took a shot at you two? And *missed*?" Wynn said.

"I think he was actually aiming at our boat motors. I think he wanted us to be stranded there," Ashe said.

"Whatever the reason for this North fellow, I'll bet anything it's also the reason Durant hired Chuck to bodyguard him," Pat said. "And it got Chuck killed."

Ashe looked at his friend. *He hasn't said much, but when he does…*

"I think you're right, detectives. There's a good deal more to be discovered," Wynn said.

"Has anyone heard of a Searl? A man or a company?" Ashe asked.

No one had. But Ashad's eyes flickered, and he tried to shrug, but it looked suspicious to Ashe.

Then Ashad looked at his watch. "Well, thank you, John, for putting this together. I have to be getting back to the capitol now," Ashad said and stood up. He motioned for Rachel's SAC to walk with him then turned and said, "John, Rachel, a minute please?"

They all walked out into the hall. Pat seemed to want to follow, but before he could, Ashad closed the door behind them.

Wynn didn't go with Ashad but walked directly over to Sheriff Jacobs and shook his hand. "Sheriff, you need anything, you call me direct. That goes for you boys too. I was a deputy sheriff myself years ago."

"Thanks, Chief," Jacobs said.

He handed Jacobs, Ashe, and Pat a business card.

"It's Jack to you guys. I mean it, anything I can do. Chuck was a good man." Then as he walked to the door, he paused. "He had kids, you know. One in college. I think you feel like me, I want the bastard that did this."

Ashe shook his hand, but held it a beat longer. "I think North was originally here to kill Durant. He missed somehow, then he began looking for him. He probably guessed Durant was still in the area, which is why he first started watching us."

"Makes sense," Wynn said. "He wouldn't hang around after all that shooting unless he absolutely needed to be."

"I think North and company *are* still around here, but they're looking for the flash drive that he thinks is still here. The one we believe Durant has, wherever he is. I'm also guessing something about it is hotter than Durant knows, *because* North is around. I can't think of any other reason."

"You damn well might be right, so as long as he thinks he can recover it, he'll be in the area." Wynn turned and walked out the door.

As he did, Rachel and ADA Price returned. No one said to, but everyone sat back down at the table and Jacobs closed the door.

Both Rachel and Price looked pissed off; Price's face was beet red.

"We never got to how Crawford and Lou Buckram were looking for the thumb drive, nor how they cleaned out the Blockader's meeting room," Jacobs said.

Price just shook his head. Ashe noticed that Pat and Rachel were staring at each other. At this point in their relationship, Ashe guessed Pat could probably read her pretty well, and vice versa.

"There are to be no subpoenas for the Foundation or the Lifenablers, LLC," Price said. "Anything we need, they will provide through their attorney, Tom Fischer."

"What?" Jacobs said. "I'm getting a little tired of this high-and-mighty Mister Ashad!"

"Those subpoenas would have filled in the gaps in these spreadsheets Durant provided," Ashe said. "So that we'd be in a stronger position without him."

"The district attorney's office will not issue any subpoenas for them, but I can get them for the Blockade Runners," Price said. Ashe noticed that with a pen in his hand, he was drawing deep circles on a pad. His knuckles were white.

"That's putting your finger on the scale a bit, huh?" Pat said.

"Anyone notice how Ashad didn't mention the governor is also on the board of directors of the Able Keys Foundation?" Ashe said.

"You said we shouldn't mention it either, Chig," Pat said.

Price seemed to have a thought. "That's actually good. She wasn't mentioned at all. So if anything connecting the governor's office comes up…"

"Don't even know that it would," Ashe said.

"John, I appreciate the position you're in, but as a Special Agent of the State Police CIB, I can issue my own subpoenas. I am only required to provide you, as the local ADA, a copy," Rachel said.

"You heard Ashad," John warned.

"I work for my SAC, and he gave me no such direction."

"Ashad is almost at the top of our chain of command in the State Department of Justice," he said.

"Well, they can fire me later," she said, and gave him a sarcastic smile.

"What the hell are we doing, then?" Jacobs asked. He lit a cigarette then looked at everyone as if to say, *whatever, I'm smoking*.

Price tapped his pen on his pad. "Dammit, we investigate. First, pick up Crawford from the bank. He's allegedly the president of the Blockaders as well, and if we turn him, he might help us with the financials. Also, we give him one of your subpoenas, Rachel. That might add some heat."

"I'm on it," she said, and began texting someone. Ashe assumed Breslin still had eyes on Crawford.

"And Lou Buckram," Jacobs said.

Price shrugged. "Okay, sure. He seems to know something about all this, and he certainly had a motive. Then also pick up Stevie Collins."

They all slowly glanced at Ashe. "Rachel, that's yours," Price added, without looking at Ashe.

"Shit!" Rachel said. Everyone stopped and looked at her. "Um, sorry, I wasn't cursing about Stevie, but Crawford is up in Metro right now. I have an agent on him, assuming we'd want him sooner or later."

"Any idea why he's there?" Price asked. "Or how long?"

Rachel looked at her texts. "Until at least lunch or later. He's at a banking meeting of some kind."

"Hey," Pat interrupted. "She and I could head back up to the city now and talk to him there."

Price thought about that. "Yeah, okay. But I want details today."

"Detective Ashe, let's me and you go get Buckram. John, you want us to bring him here?" Jacobs said. Price nodded.

Everyone filed out and headed toward the parking lot. It was hot outside, still a little overcast from the earlier rain, and heavily humid because of it.

Ashad and the SAC were talking on the courthouse steps, but Wynn was still in the parking lot, taking off his sport coat and tie off.

"Jack!" Jacobs shouted and walked over with Ashe. "One more thing if you have time."

"Sure," he said.

"We have to have Arthur North, sooner or later. Any ideas?" Jacobs asked.

"Huh! Well you and the rest of the federal law enforcement community want that, as well as the Royal Canadian Mounted Police. Good luck."

"I thought you'd say something like that," Jacobs said.

"But," Wynn said, and wiped his face with a paper napkin from his car. "You've run across him twice down here, right? Watching you, then going after Harold Marsh."

"You know about that?" Jacobs asked.

"I know Judge Harold Marsh, and I try to stay ahead of lawyers like Ashad, guys. I don't golf, I hunt, and Agent Hume and her SAC filled me in."

Ashe smiled. He was starting to really like this guy.

"If I'm right about North, he wants Durant *and* the data from that stolen thumb drive," Ashe said. "A guy like North won't leave Durant walking around. Wouldn't be…professional."

Wynn nodded. "That is an extremely dangerous idea you're having. Have you dealt with men like North before?"

"I don't know about North, but I've dealt with organized crime hitters, and out-of-state talent brought in for special jobs. I know the type, I guess."

"Ashe was almost killed by three hit men last year. He got them all. Almost killed him, but he took care of business himself," Jacobs said, and put a hand on Ashe's shoulder.

"I appreciate the confidence, Sheriff, but I don't know that I'd put the Concrete Crew in the same category," Ashe said. Then to Wynn, "Chuck had a radio and an earpiece. Who was he talking to? Who was his backup?"

"We don't know yet. I have the same question."

"You mentioned North worked for an organization that everybody has their eyes on. Does this group have a name?"

"They do. They call themselves, 'the Elite Watch.' Funny name. Must mean something in England," he said. Then he got in his car and drove away.

"The Elite Watch," Ashe repeated.

Doesn't sound funny to me.

CHAPTER 22

$\blacklozenge$

Stevie sat at a table in Roger's Café. She finished the water the hostess had given her as she waited on coffee. She was still slightly dizzy, and the powerful smells of bacon and eggs and sausage that filled the air and permeated the walls, didn't help her stomach.

She hadn't been drunk in over a year, but that accomplishment was literally washed away. She felt like crap between her head and her gut, and worst of all? She felt she deserved it. She tugged at the shorts she'd thrown on when she'd left the apartment. They weren't the longer khaki polyester ones she'd wanted, but the shorter denim ones she usually wore to the lake. She'd put on a polo and a set of dockers in the dark before Tom was awake.

Looking at it, she realized she hadn't been in Roger's since she moved out of town, and she saw there had been several changes. There were more seats inside somehow, and an outdoor patio replaced the old low brick wall that ran beside the sidewalk in front.

Then she remembered. The very last time she'd set foot in here, months ago, was the night they tried to kill Ashe. The night three men came after him, and almost succeeded. She had run outside onto the sidewalk that was no longer there, running to try and save his life. She'd held his bloody head in her hands and tore her shirt apart to try and bandage his bleeding wound.

"Well, you're just a picnic basket for my eyes this morning," Tilly said, standing at her table. Stevie jumped and almost spilled her water.

Tilly reached over and turned over a cup on the table. "Coffee?"

"Hey, Tilly," Stevie said. "Yes, and keep it coming."

Tilly looked at Stevie hard up and down. "Huh. Old problems, I see."

"That obvious?" Stevie wiped her face with her palms. She'd left the house early and hadn't showered. She wanted to talk to Tilly, but not with their usual bantering back and forth.

"Uh-huh. *That obvious*. I've worked breakfast shift enough over the years. You're still drunk."

"Yeah, I guess so. I need help, I need *your* help."

Tilly set the pot on the table and continued to stare at Stevie. "I'm not sure I can give you the help you need, hon. Aren't you in some kind of AA or something?"

"No, I mean yes, but, that's not the kind of help I need you for. It's about Ashe."

Tilly lowered her chin. "Oh boy."

. . . .

Ashe checked his watch; it was late morning. He and Jacobs had rolled around the county from place to place and hadn't found Lou Buckram. He wasn't at work; his supervisor didn't know why, or where he was, and he wasn't at home.

Jacobs obviously thought Lou was somehow heavily involved, but from what they'd discovered, the killings were a terrible result of some bad financial dealings between a bunch of rich people. He couldn't see Lou being central to that.

Ashe got a text from Pat.

CC has left city. DB thinks back your way. Heads-up.

Ol' Clarence had given them the slip? It was just as well. This way, maybe he'd get to sit in when they eventually question him.

Finally Jacobs pulled over and parked on the square outside the courthouse. He rolled down his window which quickly evacuated the air-conditioning and sucked in humidity and heat to fill the car. Jacobs lit one, so Ashe rolled his window down too. At least what small breeze there was blew the smoke away from him.

"Any other damn day, he'd be up here at the hardware store, or out at the Co-Op. Picking up parts, delivering supplies, making sales. I can't figure him not being around," Jacobs said. "Monday's a busy day for him. Farmers and self-employed workers, they can't get anything here in town after two on Saturday, or all-day Sunday.

They have to drive to McCormick. Monday is a big-rush day."

"You think he's split?" Ashe said, and realized he really didn't care. Buckram wasn't who he was thinking about.

"Split where? Lou's probably never been anywhere too far in his life."

Ashe drew in a hot, slightly smoky breath. "So, changing topics. I can't get something out of my head."

"Oh? You need a new truck?"

"Ah, yeah, but stick a pin in that. I mean, this Arthur North and Durant. Wynn agreed North's likely not gotten what he came here for, so he's still around. Said we'd run into him twice that we know of, and seemed to hint we'd see him again. Like a warning."

"Yeah. You might want to go by the old judge's and check on him. He's fond of you like he was of your dad."

"Now, I can see him staking out Roger's Café in the morning. Hell, the town circulates around that place. Tilly calls it 'Seacord Central.' But how did he know to watch Harold Marsh's house? Even had his local-hired thugs outside to run interference."

"What are you scratching at? You always go the long way around the barn, you know that?"

"Someone is in contact with North, or at least whoever hired him. Feeding him information. Someone with knowledge of this town; its people, *us*."

Jacobs threw out his cigarette and after another second, leaned his head slightly out his window and blew out the last puff. He sat there while the two of them got hotter.

"You think this Foundation has hired North, right?"

"Yeah, I do," Ashe said.

"Okay, say I agree. So who around here would be a contact for a big international foundation, *and* do all the things you just said?"

"They'd have to be able to put North onto local muscle. Birddog us, know the judge, and get them an old photo of me and…" Ashe let his voice trail off.

They sat in the hot car another second then looked at each other.

"Tom Fischer," Ashe said.

. . . .

Tilly and Stevie had moved to a small break room in the back so they could talk uninterrupted as Stevie tried to explain everything from the Blockade Runners, to her worries with Tom. Her hangover didn't help, but at least she was close to the employee bathroom.

"My God, girl, you do manage to get neck deep in some crap, don't you?"

Stevie found some aspirin in her purse, and Tilly had given her a cool washcloth to hold on her head. "I went there to Clarence's place to try and find out what my fiancé's involvement is with them, and to try to protect those children, but I think they outsmarted me. They kind of manipulated me into drinking, and I made it too easy for them. I…thought I was in control, jeez, I'm an idiot."

"No. Just a woman these sons a bitches think is stupid. They knew you'd drink."

"They used me. I think, to get at Tom."

"I don't follow," Tilly said. She reached over and wiped a lock of Stevie's hair out of her face.

"I think they were sending a message. I thought Tom was working to protect the Blockaders, but I don't think so. I think this box"—she kicked the box at her feet with the documents—"was what he collected that night, not to hide from the sheriff but to use against *them*. It's mostly records of membership, but some financial documents too."

"And Ashe needs this stuff? It's that important."

"Yeah, it has to be, because Tom thought so. Along with this." Stevie held up the digital recorder. "I have to find a way to get this to him separately, though."

"This has to do with the murder of that friend of Ashe's; the man they found in the lake. And that poor girl Carol," Tilly said.

"I have no right to ask you, I know this is dangerous, but I also know you care about Ashe. He thinks he knows what to do all the time, but, well."

Tilly nodded. "He's not young anymore. He's going to get hurt, I mean really bad again, I'm afraid. He's too old to be running around like he's thirty, or even forty, again. I want to pull the hair out of that friend of his, Pat. Always getting him fired up. And don't mention Larry Jacobs to me. I wish he'd never met Chig."

They looked at each other silently for a minute. Stevie dabbed at her neck with the washcloth.

"So you want *me* to get this box to him because…" Tilly asked.

"If it comes from me, he might not trust it. That state agent, Hume, she definitely won't trust it. Plus, if Tom knows I'm helping Ashe, I'll lose whatever chance I have left with him."

Tilly looked at the box.

"Shit, I thought when you came in here and said you was in trouble, and it was about Ashe? I figured you were pregnant."

Stevie busted out laughing at that. "Oh my God, Tilly! No! I haven't been with Ashe in…well, let's just say had he gotten me pregnant the last time we slept together, the kid would be here by now!"

Tilly's eyes went out of focus and she quickly looked away.

"What did I say? Are you all right?" Stevie asked.

"Sorry," was all Tilly could get out.

Tilly wiped her eyes and put on what looked to be a fake smile. "I'll take care of this box. I have no idea how, but you better be more careful. I'll think of something."

"Thank you," Stevie said.

"I used to really hate you; you were getting all the fun and attention from Chig I missed. But, anyway, I'm sorry for how I treated you."

"Truth is, I was always jealous of *you*. You had this decades-long connection with him, but now neither of us are with him. Funny."

Tilly turned her head again, but this time, Stevie sat closer and held her. "Tilly?"

"I have to tell somebody. You've told me so much, I guess I can trust you. Now, this cannot get out," Tilly said.

. . . .

Stevie sat in her old Beemer with the AC on and thought about what Tilly had just told her. *No wonder she hated me.* Then across the square from where she was parked, she saw Clarence Crawford pull up in front of the bank, so she got out and started walking toward him.

It was hot and humid outside the car, and soon her stomach began to roll as she walked to try and catch him.

I will not throw up. I will not throw up.

"Clarence!" She caught him as he was getting out of his SUV.

"Hey, Stevie," he said, but his face looked confused.

"We were supposed to meet today at noon, to talk about the HCCS."

"Um, oh yeah. Listen, now is a bad time," he said and tried to walk past her.

"No, it's a perfect time," she said and held up the digital recorder.

"What's that?"

"Your office?" she said, and tried for her intimidating look. She stuck the recorder in the front pocket of her shorts.

Inside, Crawford looked at her and smiled as he closed his office door. "I see you're still sweating it out from last night. Good for you not to be lying in bed all day."

"I...had a nice time. We should do it again soon," she said, although she never wanted to smell that moonshine again.

"That's a great idea! We're almost set up in a new location and...hey! You said you would be our new batch queen!"

"Oh, sure! That sounds like fun. First, I want you to make me the sole administrator of the Children's Sanctuary, and a voting member of its local board."

Crawford dropped his smile. "Um, what? I know you said that last night, but I'm thinking that would be a conflict of interest, given you load the funds into their account at Lifenablers?"

"I'm sure after our little party last night and your 'message' to Tom, I'll be fired by the Foundation any minute now."

Crawford dropped his pretenses of cordiality. "Okay, Stevie. What is that electric doo-dad you showed me?"

She took it out and turned it on to a spot where she'd paused it, and pressed play. Commissioner Jasper's voice came on.

"'Left messages, even sent a guy to go make him an offer. Two hundred thousand for that stupid little jug.'" She turned it off.

Crawford frowned. "Jasper is an idiot," he said very softly. "But that proves nothing."

"You sent a man out to the lake to meet Durant and Carol. They're dead now, and so is your messenger," she said.

"Yes, so if I were you, I'd be considerably more careful who you fuck with," he said.

"All I want is the sanctuary. Full control. In writing," she said.

"Nothing for yourself? Maybe something to help you get back in good with your fiancé?" Crawford picked up his phone and pressed a button then set it back down.

"What do you mean?"

Crawford stood and closed the blinds on the window between his office and the lobby.

"Stand up," he said.

"I beg your…"

"Beg all you like, but you've already recorded me once, damn you," he said. "Stand up, *my queen.*"

She had thought once she revealed the recording, this might happen. The younger man who had driven her home came into the office wearing a suit.

She stood, holding the recorder tightly. Crawford ran his hands over her like an imitation of a frisk he'd seen on TV. She was wearing only the polo and shorts, but he took his time. The other man stood there and stared; he was probably there to be sure she didn't try to leave.

Crawford's fingers lingered at her hips, pressing her pockets flat, then he stepped close to her, pressing against her as he draped his arms around her and ran his thumbs across her bra strap in back. Then he stepped back and ran his thumbs along the underwire of her bra in front.

The shame of the night before rushed back into her mind. *This is what I get,* she thought.

Finally, he lifted her shirt up slowly in front to expose her belly and pulled it right up to expose her bra, but she slapped his hand away.

"I'm not bugged," she said.

"You *are* beautiful, Stevie. What do you think, Walt? She'll make a perfect batch queen. Now give me that recording. I want to hear all of it," he said. With a wave of Crawford's hand, Walt stepped back out of the office, but he leaned his back against the outside of the door.

"Papers first. Today, Clarence."

"Or I just take it," he said. "With or without Walt's help."

"I'll scream and rip my own shirt. Every woman in this bank will see me run out of here."

Crawford stared at her, thinking about the scene she'd just illustrated for him.

"Plus, you won't ever know if I have a copy," she added.

"You really are taking chances, you know. Okay, I like you. I want us to be friends again, so I'll agree to your request. I don't think that sanctuary will be running much longer, anyway. One last condition. Give us all the documents Tom took from our meeting room."

"I don't think he still has them," she said, smoothing out her shirt. Trying not to tremble.

That bothered him. "Who...who does? Did he pass them on to the...anybody else?"

"I don't know. You managed to piss him off at me. Like I said, I'm probably fired, and maybe un-engaged."

"Oh no! You did *that* yourself, and by the way, it sure looked like you enjoyed it. But, back to our deal, you don't happen to have anything else? Like...our little item we discussed?"

"Your jug? Your recipe? Maybe. Papers first, Clarence. Full control."

"Come back in an hour," he said. "But bring whatever you have."

She left his office, pushing past Walt. As she got outside, Stevie caught a glimpse of a car turning sharply into a parking spot across the street from her. In its rearview mirror, she saw a face watching her she recognized from last year.

Breslin? Wasn't his name Dan Breslin?

Breslin caught her eye in the mirror and shook his head slightly. She knew he didn't want her to draw attention to him, so she turned to cross the street in another way.

Suddenly, a large man roughly took her by the arm and half picked her up. He hurriedly moved her down the sidewalk, her feet barely touching the ground, and took her to another car. Before she could scream, she was shoved inside and the back door slammed.

"Stevie, stay there!" a voice she recognized said. It was Ashe's old partner, Pat Keagan.

Oh thank God. It's only cops.

Then she slid to the other side of the car, opened the door, and threw up on the street.

. . . .

Pat texted Ashe, **We're at bank in Seacord.**

Ashe and Jacobs looked up and saw Pat park his SUV nearby.

Ashe texted back, **We're at courthouse.**

They got out and moved across the square from where they'd parked to take up support positions outside the bank, in case anyone else was interested in Crawford. Rachel and a pair of uniformed state troopers were walking in, and she had papers in her hand.

Ashe noticed a nondescript, totally unnoticeable car back out of a slot and leave. Breslin was at the wheel.

Good move, Danny. In case North and company are watching, don't get burned.

Then he saw the back door to Pat's SUV open and watched Stevie getting sick.

"What the hell? What is she doing in Pat's car?" Ashe said.

"I think they got this," Jacobs said. "Maybe we can watch from the car. Out of the heat."

"Yeah. Good idea, and away from...um, that," Ashe said, pointing at Stevie.

They were about to get in and start the AC running, when Ashe heard, "Chig! Sheriff!" from nearby. It was Tilly walking toward them with a box in her arms.

She slammed the box on the hood of Jacobs' cruiser. "Larry Jacobs! I have done told you a hundred times about people using our dumpster out back of the café for their personal trash!"

Jacobs shrugged. "Tilly, I don't recall you or Roger ever telling me..."

"People dump their damn home trash and garbage there, and that's a private dumpster for the café! We pay for that, and it's illegal!" she shouted. "*Just look at this!*"

So Ashe looked at it. The box on the hood had stacks of folders and papers, neatly packed. It looked to Ashe to be a banker's file box.

"We put up a gate and everything, but people still just dump their crap in our dumpster! *Look at that!* I bet there's private information in there, who knows. Bank records, something. Stuff that ought to have been shredded! Right out in public; in our dumpster!"

Ashe poked through the box. A name caught his eye on a register. *Anderton.*

He looked at Tilly and caught her eye for a nano second. Her "angry, complaining citizen" act became a bit more transparent to him. He'd known her forty-plus years, but she'd buffaloed Jacobs.

"Okay, we'll take a look, see if we can figure out who dumped this, Tilly. Calm down!" Jacobs said.

"Huh! Cops!" she said, "Maybe a little less time doing…stuff, and a little more time…checking…dumpsters!" Then she spun on her heels and marched back to the café.

Ashe picked up the box and said, "I think I have an idea what to do with this, boss. Let's go see what Rachel has."

CHAPTER 23

Stevie climbed out of Pat's Dodge and walked across the street to the town square. A few people had stopped to see why the cops were at the bank, but they paid little attention to her, which suited her just fine.

She felt better after being sick all over the parking spot, but she wanted to get home, get a shower, and maybe a nap before everyone started talking to her.

Everyone meaning Ashe, and of course Pat and Agent Hume; probably Sheriff Jacobs as well. But definitely not Tom. She couldn't stand the thought of him seeing her like this again.

Of course Ashe had seen it before. He'd had seen her worse than this, especially the day she'd thrown him out of her life.

The rain had broken up and there was sunlight getting through here and there, which made it muggy, and with her hangover, that was not good. In fact, it sucked, so she made it to her car as best she could, got in, and left.

God, I hope Tom isn't home.

That thought bothered her. It was the first time in their relationship she didn't want him there for her. She felt weak, and not just in the way her hands trembled and how she felt unsteady on her feet.

I've started something I hope doesn't blow up in my face.

Once home, she was relieved Tom wasn't there, but looking at her phone, she had a bunch of missed calls and messages. She stripped and got in the shower, soaking everything and lathering all over with a lot of soap.

It did and it didn't help; she still felt dirty. The soap kept washing off and then it was just her.

Is Tom just doing what he can to keep his directors happy? Does he care about the children at the sanctuary? Was he trying to get evidence against the Blockaders? Did he have anything to do with Durant? God...did he have anything to do with Carol's murder?

She got out and put on a shorty robe then rubbed her facial moisturizer in. Her eyes looked horrible, so she found some eye drops and used them. Then she padded out into the kitchen and thought about coffee but drank a diet soda instead.

She looked at the notes he'd left her and then her phone. After a long minute, she called him.

"Where are you?" he yelled over the speaker. "I've been worried sick!"

"I'm home. I needed to do some things."

"I'm on my way. Ten minutes," he said and hung up.

Then she called the sanctuary. Brie answered.

"Brie, honey, is Mrs. Franks there?" Stevie asked. She heard Brie drop the phone and shout for Franks.

"Stevie, good Monday to ya. Are you in town or over in Harmony today?" Mrs. Franks asked.

"I'm in Harmony. I'll try to get over there today. How are the girls?"

"Fine, just finishing lunch and then we're going to the elementary school gym since it's been raining. We got all the prescriptions delivered today."

"Oh, um, that's great," Stevie said. It felt like forever since she'd worked on those.

"Did you know the cops were all over here this past Sunday? They came and raided those men downstairs and hauled off some stuff. The county prosecutor was here, and they took everything out of Carol's, I mean *your* office."

"*My* office?"

"Yep, Dr. Gregory stopped by today and said we were all working for you, and if anyone gave us any trouble with anything, we needed to call him."

Dr. Gregory. The Blockade Runner.

"Ok, call my number if you need me," Stevie said and hung up.

He'd set my glass out of reach.

Thinking back didn't feel good with her hangover, but it hadn't seemed to her like he was completely *with* Crawford and Jasper.

She didn't have much time to consider this further before Tom arrived, and burst through the door as if chased by lions.

She started to give him a hug, but he turned and ran into his office. Then he came back out and took her by an arm.

"I don't think anyone's been here. Is it true? Do you have it?"

"Who's not been, oh hell, have what? Jeez, Tom! Let go of me!"

"Clarence Crawford called me a while ago. Said he'd just been with you in his office. Said you wanted to trade taking over the kids shelter for their…little moonshine jug."

Stevie jerked her arm back. "No, for this!" She went to the kitchen counter and took the digital recorder out of her purse.

"What is that? Listen, now is not the time to lie to me! *Do you have it?*" He took ahold of her by both arms this time.

"They said they were willing to pay a couple hundred thousand to Carol Buckram and Michael Durant for it! For a recipe for moonshine? Bull, Tom! What is this really all about?"

"So, you *do* have it?" was all he said. His eyes were wide and he was sweating.

She pulled her arms away. "You're hurting me!"

He stepped back and held up his hands. "Okay, okay. But…is it here?"

"Say it, Tom! Say what you want!"

He sighed. "If you had it, you'd know. It's a thumb drive. A tiny one. Hidden in that stupid jug."

"A thumb…okay, what's on it?"

"It has some financial tracking data, records, I don't know what all, but you can be sure the Foundation and their partners do! *It has information on us all!* Everything anyone would need to sink both the Blockaders *and* the Foundation. And the Foundation is tied to a lot of important people and foreign investors! You know, the one the governor is a member of the board of directors on."

"Wait…sink who? Why? What do you mean on *us all*?"

"Damn, Durant! Once he knew he was out, I mean kicked out, he collected what he needed to blackmail everybody. He knew what they'd been doing with all that illicit money, something about sending it to a big offshore company. I guess the girl at the sanctuary place…Carol? Anyway, she and Durant also found out that the Blockaders had been skimming Foundation money. They must have tripped across…but…you don't know any of this, do you?"

She felt a pang of guilt, then said, "Well there was a box of documents at the sanctuary."

Tom nodded. "I collected what stuff I could so that they'd, we'd…so *there* would be some leverage. I guess the sheriff or the state police have that now, after their search warrant."

Stevie thought of Tilly and bit her lower lip. "Yeah, I'd say you're probably right."

Tom walked to their living room and flopped in a chair. "And you *never* had it. You were bluffing Crawford. And I…shit!"

"You what? What did you do, Tom?"

"I called my contact at the Foundation and told them I thought I could get my hands on the data. Crawford said you were going to give it to *him*, and that you would be working for *him*. Being their beauty queen, or something. Said he'd send me pictures. Kind of, sticking the knife in and twisting it, so to speak. I got mad at him *and* you; I guess I wasn't thinking when I told my contact you had it."

"Well, no. I don't. You have to tell them you can't get it."

Tom closed his eyes and shook his head. "No! They won't believe that!" Then a thought appeared on his face. He jumped up and ran to the front window and parted the blinds to look out.

"Get dressed," he said over his shoulder as he looked at the parking lot.

"Why? I was looking forward to getting a nap."

"Because my contacts at the Foundation will be expecting that thumb drive."

"They're a charity, for the love of Pete! Call them back and…look, maybe I can talk to them."

"No. No, you can't. Get dressed, you have to get out of here!"

"Okay, okay, wait! Let me help. Tom. We'll go to the sheriff, together. Tell what we know. I have Crawford and Jasper on this recording. I saw Pat Keagan in town today at the bank, maybe he can help. You have to tell them everything you know."

"Just get dressed. Please," he said and went to his office.

She finished her soda and could hear him on his computer. She went and got dressed in fresh shorts and a tank top. When she was done, he was in the kitchen, staring at his phone.

"Tom, look. You are an attorney, and an officer of the court. Let's go talk to Harold Marsh if you don't want to talk to the sheriff. Or maybe that special agent I met last year. She's very good."

"It's too late. They'll send someone here. Go, just go, and do not come back unless I say... A code. Like, oh, something like *silver*. If I say it's safe or clear or anything else, don't believe it. Don't believe any text or call from me unless I say 'it's silver.' Got it?"

"No, I do not *got* it! I do not understand," she said.

"Please, Stevie, look, here's some cash, go someplace safe. I don't care, even...even if you go stay with your ex-husband in the city...or, shit, even if you go to Ashe. If *he* can protect you, then fine. At least I'll know you're safe."

That rattled her a bit. Tom would never suggest she go stay with Ashe. In fact, he'd prefer anyone else first.

"Tom, why does this stupid rich-boy charity foundation have you all worked up? Who the hell are *they* going to send that scares you?"

"The same man they sent to get it last time. At the lake!"

CHAPTER 24

Rachel stepped out into the lobby of the bank where Pat and Ashe were loitering, waiting to see what her subpoenas produced. One of the troopers she'd brought with her stayed with Crawford; the other was in the lobby.

"It's going to be a while yet, guys. But, he at least *acts* like he's cooperating," she said.

"Does he know that we may be eyeing him as somehow involved yet?" Pat asked her quietly.

She smiled. "No, but when I asked him to come and talk to John Price and \me to explain the Blockade Runners, he said he'd be happy to. Just as soon as his attorney was available."

"Who's his lawyer?" Ashe asked.

"You'll like this, Ashe. It's Phillip Crews."

Ashe nodded and rolled his eyes. "Of course."

Rachel stretched and looked around the bank. "Where's Jacobs?"

"He needed to run by his office," Ashe said. "Oh, he and I have something for you. A big banker's box full of documents from the sanctuary basement headquarters of the Blockaders. Looks like some financial records."

"Where did you get that?" she asked.

Ashe tried for an innocent face. "A local…person complained to Jacobs that someone was dumping what looked like business records, bank statements, and privacy act information in their commercial dumpster."

"Huh," she said. "Well, state CIB headquarters is sending a pair of forensic accountants here in the morning. We'll go through it, and add it to the pile of stuff for them to review. What I have so far, I think, makes Michael Durant look like a major thief of charitable funds."

Ashe told them what he and Jacobs thought about Tom Fischer being the Foundation's point man, and their theory about how North came to know so much about their movements.

"It's a decent theory, Ashe, but that's all it is. So before we confront him, I think I want to see the combined evidence from the bank and any other banks that pop up from the FINCEN report I'm expecting, as well as your Blockader's box," Rachel said.

"Well, your team found the photos of Chuck, Durant, and Carol at the cove. The men who ran me off the road and wrecked my Jeep, they had a personal photo of *me*. Somebody's helping them. I vote Tom Fischer."

"I'll add Mr. Fischer to my list *but*, you and the high sheriff hold off on him for today anyway," she said. "Hell, boys, I'm covered up."

Ashe started to say something else, but she held up a hand and jumped in before he could speak. "And I know you, hot-shot Hurrt County *Detective*. No loose cannon, lone ranger, Han Solo bullshit, Ashe!"

Ashe laughed. "You *have* to stop seeing Pat. I mean, for your own sake."

Pat cleared his throat then said, "On *that* note, if nothing else is exploding today, I'm going back to Metro. I imagine Mr. Ashad's bestest friend, Captain Speakes, is looking for me to do my job there."

Rachel smiled at Pat, and he smiled back. She looked tired. He started to say something, but she just walked over and, on her tiptoes, pulled his head down by his necktie and gave him a kiss on the cheek. She turned and went back into Crawford's office, so Ashe walked Pat out.

"Dang, Pat. You two are public now, huh? Good. I hate having to cover for you two all the time with your boss while you keep sneaking off down here to Hurrt County to canoodle," Ashe said as they stepped outside.

"Buddy, once again, I owe you," Pat said to Ashe.

"Huh?"

"Next time, put your drunk, puking, crazy-ass girlfriend in *your* car!"

"She's not my...wait, *you* put her in...oh, kiss my butt, Pat."

"I have a much nicer butt to kiss, if I was a-mind to, than your old bony one."

Without another word, Pat turned left on the sidewalk and got in his SUV and left.

Ashe watched him as he left, and standing there in the early afternoon humidity and heat, thought about going to the sheriff's office to check in with Jacobs. It was then he remembered, he had no car, and more importantly, no AC.

"I need to buy a car," he said to himself. He decided instead to go check in on the old judge. It was a ten-minute walk, but at least it was mostly shady.

· · · ·

He arrived a little sweaty at Harold Marsh's porch and rang the bell. The housekeeper answered and gave him a surprised look.

"Mister Ashe! I am so glad to see you! Thank you for that call to warn us about that man," she said. "Come in, please. The judge is with his doctor."

"Let him know I'm here, I'll wait in the...sitting room?"

"I'll bring you some nice, cool lemonade," she said.

Ashe went into the sitting room as before, but this time, he walked straight over to the Blockade Runners photo that had Marsh and his father in it. He laid the photograph down flat and using his phone, got a couple of good shots of it. By the time the housekeeper returned, he was sitting in one of the chairs.

"Thank you, I actually walked up here from the square. By the way, I never heard your name."

"Ellen. I've been with the judge for thirty years, I guess. After my kids were grown and my husband passed, I moved in here to be on hand for him."

"I see, that's nice, Ellen."

"Oh, no. Now nothing more than just cooking and cleaning, you know. We're not...together or anything," she said.

He smiled. That was not an image he wanted to explore in his mind.

"Of course not. I still think it's good he has you here to take care of him."

"Chig?" a woman's voice said from out in the hall. It sounded like Linda Ingles.

"Yeah, in here." Then as she stepped in, he added, "Hi again, Linda."

She had her hair in a huge ponytail and wore white slacks and a navy sleeveless summer blouse. Everything fit her well; Ashe had to remind himself to breathe.

"Hello yourself! I want to thank you for that call, you might have saved our lives, you know? I mean, wow, that guy broke out a window like he just *did not* care if there were cops in this town or maybe I was armed or not! He just threw an iron porch chair through the window and came in and went straight to the judge's office!"

"I'm...glad I could help. Glad you all are okay."

"Yeah, I had my purse upstairs and my little baby Ruger pistol in it. Oh, I have a permit, you know, and I can shoot. I was glad the judge had just dropped off to sleep for his nap. Ellen and I barricaded his bedroom door! The next thing we heard was that young sheriff's deputy downstairs, so I called 911 and told the dispatcher where we were, and do you think I did all right?"

Ashe smiled at her. *She's a talker.*

"Um, sure, Linda. You did great. Can I see him yet?" Ashe asked.

"I don't see why not, c'mon," she said and took Ashe by the hand. As they walked upstairs, she said, "I'll be back here in Seacord on Thursday. You promised me lunch. Heck, I figure I owe you, so it'll be my treat."

"I've never turned down free lunch in my life," he said, and smiled.

In the judge's bedroom, he was sitting up in bed with a deep-maroon robe on. Beside him was a tall, distinguished-looking man Ashe recognized as one of the doctors in town. Then he recognized him as one of the men from Stevie's Blockaders photo she'd texted before.

"Dr. Gregory? Am I right?" Ashe asked and extended his hand.

Gregory took his hand. "Yes, I am Harold's physician. It's okay, we're done here."

"I am fine. A little angry at having my home so easily broken into," Marsh said. "Come in, Chig. Ah, Linda, will you give us a minute, dear?"

"I have to be running along anyway. You take care, boss," she said. As she turned to go and passed Ashe, she mouthed "Thursday" to him.

He perfume passed him as well. Light, citrus, fresh. *I cannot see myself missing Thursday.*

"Ashe, Dr. Gregory and I have been having a discussion I think we want to share with you. I have advised him you may take notes and be required to take official action, based on your role as a sheriff's...whatever you are," Marsh said.

"Detective. Sort of," Ashe said.

"You used to date Stevie, I understand," Gregory said. "Harold seems to think highly of her, and has assured me you do as well."

"We dated quite a while ago. Almost a year and a half back."

"I am concerned about how she was treated last night at the rented house on the lake. It actually turned my stomach a little. To start at the beginning, I have been one of the Blockaders for years. Harold tells me you know about them, and that your father was a member in the sixties."

"So I have learned. What about Stevie?" Ashe asked. He put on his reading glasses then realized his brown leather portfolio was in the sheriff's car, so he took them back off.

"Clarence Crawford, you know him, I'm guessing," Gregory said.

"Oh, Chig surely knows Mr. Crawford. And Commissioner Jasper, don't you, Ashe?" Marsh said with a sly grin.

"Uh-huh. Both cohorts of *the* Mark Portals. Back to Stevie, if you please, Doctor."

"She was invited to the lake house to discuss how she came to find the Blockaders meeting room. Crawford, Commissioner Jasper, and I wanted to dispel any misinterpretations she might have about us. But I sensed she *wanted* to be there, and her reasoning had to do with the children at the sanctuary. I also felt she was there to find out how deeply involved her fiancé, Mr. Fischer, was."

Ashe sat up a fraction. *Ah, enter Tom Fischer.*

Gregory continued, "Truth is, Clarence and Jasper had an

ulterior motive. Knowing she was an alcoholic; they plied her with one of our *stronger* brews. It's much too much for me, in fact. I knew they were after something from her, and I also knew what it was. They claimed it was the small symbolic moonshine jug we keep the past recipes for our homemade whiskey in. But I know better."

"This has to do with Michael Durant, and the murders of Carol Buckram, Charles Carter, and a man named Anderton, doesn't it?"

"Yes, it does. You should know I protested their treatment of Stevie. What I didn't know at the time was, they not only wanted to find out if she or her fiancé had their…little jar. But Clarence wanted to send a message, *a threat*, to Tom Fischer. Through him, to his Able Keys Foundation. This, I did not agree to."

"Why would the Blockade Runners want to try to threaten the Foundation? I mean, no disrespect, but that's like a local Elks Lodge wanting to threaten AT&T."

"Because they are after the same thing we are, and for the same reason."

"Your 'jar' as you call it. It has a thumb drive with some damning data on it. Carol or Durant hid it there, I believe. Tell me where I'm wrong, Doctor."

"You're not wrong. I overheard from Crawford where the Foundation was going to shut the HCCS down. They discovered the breach of their accounts and how Durant had stolen from them. But the data, as you call it, was much, much worse than just that."

Gregory stood suddenly and paced the room for a second. "Mr. Ashe. You seem to know a good deal about our situation. Harold?"

"You can stop anytime you want, Doctor. But you told me you wanted to make a clean sweep of it, to get this off your conscience," Marsh said. "I will help you get the best legal arrangement possible."

"You Blockaders," Ashe started, before Gregory could decide to stop. "You sent a representative to meet Durant, who had run off with Carol by then."

"Yes. His Foundation, headed by his ex-spouse, had cut off his money. He was no longer as wealthy as he let on. So we, knowing of his state of affairs through Clarence and the bank, wanted to made him an offer."

Ashe shifted in his seat. "At the hidden cove on the lake. Your man was to deliver this offer and retrieve your thumb drive."

"We three voted to make the offer, and Clarence recommended a man named Anderton, who was a member. But this man went armed, and well, you likely know more about what happened than I."

The sights of the carnage at the cove walked across Ashe's mind. The smell, the swarms of flies around week-old corpses. The blood, the brass. Carol Buckram in his dream.

"Yeah. I do."

"Anyway, it was never supposed to go this far. No one was supposed to get hurt."

"But it did."

"What I say now, I cannot prove, but I do not believe Clarence or Commissioner Jasper actually intended to pay Durant."

"So...they instructed Anderton to..."

"By *not pay*, I think you know what I mean. I have not a shred of evidence, but I believe they wanted Mr. Anderton to get the drive then kill Durant."

"You know there was a second, interested party there at the cove," Ashe said.

"Yes, so I've heard. Clarence received word from Tom Fischer. The Foundation and its partners had hired their own men to retrieve the data. Fischer threatened Clarence to stop looking for it, surrender it if he had it, and to fall in line or risk his bank, his job, the Blockaders, all of it. All before the events at the lake."

Ashe whistled softly under his breath. *Enter Arthur North.*

"Dr. Gregory. I'm sure the state police investigator, Agent Rachel Hume, will have questions for you, as will the sheriff. I need you to come with me to the courthouse and we'll sit down with them, and the ADA, John Price," Ashe said.

"Go with him, but wait until I arrive to represent you," Marsh said, and slowly started to get out of bed.

"Judge, he's to cooperate fully?" Ashe asked.

"I will discuss that with ADA Price," Marsh said.

"Of course. But, Doc, there's a box of documents that Tom Fischer was going to remove from your meeting room. He never got it out, and the sheriff has it. Can you look through it and validate them?"

"I was the Blockaders club secretary last year. I imagine some of those are my files."

"*I'll* review them as well, Chig," Marsh said.

"Judge, I'll let ADA Price wrestle with you over that. One more thing, Doctor. I get that this data, and its potential release could be embarrassing and financially disastrous to both sides. But murder? Sending a sniper to kill everyone, hell, trying to kill *me*? Why? What is so damning on this thumb drive?"

"You know about the Able Keys Foundation? You know who is the head of the board of its directors?"

"Governor Durant. Yeah, I'm guessing this would be a stain on her reelection, but I don't buy that as a rationale for three murders."

Gregory nodded. "Have you ever heard of Searl Magnadyne?"

Ashe frowned. "No, should I have?" *Durant had mentioned Searl.*

"Well, they are a major partner with the Foundation. My assumption is, there is spillage from those records that Searl does not want public. Go research that, and you'll have your motive for all this. And more."

"Go with him, Doctor," Marsh said. He was up and putting on a freshly starched shirt. "But nothing more until I arrive."

They walked out of the bedroom as Marsh rang for Ellen to assist him. Walking downstairs, Dr. Gregory seemed depressed.

"Detective, I know you're not the DA nor a judge, but do you think I'll go to prison?"

"That's a better question for your attorney than me."

"Okay. But I cannot continue one more damn night with the thought of that poor girl, who I actually delivered years ago, dead out there on the lake. I'll go with you, but how do you know so much already?"

"Well, Doc. You're not the only one talking to us."

"But who could…my God, you mean Michael Durant is alive?"

Ashe didn't answer but started for the front door. Then he remembered.

"Uh, I don't actually have a car here. I walked. I'll call us a cruiser."

CHAPTER 25

Stevie drove around for a couple of hours, still headachy and tired. Drained was a better word. She drove over to McCormick City in McCormick County and ate a late and very light lunch, given her gut still felt queasy. She checked her phone. No texts, no calls, no messages.

She then drove to a big chain store and bought herself some things she'd need, assuming she might have to spend the night out somewhere. Tom hadn't let her pack a bag.

She looked at her phone for the thirtieth time. Nothing. Sitting out in the parking lot, she texted him.

Are you ok?

She waited thirty minutes, closing her eyes to doze here and there. She looked at her phone; nothing from Tom.

They'll send the guy for the thumb drive; the same man they sent to get it last time. At the lake, he told me.

She was too tired and a little too mad to cry yet. If Tom knew about the Foundation sending someone to go out to the lake to meet Durant and Carol, then he knew what happened.

Accessory to murder? Conspiracy? Accessory after the fact by clearing out the Blockaders place, and still communicating with his contact at the Foundation. Knowingly, intentionally. Damn, babe.

Then this. By her bluff with Crawford then his call to Tom, the people who send murderers thought *she* had their thumb drive and the information they wanted so badly.

Tom was in such a panic, so desperate. But he wouldn't let her help him. In fact, he'd sent her away to protect her. With that thought, she did cry. In a store parking lot in her car, she broke down.

After several minutes, she slowed then stopped. All her anger at Tom, as well as the self-pity and self-loathing that were mixed in her head; it all needed out. *But not now.* Venting her emotions would not help at the moment.

If they do come and talk to Tom, and he can't convince them, they might come looking for me.

Then she had another thought. She'd used her debit card at the store and diner. *Damn!* So they'd know where she was. Mac City. She checked and she needed gas, so she went to fill up.

Go ahead and use the card, they know you're here.

A motel was out of the question, and driving around in her old BMW was dumb. She decided it was time to be smart. She sighed and pulled out of the gas station and headed for Hurrt County.

She texted, Ashe, sorry, but I need to talk to you. About everything.

．．．．

"Dr. Gregory. You understand your rights as I've explained them to you?" Rachel said.

"Yes," Gregory said.

"And having your counsel, Harold Marsh here with you, do you wish to speak with us and answer our questions?"

Gregory looked at Marsh who nodded very slightly. "I will," Gregory said.

"Understanding we may choose to end this interview at any time," Marsh added.

"Of course," Rachel said and added a note to the rights advisement and statement form then slid it over to Marsh. Marsh looked it over and indicated to Dr. Gregory where to sign.

Then Ashe signed as a witness. "Okay, Doc, please tell Agent Hume what you told me," he said.

Gregory told her about the Blockade Runners and the Foundation and Durant. He answered several questions, some quite original that Rachel asked. He described that they had sent Anderton to the cove to meet Durant but added, his private belief there was an intent to never pay. Then how Crawford and Jasper had intentionally set out to get Stevie intoxicated to find out if she or Fischer had their thumb drive.

As he spoke, Rachel wrote out a lot of notes. Several pages worth. She stared at her notes for a few minutes then said, "*Detective* Ashe has told me you may be willing to review and validate some of the records we have in our possession. This may be tomorrow or Wednesday before we can be ready for that. Will you assist us in going through them?"

"I'd like to know what your intentions are with my client, first," Marsh said.

"Sure, but before we continue, let's take a short break," she said. "I'll speak with ADA Price."

They all got up from the deposition room and stepped out into the wide courthouse second-floor hallway. Marsh and Gregory walked to the men's room.

"Good job, Rach. You've conducted a master class in interviewing."

"He's not a hard sell; he wants to get this off his chest, so that gives me a big advantage. But damn, I need more time to go through all these records in their box, and I have only skimmed through the subpoenaed bank stuff. Once the state examiners get here and sharpen their pencils, we may have several more questions, and I'll possibly need to submit more subpoenas as a result."

"Until Ashad or the governor step in."

"Well, there's that," she said.

"Sorry, but I only went to just visit with the old judge, and this landed in my lap. What can I do to help?"

Rachel sighed. "Nothing, I'm going to go speak with John Price about what, if anything, we'd offer to gain his continued cooperation. And of course, his testimony. Then call my SAC."

"One other thing. Why is it every time you say 'Detective' Ashe, it comes out sounding like *Detective* Ashe?"

She smiled very slightly and cocked an eyebrow. "Because…I have a sneaking suspicion as to *how* and *why* you so suddenly became a *detective* with Hurrt County."

Ashe just shrugged and gave her an innocent frown. "Fair enough. But to change the subject back to these Blockaders, right now, I at first saw conspiracy to commit first-degree murder for the three of them. Of course, with Anderton dead, they'll lay it all off on him. They'll say he took on Durant with that AK-47 without their knowledge," Ashe said.

"Best I can do right this second, absent staying up all night reading bank printouts, is hand Crawford over to the state and federal banking commission auditors. I could maybe prove felony fraud, probably sic the IRS on him, too. But, on a side note, him using their moonshine to get your…"

"For the last damn time, Stevie is *not* my girlfriend!"

"I was going to say *former attorney*, but ok. Duly noted. Anyway, using her, getting her sloshed, just to try and intimidate the Foundation through Tom Fischer. That's not only dirty pool, that could be very damn dangerous."

Ashe felt his phone buzz. It was a text from Stevie.

Ashe, sorry, but I need to talk to you. About everything.

"Are you going to hold Dr. Gregory today?" he asked.

Rachel stretched her back and appeared to be thinking. She put one hand on Ashe's shoulder as she stood on one foot to bend the other leg up at the knee. She took off a heel to rub her toes and the ball of her foot. Then she put the shoe back on and stood up straight.

"I hate to say this, but as far as the Blockade Runners, the proof of criminal action will be in the piles of financial records we have. It's going to take weeks, not days, to slog through how they were stealing from the HCCS and by proxy, the Foundation," she said. "So, to answer your question, I don't see arresting anybody anytime soon, unless you come up with Arthur North with a sniper rifle on his shoulder."

"One could wish. One last thing. Both Durant and Dr. Gregory mentioned something called the 'Searl' and then, the 'Searl Magnadyne' company. Gregory even said they were partners with the Foundation. Ever hear of it?"

Rachel shook her head as her phone rang. "It's my boss, I'm going to Price's office to take this," she said and walked to the closest staircase.

Ashe gave her a little wave and started for the other end of the long hallway to the opposite stairs. He called Stevie once he got outside.

"Hey, where are you?" he asked.

"In my car, and not sure where to go. Tom is in big trouble," she said. "Maybe so am I."

She sounded shaky. "I think you both should get separate lawyers. Why don't you meet me at the S.O.?"

"I don't think that's wise. Just so you know, Tom sort of told the Foundation I had a thumb drive that belonged to Michael Durant. You know about any of this?"

Oh boy do I.

"Yeah, I actually know quite a bit. Why in the *hell* would he say something stupid like that?"

"Um, well I kind of tried to...*bluff* Clarence Crawford into *sort of* thinking I had it," she said. "Then he called Tom; Tom called the Foundation. Him and Clarence, they don't like each other."

Ah shit! By calling his Foundation, Tom actually sent North toward Stevie like a heat-seeking missile.

Ashe sped up his walking. "You close to town, I mean Seacord?"

"I'm just now coming in to Hurrt County on 429."

"Turn off your phone. Go to my place, you know how to get in. Put your car in my outside garage. Please!"

"Ok. You should know, Tom told me to go to you. Should I be worried?"

Uh-oh.

"Maybe. Just do what I say, I'm on my way there," he said. Then when he hung up, he looked around outside in the parking lot. "Shit!" he shouted out loud.

He limp-jogged across the square to Public Avenue and down a block to the S.O. then ran inside. Ginny was on duty and buzzed him in. He jogged down to Jacobs' office, but he was gone.

Ginny stuck her head out of the top of the Dutch door as he came back up the hall. "You okay? Larry's with the county commissioners out at the high school."

"I need a car," he said. "Is there anything I can use?"

Ginny shrugged as she laughed. "Hell, Chig, you've been needing a car for a while! There's Tracy's old unmarked car, but I think they took it for tires."

Ashe took out his phone and started flipping through names. "Who's on duty?"

"Bell, Darren, but they're out at a wreck up on Route 358. Hey, you know Larry's brother-in-law runs that dealership on Sixth," she said. "You could run go buy you a car."

Ashe looked at her then headed for the front door.

"Hey, I was just kidding!" she shouted after him.

. . . .

Stevie parked in the detached garage at Ashe's place. She'd turned off her phone right after hanging up from him, so she had no idea when he'd arrive, or if Tom had called to give her the all clear.

It was an old wood building with two outward-swinging doors. She found the old metal desk along one wall, and in the very back of the top right drawer, held up at the top by a magnet, was a house key.

She grabbed her bags from the store and went into his house. She locked everything she could think to lock; he'd left a couple of windows open, and closed all the blinds and curtains. Then she went to his office.

Under Ashe's desk, also held by a big magnet, was a Smith and Wesson J frame .38 revolver. He'd taught her how to check it, and how to shoot it. It was loaded.

It did not escape her attention that this was the gun he'd killed two men with just last year. Two of the three who'd tried to kill him. Somehow that thought made it feel heavier in her hand.

In the top drawer of his desk was a small leather pouch with six rounds stuck in the top of it. They poked out, butt first, and were separated by twos to make it easier to grab. She pocketed the pouch and slid the .38 into her waistband.

Okay. Now what?

So she checked the fridge and found a half-pint of expired milk, a pack of bologna, a six-pack of light beer with four bottles left, and a jar of mustard.

You sad, sad single man.

So to help scare off the last of her hangover, and help steady herself, she opened a beer.

Now who's sad, Stevie?

. . . .

Ashe caught a break, and a man he knew from the hardware store gave him a lift to Sixth Avenue. He walked into the small dealership, looking around at what was there that looked buyable.

"Can I help you?"

"The Ford Explorer, how much?"

"Oh, hey, Chig. Ah, you don't want that. Too many miles and not all good ones, you know. I saw them towing your old Cherokee in. I guess she finally gave up the ghost, huh?"

"Matthew, right? Matt, show me a good fairly recent vehicle with reasonable miles. Truck or SUV preferably," Ashe said. "I'll write you a check, right now, if I can test-drive it overnight."

"You like Jeeps, right?" Matt said, a huge grin on his face. Ashe figured this was the easiest sale ol' brother-in-law Matt had made in years.

Ashe left driving a three-year-old Grand Cherokee. Once out of town, he turned up Old Martin Road and then came to his long tree-lined driveway. The sun had gone down, and there was the smell of more rain in the air.

He turned off his headlights and rolled up his drive as slowly as he could, surveying his property and house for any signs that would indicate Stevie was inside. He was assuming she'd beat him here by at least an hour.

As he made the last turn in his drive, he saw a small Land Rover Defender, parked away from the house, so that as he pulled in, the trees blocked Ashe from seeing it until the last second as he approached.

He stopped. *English guy, English car?* He slid the Jeep into park.

In the front seat of the Defender, he thought he saw a tiny green glow, just for a second. Like a night vision scope reflecting off a person's face as they brought it up to their eyes.

Damn. He'll be able to see me. My dash lights will give him all the ambient light his NOD needs.

Ashe felt that old feeling. The adrenaline surge, the slight queasy feeling. He'd been in two gunfights in the last year, if you counted Arthur North shooting over his head. He took in a slightly shaky breath as he drew his S&W 9mm and held it on his lap. His hands were still steady, but sweating. The Defender was forty yards, maybe forty-five. His Smith had a 3.6" barrel, and a night sight on the front only.

Relax. The windshield is a big target, and hitting it on the driver's side will either stop him, or give me a chance to make for the woods and circle around.

Whoever was in the Defender hadn't moved. Ashe drew in a couple more breaths to try to get in a steady one. He forced himself to breathe deeply. By the fourth deep breath, he was good.

Ashe thought about backing away, maybe draw him off from his house. Away from Stevie. But if this was North, he wouldn't fall for that.

Then the Defender's driver's side door opened and a man stepped out. He reached back in and turned on an overhead light so Ashe could see him.

Danny, mother-loving, Breslin!

Ashe pulled his Jeep around and parked and got out, holstering his gun. Danny stepped around and they met on his porch. He wore dark, nondescript casual clothing but had a Remington Tac-14 shorty scattergun in his hands. Ashe noticed several slug rounds in a sidesaddle attached to its frame.

"Special Agent Dan Breslin, as I live and breathe," Ashe said. "Newest member of the stateys!"

Breslin smiled and they shook hands. He was not quite as tall as Ashe, maybe 5'10, but he was former SWAT and Vice, and was built like a fire plug. Breslin had been not only Pat's partner in Metro but had covered Ashe's ass before. Trust didn't always come easy to cops; it was earned through actions in a career where words were cheap. Breslin didn't talk much, and he'd more than proven himself.

"Didn't recognize your new ride. Rachel told me that if I didn't have a specific tasking from her, to just haunt you, and something would turn up," he said. "Stevie is inside. Rachel was right."

Ashe just nodded and quickly filled him in.

When Ashe was done, Breslin said, "So, this North, the guy I tailed and lost from Roger's Café, is a former British spy and might be on his way here?"

"Maybe. Can you cover us while I find out what Stevie knows about this?" Ashe asked.

"Mister Ashe, you're never boring. Yeah. Good news is, I've

already spent some time outside your house. I'll find an overwatch position and let Rachel know."

Ashe tilted his head. "She's…ah, not going to be happy that Stevie is involved. Let me have a chat with her first to be sure we don't waste Rachel's time."

Breslin shrugged. "I'm still on probation with the state. You get me fired, you have to get me a job," he said. He went to his vehicle and pulled away from the house.

Ashe stepped up to the front door and unlocked it. "Stevie, it's me." He slowly opened the door. "Just me, hon," he said again.

When he got inside, he saw her behind his kitchen counter on her knees with his revolver pointed at the door. She saw Ashe and quickly lowered it.

"Ashe! Crap! There's been some dude outside, he looked through a window!"

"Danny Breslin."

She slumped to the floor. "Oh, thank God."

Ashe stepped over and relieved her of his .38 revolver. "Come on. We may not have much time and we need to compare notes," he said.

CHAPTER 26

"Ashe, before anything let me say, I'm so sorry to barge in here like this," Stevie said. "Tom told me to go somewhere safe while he worked things out with his Foundation contact."

"Okay, that's smart," Ashe said. He went to his fridge for a beer, but they were all gone. He grabbed a glass of water from the sink instead.

She turned around on the couch to watch him in the kitchen, raising her voice a little. "I thought about a motel, but that's no good; credit card and all, then I thought about Metro, but somebody might know my ex-husband and daughter live there."

"Getting lost in as big a city as that wasn't a bad notion, but you're right. If I were tracking you there, I'd first stake out your ex." Ashe held up a finger for her to wait and walked to his bedroom.

He had a bad feeling, so he changed out of his light-colored summer clothes into dark jeans and black running shoes. Then he found his concealable body armor, and put it on under a long-sleeve dark-green polo. He put on a rugged leather holster and belt, and slid his S&W 9mm in to it. He grabbed a black raincoat and a dark-gray TAG ball cap, and returned to the living room.

Stevie saw him return to the living room and grab his water. By her face, she noticed his change of outfit but didn't remark on it. Instead, she picked up where she'd left off.

"Anyway, I came here. I know I had no right to."

"It's okay. This is a good spot. But we really need to…"

"No, I mean, I kind of told you last year that I wanted a new life. I wanted to cut ties and move forward. Sober, with Tom.

Maybe even children. We were planning a wedding just four days ago."

Ashe took a moment. Then said, "Stevie, you know I still care about you, but you were the brave one. You left me for yourself and your future. I'll be okay, but right now, it's *your future* we need to focus on. Tell me what you know."

She told him how through the audit and Tom wanting her to fix a problem at the sanctuary that she'd found the secret room and the Blockade Runners. Then how she'd discovered Carol Buckram had gone missing, so she'd taken care of the children.

Then she went through how Tom had so suddenly become different and had cleared out the room, then how she'd taken the box with the records.

Ashe smiled. "But, Tilly brought that box to us. Mad as anything, claiming it was thrown into the Roger's Café dumpster. I mean, I didn't buy it for a second, but it's ingenious how she got it into our hands. Totally plausible." Then he looked at Stevie's eyes. "You did that? You and her together?"

Stevie smiled. "I might just be nicer to her from now on. I get why you and she are so close."

Then Stevie told him how she'd gone to see Crawford, Jasper, and Gregory. And gotten completely drunk.

"I saw the tail end of that, on the square today."

"I wanted to be sure those girls at the sanctuary are safe, so I asked Crawford to make me the administrator. Anyway, on my little voice recorder, I got where Jasper admits he sent some dude out to the lake to offer two hundred thousand bucks to Durant for the drive. In Crawford's office the next day, I played that part of the conversation. Then he asked if I had his thumb drive. I insinuated I did, to make him sign me over the sanctuary. I know, stupid."

She took out the recorder and handed it to Ashe.

He looked at it. "You have *no idea* how stupid, but this might help. You know what's on that thumb drive?"

"Financial records or something. At least that's what those Blockaders told me."

"And you know for a fact Tom works for the Able Keys Foundation?"

"Yes, well, they're one of his clients."

"You ever hear him mention a Searl Magna-something?"

"No."

"What about a group called the Elite Watch?"

"No, why? Who are they?"

"Well, let me tell you the other half you don't know." Ashe described Chuck Carter and the cove. How a sniper had killed Anderton as well then shot at the boat with Skye aboard.

"My god, I know her!"

He told her most of it and described Arthur North and their dealings with him so far. Then from his portfolio, he took out a photo of Arthur North.

"Does that name ring a bell? How about this picture of him? Have you seen him at all? Maybe going by another name?"

She looked at the photo for several seconds then shook her head.

"Okay, now the hard part. I want you to know that *I* know, Tom and I have never gotten along. I guess I still connect him with Mark Portals, and the fact he's with you, doesn't help. But what I have to say about him now, I promise, is not colored by that past."

Stevie waited. Her face showed sadness; in that, she might know what he was about to say.

"Tom works for the people who most likely hired North. That means he knew, well before you or I, that Chuck Carter and Carol were dead. Tom withheld all that. I believe given North's ability to maneuver around here, Tom is his local 'birddog.' To what extent, I don't know, but we damn sure plan on asking him."

She took in a long breath with several stops along its way in. But she didn't stop Ashe or argue.

Ashe went back in to his portfolio; there were copies of the photos recovered from the cove and the cropped photo of him. "These first two were found where we figure North operated overlooking the cove on the lake."

Stevie looked at them. Carol and Durant, blown up from the Blockade Runner's Batch Launch photo. Then the photo of Charles Carter.

"This is how he…North, identified them?"

"Uh-huh. Next, this is a photocopy of my picture that was given to a pair of hoods North hired to watch me. Somebody cropped it, looks like on a scanner or a copier, so only I am in this version."

Stevie looked at the picture of Ashe then covered her mouth suddenly. It was obvious she recognized it.

"That's...that is from a photo of you and me! They cropped me out. I used to have it in a frame beside my bed. When I moved in with Tom, I put it away."

"Yeah, I thought something like that."

"Oh my God, Tom had to get this from my things. It's not on the internet or anything."

Ashe drank his water. He gave her a moment to process.

"You're saying Tom gave these to the man who killed your friend and Carol? Before he washed up in Hurrt County."

Ashe shrugged. "He had access to the Blockade Runner Batch Launch photos, *before* you even knew about them."

Ashe finished his water and let her go through the parade of emotions flying across her face.

Finally she said, "I thought maybe he was an accessory. But this could mean he was a conspirator to their murders, and the continued criminal enterprise after the killings..."

Spoken in true legalese. But it's how she processes.

"So tonight, he's been on the phone trying to talk to these people?" Ashe asked. "The people who might send North for you."

Stevie jumped up. "No...he said a man was coming to see *him*. Shit! Tonight!"

"I thought they thought...he said *you* had it!"

"You think this North...oh my God, he said to me, they might send the man they sent last time. *At the lake!*"

"Call him," Ashe said and went to the front door. He flashed his porch lights a couple of times and went outside, expecting Breslin to be watching, then waved his arms for Breslin to come in.

Leaving the door open, he went back to Stevie, who was furiously shaking her cell. Ashe took her to his home office landline instead and she dialed. Ashe put the call on speakerphone as it rang.

"Hello," Tom said.

"Oh my sweet lord, Tom! You're okay!"

"Of course. Everything's all clear," he said. "They understand there was a mistake is all."

"So...it's okay there? You're all right?" she said.

"Yes, my love. It's okay. Everything is fine, it's all *golden*."

"So…I can come home?"

"Of course. Perfectly safe and clear. I love you. Come on home," he said, then the line went dead.

"He sounded odd," Ashe said.

Tears appeared in her eyes, but she wiped them away. "That's because he's in danger. He said not to believe him unless he said *silver*! Not 'golden,' not 'all clear,' and nothing else!"

Breslin appeared at the office door then came in. "What's up?"

Ashe thought quickly then said, "Call Rachel. Have her get some local cops or troopers over to Tom Fischer's apartment in Carson County, and fast. Tell her he may be under duress, and North may also be there."

Breslin nodded and stepped out to use his cell, saw it didn't have a signal, then took off toward the front door.

Ashe punched in Jacobs' cell on the desk phone. He answered.

"Ashe, hey. I just heard you bought a Jeep from Matt. Look, you probably could have…"

"Sheriff! Arthur North may be at Tom Fischer's apartment in Harmony! Can you get Carson County S.O. headed that way? I have the state en route!"

Stevie had scribbled down the address and apartment number, so Ashe gave it to Jacobs.

"Done! I'll meet you there!"

"Stevie, go to the sheriff's office. I'll get someone to escort you, but head that direction and no stops!" Ashe said, then grabbed the address and ran for the door.

He and Stevie jogged outside as Breslin was backing his Defender up to the porch. He got the garage open and Stevie into her car then jumped in with Breslin.

"Where in Harmony?" Breslin asked. Ashe gave him the address. Breslin punched the gas.

"Stevie's following us as far as Route 429, then she's headed back to Seacord."

Once they were at the far end of Ashe's driveway, he took out his cell.

Two bars, enough. He dialed Jacobs and got him.

"Ashe?" he said, his siren blaring in the background.

"Sheriff, Stevie is in her BMW and is headed on 429 back to

Seacord. I told her to go to the jail. We need to protect her; I think our sniper is looking for her! Oh, and nothing by radio, please."

"You got it," he said and hung up.

Breslin got them off of Old Martin Road and onto Route 429, and headed for Carson County. About then, a red BMW passed them as the rain started again.

"Was that…"

Ashe sighed. "Yeah. Dumb, rock-headed…" He picked up his cell again.

"Sheriff, disregard my last. On her own, she's on the way to Harmony and her apartment."

"Roger," Jacobs replied. "I ain't surprised."

Ashe didn't answer but looked at Breslin.

"She's going way too fast in this rain," he said.

"Beat her there, Danny," Ashe said.

Breslin didn't say a word, but it felt like the Defender got up on its back legs and took off.

. . . .

They got to the apartment just behind a pair of state troopers in marked cars. A marked Carson County Sheriff's Department Ford pickup had pulled in at one end of the parking lot, blocking an exit. The deputy was out of his truck with a lever action rifle.

Breslin pulled the Defender around and stopped a little off from Fischer and Stevie's apartment. He got out, holding his state badge high, as he was plain clothed. Ashe did the same thing. It was now pouring rain and wind, bordering on a squall.

Signaling the two troopers and the Carson County deputy to rally, they formed a hasty plan. Anyone inside could easily know by now they were there, so they decided to immediately breach and rush the apartment. One of the troopers was state SRT, so he brought a ram for the door and a flash-bang to pitch in before entry.

Breslin took charge; the deputy didn't object. "Ashe, sorry but you're the oldest. Take rear."

The five of them moved quickly toward the apartment door, Ashe in the rear. Then Stevie arrived.

She swung in to the parking lot too quickly, and her car fishtailed in the water and one tire dropped off into a small culvert. She got out, abandoning her running car, and ran toward the stairs to her apartment.

"Tom!" she screamed. Ashe broke with the group and ran back toward her, grabbing her before she got across the lot.

"Let me go! Damn you, Ashe, let me go to him!"

"No! Stevie, wait!" Ashe held her hard then lifted her off her feet. He did his best to hold her back, but she was fighting him to run to Tom.

"Danny, go!" Ashe yelled over his shoulder. He spun her around so she couldn't see them.

He saw the trooper swing the ram, the door fly open, then the other trooper deployed the bang. It went off with a brilliant white flash and a huge explosive boom. The four men rushed in.

The sheriff of Carson County and another of his deputy's arrived. They ran to Ashe who was holding up his Hurrt County badge.

"Chig! Is that you?" the sheriff said. "I'm Sheriff Will Minor. Larry told me to find you!"

Stevie went limp in his arms. She wasn't fighting him to get loose anymore. Her strength was gone and she was openly wailing, terrified by what she thought had happened.

The newly arrived deputy jogged over. "Take her, keep her outside," Ashe said, and passed Stevie to the deputy. Then he jogged as best he could up the stairs and into the apartment.

The men had cleared the apartment and hadn't found North. The troopers were standing around, silent. Everything in the place was turned over or ripped open. Every book off the shelves, vases busted open, pictures off the walls. The bang hadn't done that. Someone had been searching the place.

Breslin turned on some lights. Sheriff Minor entered, a big revolver in his hand, and right behind him was a soaked Sheriff Jacobs.

Ashe stepped to the master bedroom; more bedlam. The bed was thrown off its frame and ripped open. The first deputy stood there, looking into the master bathroom. He had a pistol in his hand but holstered it as Ashe stepped around him.

There was smeared blood on the walls and the floor. In the tub was Tom Fischer, nude, a plastic bag tied tight over his head.

His face was frozen in a permanent, now-silent, scream. He was bruised and had bled a good deal. A wine opener was screwed into his thigh. There were several small cuts on and around his hands, feet, and his groin.

Outside, down in the parking lot, they all could hear the frantic, anguished screams of Stevie.

"Tom! Tom! Somebody tell me about Tom!"

Ashe turned to leave. This was not his first gang-style murder scene, but it hit him harder than the others. While he'd been talking to Stevie, Tom was being tortured to death. In his last seconds of life, he'd warned her not to come home. He hadn't given his tormentors his fiancée.

In his last seconds, he'd made a choice. Knowing he was going to die, he chose his last thoughts, his last words to purchase a dream they were there to steal. He died saving her.

Ashe drew a shallow breath and let it out. Whatever Tom had done that led to Chuck Carter and Carol Buckram's death, he'd atoned for it.

Ashe walked, still half limping, past Jacobs and the rest, outside and walked straight to Stevie. The deputy holding her let her go, and she ran to Ashe.

She looked into his eyes, and in that instant, it was if she could see all the horror he had just witnessed.

"Tom?" she said, and threw her arms around Ashe.

CHAPTER 27

Police and EMS lights flashed off pooled rainwater on the street, as yellow crime scene tape strung across the apartment parking lot blew wildly in the wind like the tail of a kite. The loud staccato of noise made from the mix of emergency radio chatter and idling engines drown out everything. Ashe had spent his life walking through this kaleidoscope of chaos, often expected by everyone to make sense of it all. This was different; this felt different. This was harder.

And of course, just on the far side of the sheriff's line, stood the horde of onlookers. They were just as all the others Ashe had ever seen; made up of the frightened, the concerned, and of course, the morbidly curious. They moved as a swarm, increasing by the minute.

One of them would make incidental eye contact with him then turn to say something to the person beside them. Many tried to maneuver to where they could see in the back of the ambulance.

For years, he'd generally ignored them, but sitting there in the rain, they got under his skin.

For Stevie. You people keep your damn eyes off of Stevie.

The rain had reduced itself to an annoying drizzle as Ashe sat in the open hatch of Breslin's Defender. He looked at the open rear of a white-and-orange ambulance where Stevie sat. A female medic had a blanket wrapped around her and was taking her vitals. Every now and then, their eyes would meet. She looked as if all her spirit was lost, her eyes dull and bearing only the one emotion she had left. Anguish.

Another ambulance, dark blue in color, was backed up to the

apartment stairs close to where Tom was. In a few minutes, once the crime scene technicians had finished, they'd bring him out for his ride to the pathologist in the city.

Rachel Hume walked over to Ashe; Pat was with her and handed him a large black coffee.

"Where did you come from?" Ashe said to Pat.

"Heard about your…um, about Stevie. Tom Fischer."

"Yeah," was all Ashe said. He gestured at the ambulance then took a long pull off the coffee.

Rachel came over and sat beside Ashe in the Defender. She actually leaned her head over against him a little. "You gave a statement to the Carson County Sheriff?" she asked.

"Uh-huh."

"I've spoken with everyone else here, I guess I need to go talk to Stevie," Rachel said, looking over at her. Stevie, still being fussed over, was looking at them as well.

"Rach?"

"Yeah?"

"Give her a while, please?"

Rachel looked at Ashe then Pat, who nodded.

"Well, this is Carson County, and technically not my beat. My SAC is on route and he will likely talk to the sheriff and DA here. They'll request the state CIB take this one, so the boss will assign another agent to this investigation. That'll be tomorrow probably. Maybe wait until then."

Ashe took out Stevie's small digital recorder. "Have a listen. I have. It will be corroborated by Dr. Gregory."

"This is?" she asked.

"Stevie sent herself undercover. Blockaders sent Anderton to the cove."

"You…you did this?"

"Nope. First heard of it tonight."

"C'mon. I'll drive you home, buddy," Pat said.

Ashe ignored the offer. "Anybody else see anything? We have a description of anyone? Do we know for sure this was Arthur North?"

"One neighbor across the breezeway heard a commotion. Saw a tall black male and another man leaving. That's the best we have," Rachel said.

"Vehicle?" Ashe asked.

"No."

Without saying anything, Ashe stood up and walked over to the ambulance. Stevie watched him approaching, but not until he climbed in beside her did her eyes finally register it was him.

"Ashe?"

"Stevie. Agent Hume is going to see to it you're protected until we catch the ones who did this, okay?"

"Tom's dead?" she asked. She already knew it; he'd told her before as gently as he could. But she kept asking, somehow hoping for a different answer.

The medic put an IV in, most likely Ashe assumed to combat shock.

"Yes. And he was brave for you. He's a big hero in my book."

"Ashe?"

"Yeah, honey?"

She took his arm and gripped it hard, her eyes back into a dark focus. Her lips trembled, but her voice was suddenly louder.

"Ashe, I want you to find them. Find anybody that did this. I want you to *kill* the motherfuckers, Ashe. You know how, so for me, go kill them!"

The medic turned from whatever she'd been doing and looked curiously at Ashe and Stevie.

"Yes," was all Ashe said. Stevie let go of his arm and flopped back with her head against the wall.

"I…think that…" the medic started to say.

"Yeah," Ashe said and got out.

He walked back over to Rachel and Pat, and Breslin had joined them. Ashe stuck out his hand and shook Breslin's. "You're a damn good man, Danny Breslin. Thank you."

Breslin shook his head. "Ashe, I'm just sorry that…" Then he turned and walked off.

"Chig, Sheriff Jacobs said for you to go home, and that he'd check on you in the morning," Pat said. "Come on, I'll drive you."

"Rachel," Ashe said. "All this? Over some financial records?"

She shook her head slowly.

"Yeah, me neither," Ashe said, and walked over to Pat's Dodge.

. . . .

The ride back to his house was just as manic as the one leaving it, but that was because Pat was behind the wheel. Whereas Danny Breslin was skilled and precise, Pat's driving was more like wild and unruly. You got in, you hung on, you shut up.

Ashe didn't feel like talking anyway. After what Stevie had said to him; seeing her pain and anger, his mind was churning it all over, hoping something made sense to him. But nothing sat right with him. None of this made sense.

"I watched you with Stevie. I didn't say nothing to Rach, but I can imagine what she said to you," Pat said, breaking the silence.

"We've...both heard it before. The family of victims often..."

"Can it, Chig. I know you, twenty-four years or so. You're not going to stop, are you?"

Ashe didn't answer.

"Before it was about Chuck, and don't say it wasn't, because it was for me. But now...now it's your Stevie."

Ashe clenched his fists. He drew in a breath and tried to hold it for a few seconds then let it out slowly, relaxing his hands.

"By you sending her to your house, having Danny outside, you saved her life. She'd have gone back there sooner or later, you know her. Then they'd have done her too."

"Pat, I can't just not... This guy will slide out of here soon and be gone. Overseas. As soon as the damn money says to, he'll vanish."

They rode for a long while, quietly. Both men thinking.

"Whatever you're thinking, I'm in. For Chuck and, yeah, now for Stevie, too."

"You may not be able to."

"Shut the fuck up. And I already talked with Danny, too. He's in. He's young, so maybe part-time after work or something, but we want this damn North guy."

"Me first. We'll talk later." They pulled into Ashe's driveway.

"Rachel will take care of her. They'll get her far away from here and safe. You want me to hang around?"

"I imagine Rachel needs you more than I do. See ya, Patrick."

"No smart remark?"

Ashe looked at his house, all dark. "No, I'm all out," he said and walked to his porch.

They'd left in a hurry so the front door was unlocked. Ashe locked it behind him and snapped on the foyer lights.

He went to the kitchen and found his bottle of Darkthorn Irish and poured himself first two then three fingers. Straightaway, he downed one of them.

Tomorrow, the state accountants arrive. It'll be a sit and wait deal while they...

He didn't finish the thought. An angry tingling seized his body. In the dark far corner of the living room, he was drawn to a pair of barely perceptible eyes. There was no figure there in the shadows, just the eyes that looked mad as hell.

Do something! He heard in his mind.

Then by the foyer light, he could see his living room had been tossed. Furniture overturned. Ashe dropped the whiskey on the counter and went for his gun.

"Please don't, Mister Ashe," a British voice said. "You'll never make it."

After a second, Ashe took his hand off his gun. It was half out of its leather holster.

"Arthur North," he said.

North stepped over and turned on a lamp. The living room became bright, and the full effects of the search came into view. Ashe looked to the previously dark corner, but no one; no eyes were there.

"Please have a seat, Mister Ashe. The only reason I didn't shoot you five minutes ago is, well, you intrigue me," North said.

He was tallish and wore a dark-gray raincoat. He looked very much like his picture; fit, short hair, clean-shaven. He wore gloves and in his left hand he held what looked like an HK 45 with a suppressor attached.

North held it somewhat casually but definitely aimed at Ashe. Ashe let his right hand drift away from his own, holstered pistol.

"You're the one who killed my friend Chuck Carter," Ashe said. "And a lot of others, not to mention Tom Fischer tonight."

"Carter was a friend? Ah, that explains a good deal. Please, come. Sit."

Ashe stepped from behind the counter and down to his living

room. North righted Ashe's old leather chair, and sat himself.

"You won't find it here," Ashe said, still standing. "I see you've looked."

"We're not done looking, but first, I thought perhaps I could convince you to tell me what you think *it* is? Maybe *where* as well."

"I'm in no mood to chat, and you won't find a wine corkscrew here."

"You're a little old to be so sure of yourself. The people I represent have enormous reach and are very dedicated to this project. If after our 'chat' as you call it, I'm dissatisfied, I'll move on to the next likely person."

Stevie.

Ashe tried to not let his face reveal is thoughts. *No, Arthur I am going to see to it you won't.*

"You're not as bright as the feds say you are, Arthur, may I call you that? See, I assumed by your going after the judge's computer, probably Tom Fischer's computer, you might have learned that we believe Michael Durant has it."

North furrowed his brow a bit. "Actually, I believe, and yes, you may call me Arthur, that Mr. Durant *does not* have it. He is a consummate liar and thief. I'll eventually get the okay to take care of him, but it is still *here*, somewhere." He set the HK 45 on the left arm of the chair, still pointed at Ashe. "You want to finish your whiskey?"

From down the hall, Ashe heard an almost imperceptible sound of a bump. They were not alone.

Of course not.

"Sloppy, losing those photos at the cove."

"They must have fallen out; I *was* being chased by a helicopter."

"Just a question, when you fired at us at the cove, were you aiming at me, the girl driving the boat, or the engines?"

North gave a small smile. "You do have a curiosity! I was trying to hold the three of you there. See, the last place I knew where the small data button was, was with Ms. Buckram. They were about to sell it to those...whiskey runners. We could not allow such a small, *rural* group of people to have an advantage over us."

"Us?" Ashe wanted him talking. Hard to talk and shoot. "The Elite Watch? The Searl Magnadyne people?"

North smiled, but it wasn't cheery at all. Like a Doberman before it leaps at you.

"Yes, you know..."

Ashe drew his Smith 9mm and shot North, just as North's hand flashed to his pistol and fired.

It felt like someone had a ball bat, and hit Ashe rapidly twice in the chest. Every cell in his body went electric and he couldn't breathe.

Front sight!

Ashe brought his gun up again and snapped off three more shots at North; his orange front sight danced in a small circle against his chest. North fell backward over the leather chair and hit the floor hard.

The room started spinning, but Ashe held the counter.

Hallway!

A big man stepped from the guest bedroom, a shotgun in his hand. He was very close but stupidly took the time to yell something. Ashe fired twice more; one shot hit the man's upper chest; the other hit his head. He collapsed on the floor.

The eyes he had seen in the dark corner were staring at him again from the kitchen and conveyed extreme anger. Ashe heard something from the living room. He started to turn, but the floor slid out from under his feet and he went to his knees.

North had gotten up but was crumpled over as he moved. He looked around, shoving the chair and an end table around, probably looking for his gun. Then in a crouch, holding his chest, moved toward Ashe.

As he got close, Ashe saw he had a knife. Suddenly from the kitchen, a heavy barstool shot across the floor and hit North, tripping him.

Ashe lifted his gun, but North got up and ran out the front door.

Ashe finally got a breath in. He tried to get one foot up, but his chest began spasming. White hot pain—he couldn't breathe. The floor ran up and slapped him in the face.

Laying there, falling through the floor into unconsciousness, he heard a car outside. A door opened, loud talking, then the door closed, and the car drove off.

North. Had a guy in here, and a man outside. I'm very lucky.
Then darkness.

· · · ·

He felt his mother beside him. She petted his hair, and with her fingers pulled it back from his face. She bent down and kissed the top of his head.

He felt Stevie holding his head in her lap. He could smell her perfume, the one he loved. She tore her blouse to make a bandage and pressed it gently on his wound.

"Chig!" he heard a man say. His dad. The eyes he'd seen were his father's eyes.

"Chig!" Louder, not his dad.

"Chig! Ashe!" Sheriff Jacobs yelled. He was running his hands all over Ashe's torso and limbs, looking for blood, like the Army had taught him.

"I'm here, First Sergeant Jacobs! I'm alive," Ashe said. He opened his eyes. It was daylight.

"Don't move," Jacobs said. He tore open Ashe's polo using the bullet holes. "Body armor! Thank God."

Ashe tried to get up on one elbow, but that caused the spasms to return, so he took the sheriff's advice and stayed still.

Over his head, he heard another car fly in, siren screaming. Deputy Ed Bell ran in, gun out.

"Clear the place!" Jacobs barked to Bell, then on his radio said, "Dispatch, send an ambulance to the thirty-eight-hundred block of Old Martin Road! Ashe residence, first drive on the left, about a mile up!"

"We got a body!" Bell yelled from the hall.

"I... was trying for two," Ashe strained to say, but the spasms in his chest seized his breath and silenced him.

CHAPTER 28

Three Weeks Later

Ashe was outside in the backyard of his house, splitting wood. It was hot, but the sweat on his body felt good, so he peeled off his T-shirt to get some sun.

His doctors had told him despite the body armor, his heart had been bruised. *Contused.* They said for him take it easy, especially at his age, so he was using a wood splitter.

He heard a car crunching on his gravel driveway, approaching, so he picked up his .38 revolver off a stump and stuck it in the front of his pants. Walking to the corner of his house, he grabbed his shirt.

It was a Hurrt County cruiser. Despite Ashe's protests, Jacobs had his people checking on him almost every day. This morning it was Ed Bell.

"Big Ed Bell," Ashe said, pulling his shirt on.

"Mr. Ashe. The sheriff wanted me to come out and check on you, and to tell you to answer your phone."

Ashe grinned. "Go tell Larry Jacobs when I'm on suspension for a shooting, my damn phone is too."

Bell nodded, obviously appreciating Ashe's humor. "Okay, also there's a big meeting at his office, he'd like you to be at. One o'clock today."

Ashe looked around. He didn't have a watch handy and his phone was inside. "What time is it now?"

"Eleven-forty-five."

"Great, fine, sure." Ashe took off his work gloves and pitched them over at the wood splitter. "Tell him I'll be there."

. . . .

Ashe arrived at the S.O. about ten minutes early and was buzzed in. He walked through to Jacobs' office and saw Rachel was there with ADA Price.

"Okay, *I* want a lawyer," he said as he walked in.

They all laughed at that and greeted him, shaking hands, then sat at Jacobs' office table.

Price started, "Detective Ashe, despite my objection, I accepted your request and took the case of the shooting at your house to the grand jury this morning. They returned a No True bill. The state has reviewed it as well, and we find no cause for any charges."

Rachel went next. "You'll be happy to hear that we have Clarence Crawford and Commissioner Jasper in custody. Based off all the evidence from our subpoenas, and the box of records that Dr. Gregory validated, the Blockade Runners operated what we are describing as a *criminal enterprise*. There's evidence of payoffs, misappropriation of charitable funds, plus a hundred banking law violations. Feds are coming to indict them soon, too. Wire fraud, tax violations."

"*Taxes*? They sent Anderton to the cove to kill Durant and maybe Carol," Ashe said.

"We can prove they sent him, even paid him. But we cannot, *as of yet*, prove what Dr. Gregory says; that they sent him to kill Durant and Carol Buckram," Price said.

"Murder has no statute of limitations. It's not off the table if I can find new evidence," Rachel said.

Ashe nodded at that. "And no further word from Durant? By Marsh or otherwise?"

Rachel shook her head. "There's a warrant out for him. And the Able Keys Foundation is doing some dancing. There are about a dozen of their contributors raising hell, and the IRS and FBI are involved. Oh, and the governor is holding a press conference soon. She'll deny knowledge of everything, of course."

"That's not the whole deal, though, right?" Jacobs asked.

"Oh no. The state legislature is opening an investigation, and worse? The big news media are 'looking into allegations,' you know the story," Rachel said.

"The Cover Up at the Cove, they'll call it," Price said, mimicking a local newscaster. "What *did* our governor know about her foundation sending an assassin to kill her ex-husband?"

"Well, I guess it's good I don't watch TV much," Ashe said.

"I'm trying to avoid being *on* it," Rachel said. "Oh, and you mentioned a Searl Magnadyne, Ashe."

"Yeah, something Dr. Gregory told me to look into. Durant used that, too; *Searl*. What is that?"

"Well, the Searl Effect is power generated by magnets and no fuel. That company you mentioned, Searl Magnadyne, is a British corporation."

British. Like North. "Any ties to Durant or the Blockaders?" Ashe asked.

"Not so far," she said. "But there has to be, so the accounting ninjas are on it."

Then they all sat there quietly. Ashe waited. He wanted to hear one other thing. They had to know it, too.

"Well," Price said, breaking the silence. "I'll be on my way. I have a lot of work to get after now, thanks to you three." Everyone said their goodbyes and Price left.

A full minute after he was gone, Rachel breathed in deeply.

"No one has seen him. And everyone is looking harder. The feds are squeezing every contact they have as hard as possible. The Brits, the Canadians, Interpol, everybody is hunting him. There's an interagency task force that was organized last week, specifically to get him."

"Sheriff, am I off suspension?" Ashe asked.

"I want to talk about that," Jacobs started. Then his phone buzzed. "Sheriff, you have visitors. A lawyer and Lou Buckram," the dispatcher said.

"Send them back!" he shouted over his shoulder at his phone.

Ashe scooted over beside Rachel, and down the hall saw Linda Ingles and Lou Buckram approaching.

Jacobs stood, introduced everyone, then shook Lou's hand. "Lou," he said, a hard look on his face.

"Larry. I want to apologize for the trouble I caused before. I had no call to shove that deputy or wrestle with you."

"You were grieving, I gave you a pass," Jacobs said.

There was an awkward pause. Then, "Go ahead, Lou," Linda said.

From a paper sack he'd brought, Lou pulled out a small ceramic moonshine jug.

"Is that…" Larry started.

"From the Blockade Runners?" Ashe finished.

"Yeah. I reckon my Carol wanted to keep it safe. She hid it out at my place. I didn't know, but she'd told me she had something on these men. You'd have never found it, hell, I just found it. Anyway, after everything in the news, Miss Linda said I needed to turn it in."

Larry started to pick it up, but Ashe said, "Wait. Fingerprints, DNA, Sheriff. We have to be able to prove this is *the* jug North and everyone else has been hunting for."

Rachel pulled a set of nylon gloves from her purse and pulled them on. She removed the cork stopper, picked up the miniature jug, and began to invert it. Ashe grabbed a couple of sheets of copy paper and laid them out below the jug.

A rolled-up piece of paper tied with twine slid out. "That's my daddy's recipe," Lou said.

Then, rattling around inside the jug as Rachel shook it, fell a tiny flash drive.

"It's been there all this time?" Ashe said. "So, Michael Durant doesn't have it."

"I guess. I don't know for sure when she put it out there, but I found it a couple days ago. My fingerprints will be on it," he said.

"Given we are cooperating fully, will there be any charges pending against Mr. Buckram? From this…or before?" Linda asked.

Rachel set the jug down carefully and looked at the small USB drive. It was less than half an inch. She held it so that Ashe and Jacobs could see. On top it read, "728GB USB-C+." Then she realized they were waiting on her to answer.

"Oh, um. He'll give us a statement as to how he came into possession of this, and be available to testify in court?"

Lou nodded vigorously. "If it helps barbeque them son of a bitches, I'm glad to."

"Then, no," she said.

"Ah, hang on, Lou. Sheriff, are you investigating any unlicensed local distilleries?" Linda asked, and tilted her head slightly toward Buckram.

"They still in operation?"

Everyone looked at Lou.

"Uh…no," he said.

"Then we're good," Jacobs said.

Rachel packaged everything up as evidence and escorted them out. "We'll be over at the courthouse," she said. They all got up to leave and as they started down the hall, Ashe caught up to Linda.

"Sorry about, well, that Thursday lunch," he said.

Linda smiled at him. "I saw the news; you had a good excuse. Rain check?"

"Absolutely," he said. As they cleared the hall into the lobby, Rachel turned around, made a sarcastic *kissy* face at him, and cut her eyes toward Linda behind her back. Ashe smiled back.

Pat is ruining that woman.

Ashe walked back to Jacobs' office. "So, Sheriff. There's a task force for North. I was thinking…"

"Close the door, Ashe," he said. His face was sullen and also irritated looking.

"What's up?"

"I'll just say it. Jasper was a very popular county commissioner. Crawford has been here all his life. Several other people here, business people, are, or have been, with the damn Blockade Runners over the years. They're hollering that all this attention, it's bad for the town and the county."

Then Ashe got it.

"You're *firing* me? Damn, Larry, have I not done enough?"

"I know. You've even bled for this county, Ashe. I'm pretty damn mad myself. I have half a mind to tell them to kiss my ass."

Ashe sat and thought for a second or two.

"They would cut off your money, starve the department, fight you at reelection. I guess I should have seen this coming, even as far back as Mark Portals."

"It's not like…hell, I haven't even been *paying* you; they can't claim it's about saving money."

"They probably told you it was about insurance. They always do that."

Jacobs nodded. "You know there wasn't a murder or shooting in this town for twenty years."

"Well, there was that one, *undetected* murder a couple of years ago," Ashe said, referring to Georgia Murphy. It was how Ashe had first met Sheriff Jacobs.

There was a long and awkward pause. Then Jacobs said, "Listen, you are not an outsider around here. You just get to go back to being retired, is all."

"Sure, hey grab me for coffee every now and then."

Jacobs nodded then stood and grabbed Ashe's hand. The big man had a lot of emotion running across his face, but his words seemed trapped by them.

"Dammit...Ashe. You've...more than once... I know. Just, you know that I know."

Ashe took out his Reserve Deputy badge that was mounted on a leather belt clip and slid it across the table to Jacobs.

"I...never had an ID card," he said. Then he turned and left.

. . . .

Ashe walked out into the sun and then, leaving his new Jeep, walked up onto the Seacord town square. He'd just been canned, but he wasn't sure it actually bothered him. Irritated maybe.

People were everywhere. Even the tourists were back shopping at the antique stores and craft shops, probably oblivious to the recent events. He walked around and considered an iced tea in Roger's, but he walked over to the shady courthouse lawn instead.

Linda and Buckram were walking out on the other side of the square. She gave him a little wave, so he returned it. He started inside but ran into Rachel coming out.

"Well, *Detective*, I think I am going to enjoy giving you back the guff you gave Pat and me," she said, pointing her thumb over her shoulder at Linda.

"Hey, have at it. Oh, and it's not detective anymore. I'm retired again."

"What? Well, we still need your testimony...is that what Jacobs wanted to... Ah, shit, Ashe."

"It's okay, it wasn't his idea."

Thoughts paraded across her eyes, but she settled on the right one. "Fuck local politics!"

"My thoughts exactly."

They stood there; neither knew what to say further about that. Then Ashe said, "One favor. That flash drive. If it's what we think it is, get it on the news that the state police have it. That will make a lot of folks relax not having to worry about North."

"Ah, yeah, Stevie, sure. But what about you?"

"I shot him. There was some blood, but he was likely armored up like me. No, I think somehow he'll make time for me."

"I know you're retired again and all, but just so you know, we have a solid lead on Michael Durant. The feds will get him."

"I hope so." But secretly Ashe didn't. He wanted to find him, or maybe someone else.

"What are you going to do?" she asked.

Ashe saw Lou drive away, but Linda was still sitting in her car, looking at her phone.

Ashe smiled. "I'm thinking of asking someone to lunch."

CHAPTER 29

Two more weeks later

The man on the TV news said, "And the mysterious data drive that was at the center of the deaths in and around the lower middle counties of the state, is in the hands of the State Police Forensic Accounting Unit, which is being assisted by the Cyber Crimes Unit of the FBI. According to a source familiar with the investigation, it is expected to yield significant evidence of massive fraud with charitable contributions."

Then they showed a photo of Arthur North, warning people to not try and apprehend him, but to report any sightings to the local police.

Stevie turned off the television and stood up to stretch. It'd been a long day, but she had found trained and stable foster parents for three of the girls at the sanctuary. It was after seven, but she was in no hurry to go home. Rain had begun to fall heavily outside. She sat back at her desk.

Home? Where? The sanctuary felt as much like home as anywhere. She'd moved out of the apartment she'd shared with Tom. Ashe himself had hired a cleaning company for her, to ensure she never saw any part of what happened to Tom, and packed up Tom's things for her.

She'd found a place back here in Hurrt County, out of town but close. She felt like it was temporary, though.

Brie stepped in with a cup of hot tea for her. "Suzie, Kim, and Kelly are so excited. They like the people they're going to live with." Little Marie followed her and leaped into Stevie's lap.

"I made sure they'll let them see each other every now and then. You kids here are like family to each other." Marie had a tiny plastic horse and playfully made it trot all over Stevie's chest and shoulder.

Brie was twisting her hair again. "Um…what about me, Stevie? If you get all the kids into foster care or adopted, what happens to me?"

Stevie held an arm out, and Brie stepped over and embraced her and Marie.

"You are special, my Brianna. But you're eighteen now. We have to find out what your future looks like, but we'll do it together. Maybe I'll figure out mine along the way."

"I'd like that. I can't imagine not knowing," Brie said, then finished their hug and ran after another girl down the hall. Marie popped off her lap and gave chase.

Not knowing. Stevie thought about that as she sipped her tea. So she picked up her phone and texted Ashe.

It's time, she thought.

· · · ·

Ashe sat in his new Jeep and watched the windshield wipers slowly move the fat sheets of rain from one side of his windshield to the other. They were set too slow to provide him a clear view, but he stared straight ahead anyway as Stevie talked to him.

After she finished telling him what he'd never known, she leaned over and kissed his cheek, holding it for a few seconds. Then softly, as if she were afraid of hurting him even more, she touched his face.

Stevie got out, took off her shoes, and ran through the rain barefoot, pulling her jacket hood up over her head as she did. Ashe watched her as she seemed to melt into his windshield as she ran, and then be washed away by his wipers.

After what felt like a long time, Ashe drove to Roger's café. It was after ten, and Seacord was mostly dry, indoors, and asleep.

The lights went off in the café, and she came out to lock up, just as she had for nearly forty years or more. Tilly had on her short denim skirt and a Roger's Café T-shirt under a clear plastic raincoat with a hood. Ashe got out and walked to her; watching her for a second before letting her see him.

She still looked so good to him. She was nearly sixty and worked on her feet all day, but she never looked more beautiful than right this second.

There was no future between them beyond this; what they had as old friends who loved one another. She belonged to another man, another high school sweetheart. And through the years, that man had more than proven his devotion to her.

She turned and saw him, and jumped at first. She smiled then her expression became curiosity. "What…" she said, but he held up a hand.

Ashe took her in his arms and held her. Quietly, firmly, in the falling rain, he held Tilly close.

After a few seconds, she put her arms around him and held him closely too. He felt her small body begin to shake. He held her tighter. Then without wanting to hold back, he cried with her.

They would not be together; oceans of time had robbed them of that. But he knew by his heart that should she or her family ever need anything, he would not be far. And some day, should time take her away from him, or him away from her, they would both live on through a lean, blue-eyed man far away.

A man Ashe had never met, and Tilly had only known in his very first hours.

Ashe was Tilly's first, and she was his. Then he'd left home for the Army, and forty-two years ago, she'd had their child. A child she'd surrendered to a better destiny than she could provide. A secret she'd held in her heart all that time. He'd written his birth mother several times, and so Tilly had told him about his father.

He was a grown man with a good career, a house, and a family.

And a little five-year-old boy everyone down in Texas called, *Chigger*.

CHAPTER 30

Across the Atlantic, in a small village in Portugal, called Ferragudo, Michael Durant sat at an outdoor café that overlooked the ocean. He was tan and relaxed, and looking forward to his dinner as the sun began to go down.

A waiter came over with a phone in his hand. "*A chamada e' para voce, senhor*," he said in Portuguese.

"I have a call? There must be some mistake. Um, *Voce cometeu um erro*," Durant said.

The waiter shrugged at Durant's poor effort at Portuguese but left the phone.

Durant picked it up. A man's voice, possibly recorded, gave him a message.

"You have been selected for observation by the Elite Watch. You know the reason; this is your only warning. Any action you take as a result of this notice is your responsibility. This is not a threat; this is not a hoax. You are under enhanced surveillance. If this changes, you will not be notified, but you will be…*contacted*."

Durant dropped the phone. A cold chill ran down his spine like an ice cube had been dropped down his shirt. He started to get up, when he was stopped.

He felt a man's hand over his mouth and immediately a terrific sharp pain in his upper back. Centimeter by centimeter, he felt the steel of a knife sliding in. Slowly, surgically.

As he felt himself losing consciousness, he heard his assailant's British accent whisper in his ear.

"Michael Durant. Consider this…your last *contact*."

. . . .

Ashe packed the last of the boxes of what he'd need from this house in Metro. He reached over, grabbed a beer by the bottle neck, and finished it off. He still planned to be here when he could, but for what he saw as his immediate future, a small apartment in the city worked best.

He'd spent most of his life there as a cop. He figured minus any changes in the last three years; he knew every inch of it.

I'll need every advantage for what I have to do.

He heard his phone buzz. It was a text from Linda.

See you in the city!

Just then Pat walked in and grabbed the box. "This it?"

"Will it fit?"

"Yeah. In your Jeep."

"Okay, go ahead and take off, buddy. You have a key. I'll meet you there after I finish closing up here."

"You stopping by the S.O. or Roger's?"

Ashe thought about that. "No."

"Ah… you going to go say something to Stevie?"

Ashe thought about *that*, then said, "No."

Pat set the box back down. "Hey, Chig. What all do you suppose was on that little thumb drive? I mean, to be worth all this?"

To be worth all this?

"I don't know. Hell, Pat, we've seen people killed over damn running shoes or phones before. Truth is, I don't care anymore."

Pat nodded. He picked up the box and left. In a minute, Ashe heard Pat's personal pickup truck pull off.

Ashe looked around his place. The place his grandfather and father had built themselves; the place he had been raised. The home he had restored. After a deep breath, he grabbed his keys and sunglasses then paused at the door.

"I'll be back," he said out loud to no one.

Or maybe…someone.

Then suddenly, Ashe's desk phone and his cell rang at the same time. He jumped a little, not expecting to have cell service, and was momentarily confused by both phones going off. He answered his cell.

A man's voice said, "Answer the other phone, please." And hung up.

The desk phone continued to ring, so Ashe stepped into his home office and answered it.

What sounded like a pre-recorded voice read a message.

"You have been selected for observation by the Elite Watch. You know the reason; this is your only warning. Any action you take as a result of this notice is your responsibility. This is not a threat; this is not a hoax. You are under enhanced surveillance. If this changes, you will not be notified, but you will be…*contacted.*"

Then the line went dead.

So, it's begun, Ashe thought.

ABOUT THE AUTHOR

David C. Reed is a retired criminal investigator with extensive experience in major crimes cases, including homicide, fraud, and missing persons.

As a veteran, writer, analyst, and division chief for the DoD, he wrote and conducted courses in special tactics and policing management worldwide.

www.amazon.com/author/david-c-reed
WriteDCReed@gmail.com

If you are enjoying these stories, please leave an Amazon review!

Other Chig Ashe series novels by David C. Reed
COLD, DARK AND SILENT, and (coming Fall 2025)
THE ELITE WATCH